The Shareholders

H.S. Down

Published by Hunk of Junk Press, 2022.

This is a work of fiction. Similarities to real people, places, or events are entirely coincidental.

THE SHAREHOLDERS

First edition. March 31, 2022.

Copyright © 2022 H.S. Down.

ISBN: 979-8201045173

Written by H.S. Down.

To Bean and Bear, I have written this future, so that perhaps yours can be written otherwise. To my wife, thank you for the encouragement to finish what I started.

The Shareholders

By
H.S. Down

We are defined not by what we have, but by that which we believe is ours but cannot possess. The 21st-century will be defined by the 'politics of letting go.

Chapter 1: THE PARTY

THE DOOR TO THE ROOFTOP patio was ajar; orange shadow leaked around its edge and pooled around Alex Gateman's sneakers as he watched his parents dance. With her shoes off, his mother swayed, barefoot and unsteady, as she fought for balance against his father's rhythmless lead. With his hand pressed to the door, Alex could feel the pulse of the apartment's community jukebox in his palm. The other residents of the apartment danced in a ring around his parents, careful not to break from their orbit.

Yellow, blue, and green strips of bunting hung loose and ran from wooden trellises, erected at each corner of the roof, and terminated in big lazy bows in the arms of a gazebo planted at the rooftop's center. The bunting somersaulted in the wind, and in the arches of the gazebo he glimpsed the faces of children bowed with laughter. In that gazebo, its bone-white paint now peeling in leprous curls, he had sat on his father's knee and the three of them traced the fiery tails of the rockets headed for Mars, their narrow payloads flying away from Earth like inverted shooting stars, receding into the dark of the heavens.

In remembrance of his childhood, he leant too far through the door and his father, in completion of an awkward shuffle on the spot, spotted and beckoned him with a smile and wave. With a sigh, he obeyed.

"Alex! Where have you been, son?" And as his father spoke, his mother leaned out and cradled his face in her hands; the tremors in her fingers fluttered like butterfly wings on his cheek, but he forced a smile.

THE SHAREHOLDERS

"Oh, you know, around," he answered.

"Well, get in there while the going is good," laughed his father as he tipped his head at the three tables set by the gazebo laden with food. Alex had recognized the smell: a rich metallic aroma that reminded him of the taste in his mouth when he bit his lip. They had served real meat when Debbie's father checked in, too. Unentitled meat served in thin, charred strips, accompanied with a murky oily dipping sauce in little white dishes. He made out a quarter of a chocolate cake, too. As he approached the tables, the scent of chocolate eclipsed the smell of meat as a heaviness and sweetness filled the air. His mother knew a word for the rich smell of real dairy and flour. Decadent was the word she used. 'That's not a word for food,' he had replied. 'That's how they describe the old nations, in school. Not a word for food.' But as she often did, she merely smiled and shook her head.

Two children chased after one another and darted under his feet before running beneath the tables of food and then back around the gazebo. Behind him a piece of the dancing ring broke away, and a red-faced man stumbled into chase, bellowing over the music about the dangers of running on a roof, "Guardrails be damned, you two will run right over the side!"

In the commotion, it took Alex a moment to realize that his wrist was chirping at him, spewing lines of text across his forearm. *Remember, it is custom for the child of a parent checking in to congratulate them with a piece of cake. Based on your mother's latest neurological and digestive data now is the optimal moment to serve her.* Without hesitation, he cleaved a hunk of chocolate cake onto a graphite plate with the serving knife and turned to go.

Fork? His forearm queried. With a sigh of exasperation, he fumbled for a fork on the table setting and placed it in the shadow cast by the mountainous slab of cake he had cut. It was easier to let the retinue of digital curators and self-help genies wire themselves into your limbs, to surrender and let them mesh into the nervous system as digital sinew. Didn't they say, after all, that the auto-self was more reliable than muscle memory?

The cake wobbled and then fell on its side as he approached the ring of dancing couples to his mother and father. He smiled but cursed the numb ritual of all the check-in parties. Same bunting. Same stupid happy faces and cheery shirts and dresses. The same rarified food, and the same stench in the apartment's communal bathrooms afterwards when everyone's guts tightened and wrung the morsels of mystery meat out from their bowels. But it wasn't the same. Not this time. It's not every day your mother has her check-in party, he thought.

He waded through the outer ring of dancers and waited at her elbow for her to notice him; and something about waiting beside them, expectant and almost desperate for them to take notice of the outstretched cake in his hand, made him feel like a little boy again.

"Oh," his mother whispered. "Oh, thank you," she said as she gripped the plate with trembling hands and his father gave him a slow, daft wink. For a moment, Alex felt his lip twitch, and had to fight a scowl from his face. His father. With his empty winks and unshakeable conviction that they'd all make it to Mars. *Mark my words, son. We'll get there sooner than later. I will sleep amongst the red sands of an alien world, there is wonder yet, my boy. Don't let them tell you there isn't wonder out there.* Suddenly, his consciousness streamed all the times his father had winked at him. Stupid, dumb, pointless winks. As if they were both in the know of something greater. His vision grew red and narrow with the thought that, despite all the winks, here she was with a slice of cake at her check-in party. The tremors had come faster than his father's winks and far faster than the promise of a rocket ship to Mars. The twitch in his lip crept up into cheek.

THE SHAREHOLDERS

In response, his auto-self issued a soft coo and a sudden sense of calm trespassed upon him and his disdain for his father loosened, sinking away within him like a stone vanishes into the inky black bottom of a pond. He thought of his mother, her body restored by a state of permanent immateriality, venturing through a series of bright, cheerful, simulated worlds. The image came with a pang of joy.

"Cake speech, cake speech," shouted their observers, and the rooftop broke into random clusters of applause. He watched his mother hesitate and her eyes widen as they moved from his father to him in a succession of panic. She grabbed his arm, and Alex noticed, as if for the first time, how much taller than her he had become. Her grip on his forearm and bicep was tight, though he could not tell if it was an embrace of love or fear. Perhaps it was both. She pivoted on her toes as if unsure of how to best address the ring of dancing couples that had formed around her.

"Thank you all for coming, it means the world to me."

"Which world?" called the crowd in jubilance.

"Our world," she replied, as had become the custom. "I am as scared as I am excited. The journey into immateriality is one we don't make alone. I want to thank my husband, Ian, and my son, Alex, for helping me make this choice. As so many of you know, it is not an easy choice. I don't think it is ever quite possible to gain what we leave behind. Promise me we won't lose touch. I can't wait to be on your wrists, sharing worlds with you that we can't imagine, worlds that seem impossible from this rooftop. We don't need to leave an imprint on this world to be whole." And Alex felt her grip on him tighten. She took a deep rattling breath and her eyes became fierce, glistening in the cotton candy sunset of the descending northern sun. "Next stop, Lotus!" And the rooftop broke out in waves of applause and soulful cheers.

Alex stepped aside and watched as the ring of dancers approached his mother with their arms outstretched, their voices becoming a cacophony of ecological psalms. *'Preserve the material, become immaterial'* and *'There is divinity in the sequestered self'* were refrains Alex recognized from other check in parties. His own words, 'love knows no form,' remained lodged in his throat as a tsunami of hands, small, delicate hands, hands with crooked fingers molded by taps and swipes, skimmed her face, leafed over her titan hair and ran over her body. Alex drifted to his mother's side and watched as she closed her eyes and surrendered to the crowd's embrace. Serene. Calm. On the edge of the gathering he found his father, awkward and apart from his mother. Alex watched him fold his hands in a tent in his lap, and then tuck them behind his back, only to throw them to his sides. Alex watched his father scan through the crowd for him, watched as he bobbed on his toes to see over the fray of hands that continued to cocoon his mother. Without hesitation, Alex slipped back into the apartment building, murderous with the thought that, behind him, his father was no doubt smiling and still winking to himself as the plotted their future. As he descended the stairs, Alex could not shake the feeling that whatever future came to pass, he would meet it in the wake of his father's ungainly footsteps.

IAN GATEMAN LAY WITH his wife. The party had ended and though they had retreated together, she lay with her back to him. Ian knew it would be the last time he felt her, the last time her presence would have physicality, the last time he would breathe in the smell of her flesh, the pheromones in the top of her head. The heat of a heavy and oppressive March evening leached into their room and beaded on their flesh, and in the descent of climax, their bodies were still and loosened. Anne's auburn hair cascaded over her shoulders and then branched into tributaries across her soft and dimpled back.

THE SHAREHOLDERS

No words passed between them and Ian welcomed the silence, because he longed to be sated by her presence. Desperate to hold onto her, to form a solid memory of her, he immersed himself in the constellation of freckles that dotted her lower back; freckles he had been intimate with for over eighteen years. Freckles that had come to live on the edges of stretch marks that had appeared as pale lacerations when Anne had cocooned Alex against the world.

As Ian lay behind her, Anne spelt with her lips the one needful thing of which she was certain: their world could not possibly support new beginnings. 'We live in the age of the epilogue,' she reminded herself and nodded perceptibly at what she felt was a succinct and elegant presentation of the problem at hand. Faint as it was, Ian noticed her nod.

"Anne," he whispered; his words were hoarse, and he could taste his breath as it bounced off the back of her neck. She turned her body into him and let her breasts fall against his chest. Her breath, still flavored by the strawberries they had eaten, fell hot against his chin in a slow suspire. Hours ago the smart shades in room had deployed themselves to hold off the heat, but now the sunset managed to curl in through small gaps at the windows' borders to lay a tangerine shadow across her face. Ian dared not utter another word, but let her gaze find and subdue him.

Anne's eyes often seemed cast in a state of heightened permanent alertness; a state too intelligent to be described as fidgety, but fixed in a blue restlessness. Yet tonight, Ian thought her eyes had changed. They looked calm and disarmed and Ian wandered within them into the borderlands of their early twenties, back into the half-walked trails of their conversations about having Alex, and what would lie ahead of them thirty years from now. Later, they shared cloistered and sullen murmurs about the meaningful actions they could take as the planet tumbled into its terminal years of habitability.

Anne ran her fingers softly up and down his forearm, coaxing him back into her gaze. Beyond their room, down the hall of their Cargo-Condo, he could hear Alex's laughter, coarse with the onset of adolescence. Her eyes remained calm, but her body felt rigid next to his, braced in faint anticipation of some possible rebuff.

"Thank you for understanding," she said. "I am so sorry, so sorry to leave you both. You know ..." But Ian stopped her with a solemn nod and the promise that at some point, when Alex was safe on Mars, that he would join her. Who, after all, would turn down the opportunity to join their soulmate in infinite simulated worlds? 'he'd asked.' She offered only a smile in reply. That evening he watched her clear out her section of the closet and pack her clothes into several blue containers. With her usual surgical precision and economy, she reduced herself to a small collection of luggage at the foot of their bed.

In the morning the three of them ate breakfast. Though Ian tried several times to convince Alex to accompany them to the Lotus Hotel for his mother's big send off, he remained intransient; again and again he professed that he would wait to see his mother as soon as she checked in. Anne relented, bent over the sofa where he lay and planted a long kiss upon his forehead; a scene reminiscent to how she bade him goodnight when he was a toddler.

It was not a long walk to Lotus, and once they entered, the opulence of the lobby took them both aback. A white marble floor, immaculate of the usual dusty footprints that haunted most buildings in the Enclosure, flowed to a crescent-shaped reception desk. Above the desk, etched into the pale wall in black lettering, was the phrase, *Become Immaterial for the Preservation of the Material.* From behind the reception desk, a slender woman in a black sheath dress eyed them with an alert curiosity. She flashed them a shadow of a smile as they marveled at their surroundings.

THE SHAREHOLDERS

Interspersed throughout the room were screens: each cycled through the images of the ubiquitous program *Lost and Treasured Places*. A montage of scenes of the natural wonders and ecologies that had been lost throughout the 21st century. Ian glanced at lush canopied forests of the Amazon, oceans, and snow-capped mountains. Beneath the screens, several men and women stood motionless, their arms folded behind their backs, and opposite them was a live orchestra playing the violin, the flute, the cello and brass accompaniments. A small plaque to the left of the orchestra informed them that for their enjoyment the string instruments had bows made of authentic horsehair.

"Beethoven's ninth! Ian, how lovely," said Anne and she cast him her familiar smile of reassurance, which always seemed to outrun him. Ian nodded, although he could not recall which one was Beethoven. They paused in mid-step, and he squeezed her hand a little tighter, as the woman broke away from the reception desk to greet them.

"Welcome to the Lotus Hotel!" she smiled and clasped her hands in approval. "We took the liberty of scanning your auto-self so that we would be able to provide you with your favorite music, Anne."

"You're so kind," said Anne, her cheeks flushed with embarrassment.

"That's simply how we do things at Lotus. Everything is personalized to your taste. But, I am getting ahead of myself. I am Edna, your onboarder. Are you ready to check in?"

"This is my husband, Ian, he wanted to be with me for my departure. My journey to the undying lands, as it were," she added, but Ian could not place her reference.

"Of course, of course, Ian, it is a pleasure," smiled Edna, revealing a mouth of pearls whiter than the marble floor. She used the smile to direct them to a hallway to the left of reception. Her smile continued in her office as she sat in front of them, her fingers clasped in a delicate tent. Behind her lithe figure, a touchscreen flashed basic information about Anne, no doubt downloaded from the archives of her auto-self.

"Now, when we last spoke, you had confirmed today as your check in. Would you still like to proceed with a permanent stay?" asked Edna.

Anne nodded. "Yes."

"Excellent. Now, I don't want to be too intrusive, but I am required to ask you a few questions." Anne bit her lip, but shrugged her approval. "Why have you decided to join our community? What is it about life in the Enclosure that has made you want to choose Lotus Hotels?" asked Edna.

"I suppose ..." Anne started, but then paused to inhale the room. "I am just too tired. Too tired of the gray, and the heat. Too tired of my failing body. Tired of worrying about when *things* will turn on us? Our son Alex ... when he was born ... well ... I just don't know how to raise a new life as I try and learn to embrace the end of the world," confessed Anne.

Edna leaned in and held Anne's hand, coaxing her to draw on some near-tapped reservoir of perseverance.

"Does this make me terrible mother and a bad wife?" Anne asked. Although Ian was sure Anne directed these questions at him, her gaze remained fixed on Edna.

"Of course, not Anne, of course not," whispered Edna with a familiarity that irked Ian but seemed to further disarm Anne.

"Really?" begged Anne, tears now spilling down her face in great drops from her luminous blue eyes.

"Really. This world is too much and, at once, far too little. It makes one so very weary. There is no scarcity like deprivation and being trapped in an ill body. Ian understands, don't you Ian?" Before Ian could respond, Edna continued, "Checking in permanently isn't

THE SHAREHOLDERS

the end, of being a mother or," she said, arching her eyebrow ever so slightly in provocation, "a wife. We are giving you the opportunity to enjoy an eternity of ecologically sustainable living. Think of it; as a resident of Lotus you will live for as long as you wish in a virtual community of your choosing. Here you can explore seamlessly simulated worlds. The very depths of human experience will be forever at your fingertips. It is a world without limit. Can you imagine a world without limit, without scarcity, without restriction? Oh, of course you can't! How can any of us living in times such as these? After what you have been through, all the upheaval your generation has faced, don't you deserve a chance to experience the life you were promised? And think, admittance to Lotus will reduce your ecological footprint to nearly nothing. By making this choice, you will be conserving resources for your family."

"Ian, are you still okay with this?" she asked, and averted her gaze to the sleek white empty space of Edna's desk.

With as much force as he could muster, Ian replied, "Of course. You know that. I am sure we will be together again like that." And he snapped his fingers, but when she turned from him, he deflated and frowned into his lap. The conversation shifted quickly from the unrivaled opportunities of life in Lotus to a stiff discussion of the fees. The savings they had put aside was enough for a 25% down payment. With a nonchalant wave of her finger across Anne's auto-self, Edna took the funds. She assured Ian that they would work through the details of the financing after Anne's admission.

"I can check you in today as planned. Do you have any business or personal matters you need to attend to first, though? There is no going back, and we want to ensure the transition is seamless for employers and families." This last little epilogue came quick and in a perfunctory tone, which left Ian with the impression that it was perhaps the final question before they moved on to Anne's admittance.

"No, I have let my employer know and Ian and Alex threw me a lovely check-in party. I am—we are—" she coaxed Ian by rubbing his arm "—ready."

"Splendid, let me show you both to the transition room," said Edna.

THEY CAUGHT AN ELEVATOR in the lobby and journeyed up through the building in a brittle silence, spare the ambient elevator music, which Anne informed them was Bach. With a lackadaisical halt, the elevator doors peeled back to reveal a brightly lit yet expansive chamber. As his first steps clattered against the metallic tiled floor, Ian realized he was walking on chrome. Some hundred meters away at the room's center, a white spherical column ascended from the floor to a vaulted ceiling. Nestled in the center of the column was a darkened screen. Below the screen at the base of the column was body-sized port that faced out into their approach like a wide-open mouth. To the right of the column, suspended from the floor by black steel rod, was a large touchscreen console.

"Welcome to your room," squealed Edna, and she swept her arm towards the column as if making an introduction. While Anne inched forwards, catching Edna's enthusiasm, Ian inspected the room further and saw that it was composed of many overlapping white metallic tiles. Each its own port, and he presumed each was a little window bay upon which to look on the intangible fuzz and hum of each resident's digital upload. Consciousness preserved and stored, and he could not shake the image of thousands of little pickle jars, their contents jostling about in the brine.

"It looks cold," said Ian.

"I can assure you that only the room itself is cold. Once Anne is transferred into Lotus she will only ever be as cold or as warm as she would like to be; if you so elect, Anne, you can choose to be neither.

THE SHAREHOLDERS

You choose from an unlimited number of experiences," and as she spoke Edna seemed to fall into her own private reverence. "Limitless choices in a time of such scarcity, what ingenuity, what a gift." She clapped as she gazed into the blank screen that peered down upon them from on high. The words "limitless choice" conjured for Ian an image of vast emptiness and for the first time in a very long time, he felt fear; he reached out to hold Anne's hand, but she was already too far in front of him, her head craned upwards in silent worship, to notice him and reach back.

Edna moved ahead them and strummed the touchscreen console to live, making the screen flicker into the image of a blue orb superimposed against an inky galaxy. Her well-made hands moved about the orb with adroit precision and drew from it green threads that soon appeared like ivy on the touchscreen; each strand featured its own heading, things like birthplace, art, love, travel, genealogy, fears, interests. Without looking up, Edna informed them that she was building Anne's Lotus profile and that the admission process would be initialized momentarily. Ian and Anne both gave mute nods of assent.

A burst of static erupted across the screen held by the white spherical column in the center of the room. The uniform darkness of the screen was split in half by a very thin horizontal red line, which crossed through the screen's center. Then, with the speed and motion of eyelids stung by dawn's first light, the red line expanded up and down as the black space receded until the screen became fully red. The word Lotus appeared in white lettering down the left side of the screen, and running horizontally from each letter were the words:

Life
Outside
The Terrestrial
Universe
Systems

Edna put her hand on Anne's shoulder. "Lotus is ready to receive your upload now. We just need to construct a life narrative, so the system knows how to receive you. Please let me assist you in creating your life narrative." Shepherded by Edna, Anne approached the base of the column, and then Edna broke stride from her, withdrew from a drawer concealed amongst the tiles an ivory crown, which she informed them would transmit Anne's consciousness into Lotus.

Edna turned the crown over in her hand to reveal four narrow, needle-like chrome pins positioned at the crown's front, back, left and right sides. With only gestures, Edna beckoned Anne to kneel before her as she carefully fitted the crown to her head, until the pins connected to her scalp. Confident the crown was secure, Edna instructed Anne to begin her life narrative.

I was born ...

Ian did his best to listen to the last time he would hear his wife tell a story with her own vocal cords, but he found himself focusing more on the gentle cadence of her voice than her actual words. Occasionally, though, he managed to trespass upon her last earthly confession:

"I know that there was a time before the division of arid earth, thirsty pale valleys, and emptying oceans into the thousands of lays doled out to the Shareholders for safekeeping, but I can't feel it. There are videos archived on timelines from the days before the Great Partition, but those days have become placeless things, moving through this world like lost ships without anchors.

The algorithms, I suppose, seek to remind me. But they remind me less about the exact events that led to the splintering of the old nations into thousands of lays, and instead the words that were used to clothe those days: confusion, ecological breakdown, Anthropocene, deniers. My father use to say that a people unable to take action are often blessed with the largest vocabularies.

THE SHAREHOLDERS

I don't mind that the algorithms today have let the days before partition slip away. I just know that we have now established an order to the end. Everything, we are told, will be well managed down to the last fertile field. I suppose this how we make civilization compatible with the end of the world.

I join this august walk as the only child of a middling sort of family. A family of professionals, my mom would say. She ran an agency dedicated to the relocation of ecological refugees and my father was a professor of political theory, one of the last of his age, before the educational reforms. I was their only child, and they brought me into a marriage that was well worn and comfortable when they entered their early forties.

By the time I was old enough to really travel, it was well beyond our means. Like most of my generation, I was raised under the new directives from the shareholders that ensured human mobility was fully ecologically sustainable.

I've visited Paris in virtual reality. Crept through the London Underground and snorkeled off the Great Barrier Reef, all without ever travelling beyond my living room. We fast became time travelers, voyaging back and at all costs averting our eyes from the event horizon that yawned ever wider ahead of us. I was lucky. The simulated reality programs left many of the first generation of virtual voyagers dizzy and nauseous. For some it was so bad they couldn't use them; their world was just that much smaller. Experience is the best palliative to scarcity and being governed by a class of immortal men and women makes you nothing but attentive to the scarcity of life itself.

What else about me? I dream of emerald oceans, and fresh air. I savor what I think it would feel like to have my cheeks kissed by breezes cast from wind-roiled seas.

Though the old world is consummately aloof, I do wonder if the world felt different before it was divided into shares. I believe it must have felt less tight. *Our steps wider, our passions and bonds with others less claustrophobic.*

Ian smiled and willed himself to imagine that he had seen Anne smile too. Her words took him back to when they had first met and would talk in excitement late into the night about the world before the great partition.

When I was young, I snuck into my father's study. I was not sure what I was looking for, but I found the videos from the early days after the release of the treatment. I can still remember the way the pandemonium bled out of the screen and into me. Its contagion.

There were clips of the old cities; London, Bangkok, Vancouver, with road after road alit with for sale signs. Stories of robberies from treasuries and banks. Hedge fund managers absconding with all their clients' assets for the chance to extend their lives for hundreds if not thousands of years.

More than anything, I remember seeing the riots. The buildings red with flame. The throngs of people in the streets demanding to join a limited edition utopian undying world. I remember children falling under the crowds as they ran from men with guns.

I cried in my father's lap and after he scolded me for snooping, he told me what made those days so ugly was the mistiming of it all. A hand's worth of decades earlier, back when the rich wanted the poor to work, the treatment might have been offered to the poor. 'Imagine the immortal, disease-free worker, imagine how profitable that would have been,' he claimed. However, the treatment came just when it was truly apparent that too many of us were surplus to requirements. What was to be done with the new dispossessed? Nobody knew, but extending their lives indefinitely certainly wasn't the answer.

I can't remember when, but shortly after that the tipping points finally tipped for real. The tipping points. The big horizons, incomprehensible thresholds, and yet they never once touched us with any real permanence. They came like waves from a nameless shore

THE SHAREHOLDERS

adumbrated by distance and by our habitual and weary attendance to our own mortality. What would make it real, we wondered? Then the great thaw came, the permafrost and northern ice gave way, and the world ran away from us.

My mum's sullen reminisces of the three years when summer just refused to end. But for my parents it was three years of homegrown raspberries, Pimms, and galas on patios. New styles of clothing were made like beach formal dress-wear. That was here. Elsewhere it was floods and famine.

I often feel a sense of disgust that we profited from the birth of an institutionalized nomadic class of workers. The old powers did their best to stem the tide of people that dead fields, parched streams, and burning jungles, threw asunder. They introduced temporary land leases to foreigners who farmed and built colonies only to be moved from place to place on non-negotiable itineraries. My mother knew of a family that spent fifteen years moving, from Uganda to Turkey, to France, to England, to Iceland to Timmons, Ontario. In their wake they helped erect the infrastructures for what eventually became today's Enclosures.

As benefactors of the ecological divide, we ended up with a cheap cottage near Yorkville, our plan B. Every middleclass family had a plan B towards the end. I suppose those cottages are still out there, derelict and overgrown. An homage to the hierarchy of escape plans that emerged as every family began to hedge their bets. Is there a better epilogue to the human experiment than that? Even in the face of the systemic, brutal ecological collapse, individuals held firm that they could untangle themselves from humanity's extinction with getaway cottages, solar panels, and rain barrels?

But, that is what we did. What we still do. We exchanged rain barrels for the long-sought hope of transplantation to Mars. To think that my migration was defined by a move to the outer reaches of Northern Manitoba, but to avoid the brunt of ecological decline Alex may move to another planet. How's that for progress?

H.S. DOWN

My father never adapted to the lifeline of the Shareholders. Life, he said, was a primeval form of power. There was a reason, he said, Hobbes had written physical strength, endurance and stamina out of the first social contract. After all, how can those who possess absolute biological, political, and economic power withstand corruption? His colleagues laughed at him, called him paranoid. Nobody laughed, though, when all the shareholders moved to Mars to govern from the heavens. Prometheus may have given us stolen fire, but in the end, we would let the designers rebuild Mount Olympus.

Then I met Ian and we had Alex. Sweet, gentle Alex. When he was little the three of us would climb to the roof of our condo to watch the rockets to Mars fly. Alex's eyes would grow wide with wonder as the ships sailed over the stars, his little fingers tracing their flight until their amber fires outpaced him and flew higher, beyond his reach. I know Ian found those evenings reassuring, but they are memories I cannot..." Anne stammered and went silent. After a long pause, her words returned to her, but she closed her eyes as she spoke. *"I don't have anything left to say. Not anything that will make a difference, anyway."*

Edna placed the ivory crown on Anne's head. Anne motioned Ian to her, they locked eyes and fell into their familiar embrace. Ian tasted her breath; the salt of both of their tears burned on his tongue.

"I love you," she uttered, and then the four chrome pins in the sides of the helmet pulsed and hummed. Her eyes closed and the screen grew bright and became a taskbar informing them how much of her consciousness had been downloaded. Ian watched the bar move towards the right of the screen in small increments.

"That was very sudden," he murmured, unsure of whether he was speaking to Edna or himself. "I didn't feel like I really got a chance to say goodbye," he added.

"There is no need for the sentimentality of a final goodbye," stated Edna. "Goodbye is a phrase that belongs to a world with

THE SHAREHOLDERS

endings, a world with edges. Life in Lotus is limitless," murmured Edna. "But, of course, you can stay with her material residue," and she stroked Anne's arm gingerly as she spoke, "for as long as you wish."

Ian looked upon Anne and was overcome with the strange thought that she was untouchable, in some place of far-off belonging. To graze her cheek with his fingers would be to scrape the surface of a distant, cold, winking star. He stifled a gasp when he realized he had marooned himself here, on the side of time and space which, with their mutual covenant, offered only the promise of the loneliness of the in-between. The giant screen overhead gave an electronic burble as the taskbar completed. In its paling neon glow, Ian's auto-self chirped to life with his first message from Anne:

All checked in. I've let Alex know, too. Thank you. Thank you. I love you both to Mars and back!

As he read her text, Ian rubbed her cheek and was alarmed to find it still faintly warm to the touch. It was too much, he thought. Too much terror, too much wonder and too much possibility. Nausea cut through him, and his knees buckled.

Chapter 2: CHANGE OF SCENE

AN HOUR AFTER ANNE'S dematerialization, Ian was seated at his office at the Department of Sustainable Ecological Refugees. With his ability to focus on where he was or what had just transpired obliterated, he tried to distract himself by clearing his desk, but his white little taskbar was spotless, barren of any notifications or memos. His attention drifted to his auto-self where he repeatedly read the chain of numbers and letters that was the link to Anne's new address inside Lotus Hotel.

It all seemed so clean and effortless. The only task she had left him was to collect and recycle the luggage she had left at the foot of the bed. The nausea had subsided, and so he tried to turn his attention to the pamphlet Edna had handed to him as he left, *'Our patented, simple, elegant design of dematerialization*, but the rest of the sentence escaped him. Alone in his office, he tried to build a clinical assessment for the disjointed feeling that had come with the new borders of their arrangement. He rubbed his temples and his auto-self suggested he embrace his good fortune of being alive in an age when it was possible to be spared the sentimentality of a final goodbye. Finding the solace wanting, he returned to the pamphlet and pondered the terms and conditions attached to their new marriage at the bottom of the last page in tiny print. *Lotus accepts no responsibility for relationship breakdown or marriage dissolution in relationships where one spouse remains physically constituted ...* There was a knock at the door, and Grayson, the Department Deputy Minister, huffed into his office, red-faced and beaded with sweat.

THE SHAREHOLDERS

Grayson always appeared in a perpetual state of perspiration and mild heat exhaustion, which Ian thought to be consequence of Grayson being heavyset and pensive. Whenever Ian came across him, he appeared at pace, a bulbous droplet of sweat forever swinging at the end of his nose. The antiquated climate controls in the building did neither of them any favors nor did the fact that he and Grayson were the only permanent employees of the department.

"How are you holding up?" asked Grayson as he completed a lap in front of Ian's desk with his arms tucked behind his back, which only extenuated his belly.

"Fine, I suppose." Ian grimaced.

"Not an easy decision for a family, but as you said the tremors were getting worse, weren't they?" puffed Grayson. Ian felt his shoulders jump up to his ears; Grayson had been one of the few people he confided in about Anne's failing health. Yet, hearing him speak about it somehow felt like a betrayal.

"We had reached the point where there were more bad days than good days," said Ian.

Grayson gave a solemn nod, "Will you check in after her?"

"Not until Alex is fully grown and off this rock."

"I remember when Debra checked in permanently. It wasn't tremors. It was something else. Something invisible and unshakeable. Mind you, we never had any children, but it was very hard," said Grayson in a sympathetic wheeze as he stopped to steady himself in the corner of the room.

"I have no idea how Alex is going to cope. I mean, when the reality sinks in that his mother will never be able to hold him again."

"Kids these days are goddamn resilient. He started piloting this month, didn't he?"

"He did. He sends me screenshots of the Ash Deserts, or what might be the Ash Deserts. He's already earned us a few loyalty credits with the target acquisition missions he's completed."

H.S. DOWN

"Those were the days, eh? Pacifying the south. Not bad way to sublimate that teenage libido, to think our great-grandparents had to settle for drugs and shit stain moustaches." Grayson laughed.

"You were in the top 20 in the district, weren't you?" Ian asked, though he was wary of where this well-practiced conversation was headed.

"Until my retirement at 17. If I recall you weren't all that good at it," said Grayson, with a sweat speckled smirk.

Ian tried to laugh. His lousy performance as a drone pilot was a perennial cause for ridicule or, worse, distrust from his colleagues. He quickly fired off the answer he had rehearsed since he turned fifteen.

"I never got my head around the fact that I'd never know if what I had done was real or simulation. I mean, I had no qualms about blowing up southerners," Ian said emphatically, unsure if he had inspired the err of assurance he desired, "They're an existential threat, after all, but not knowing if they were real or just part of the simulation always made me pause. Anne was incredible, though."

"Oh god, yes, if Alex takes after her." Grayson whistled. "Did you know that before we were logged, they ran it a few times without any simulations, but too many pilots started to miss their targets? Anyways, I never felt the need to get bogged down in the details. You know, it is what it is." Grayson shrugged and cocked his head to the side as he often did when he waited for Ian to reciprocate his sentiments.

"It is what it is," replied Ian as he attempted to conjure an expression of resignation in place of his squeamishness.

Grayson appeared unconvinced, "Well, anyway, it is his first month, chances are he hasn't been logged into a real drone and won't start on IRL targets until he's requesting to wash his own sheets."

"Things to look forward to."

THE SHAREHOLDERS

"Simulated reality, material reality, it's all zeros and ones ... I think the only reason we're charged with protecting the environment is because we need a material world to house our simulated one."

"Would you ever check in to Lotus?" Ian diverted.

"Me? No," he said flatly. Perhaps seeing Ian's puzzlement, he continued, "An infinite number of experiences and an endless customization of reality is just too much for me. I'm small-minded, I suppose. Too old to come to grips with it all, honestly. I just can't see what it really offers, a non-tactile infinite experience just doesn't sit well with me. Too overwhelming, can only imagine it is like dreaming forever," mused Grayson as he raised his arm to give his sweat-dotted brow a surreptitious dab with his sleeve.

"Do you miss her?" Ian ventured, yet he knew it was unlikely Grayson would give him an honest answer.

"We eat dinner together every other night, and I get messages from her a couple times a day." Perhaps pressured on by Ian's incredulous stare, Grayson continued, "Well, it's certainly not the same as being with someone who's still material. We have an agreement. You know, the occasional liaison with a real-life woman." Noting Ian's raised eyebrows, he added, "Trust me, she does the same too, I think. You know, in her own way. It must be a non-stop orgy in that thing. You can, of course, interface with each other, too, but the whole apparatus is a little embarrassing." Perhaps seeing Ian's visible discomfort at this last confession, Grayson made haste to lead the conversation in another direction. "Anyway, I have something that I thought might cheer you up." And he tapped his auto-self several times and then flicked his wrist at Ian. "It is an important assignment. I wanted to do it myself, but I figured some time out of the Enclosure might do you good," he added.

Ian sat down in his chair, inserted his earbuds, and accessed the request through his auto-self. Eventually his digital guide kicked in and started to translate the text of the assignment into an audio file, delivered with a deep masculine cadence optimized to his identified listening profile. Ian shut eyes and let the voice of the digital guide wash over him.

Upon the advice of Chief Factor Trimalchio, the Enclosure has decided to continue to capitalize on its carbon sequestration assets. We are now seeking a buyer to support the Egg Island colony. Egg Island is a colony comprised of several hundred relocated ecological refugees. However, a few bad harvests have landed the colony in crisis, but the opportunities for carbon sequestration are incredible, especially in attempts to further extend peat bog. If a buyer can support the colony with new infrastructure and supplies, the Enclosure will entitle the buyer to 80% of the carbon credits generated by the colony. You will travel to the seven estates in our region and receive assignment pay at a 1.5 bonus level credit upon completion. The trip is booked for one month from today. Swipe right to confirm your itinerary; your opportunity to accept this assignment will expire in ten minutes.

Ian lay back in his chair and drummed his fingers on the spotless surface of his composite-plastic desk. His mind flashed to the containers of Anne's clothes waiting for him at the foot of their bed and then the memory of her, of her taste on his lips, plunged him, unaided by the prostheses of digital timelines or archived videos, into an organic memory. Twilight grew over his office and the memory grew stronger, blotting out his desk and the pamphlet he had forgotten remained in his hands.

They lay on their backs in the small, curated park opposite their building. A July heatwave had overwhelmed the cooling mechanisms of most residents' apartments in the Enclosure. Starting in the midafternoons, when the heat had stormed past the climate controls of most buildings, people came out and lay quietly in parks, to have mist sprayed upon them by water-carrying drones, until the heat broke in the early hours of the next morning. The young held midnight picnics and listened to music. Not far from them, down

THE SHAREHOLDERS

the gradual slope of the park's hill, the elderly lay on their backs, torpid, their mouths open, biting at the air, waiting in desperation to be renewed for another twenty minutes by the next round of misting.

The frenetic buzzing signaled the arrival of the next wave. The blast of the cool mist enveloped them. In the aftermath of the relief, Anne rested her head on his bicep while she guided his hand across her expanding waist in search of the palpations of Alex's feet, so Ian could greet their son in utero. She moved him over her belly, her grip a tender mediator between them, though she did not smile.

"What does it feel like?" he had asked.

"Fluttering," she responded, in way Ian knew she had no intent on elaborating further. "Another record long heatwave," she tightened her grip on him as she spoke. "I wonder how long the heat waves will be when he's our age," she asked. "I'm not sure we will be able to keep up the dewing evenings."

Ian said nothing but squeezed her hand back. He felt perpetually disarmed by her comments about the future. In keeping with the ritual that had formed between them, he offered up a solution.

"There is so much time left. Another six hundred years by some estimates. We'll find an equilibrium. And, of course, there will always be Mars." Mars had fast become his go-to in their discussions of the Earth's failing habitability. The colonization of Mars would insulate their child's adulthood and give him leave to take refuge with the shareholders. In his opinion, Anne had never weighed this option with the significance it deserved.

Without acknowledgement, she continued, "I wonder how knowing our species has a fixed expiration date has changed us? What would the Aztecs have done differently had they known it was all going to come down to 1521?"

"1521?" pressed Ian.

"The year Cortez arrived. Would they have done anything different had they known it would end in a few generations? Would they be kinder, more self-reflective? Would they still bring babies into the world? Would they make art?"

"I would hope they would find a solution," pressed Ian.

"Sure, but what if there wasn't one? Would they make a new set of ethics?" She webbed her fingers around her belly and swayed her hips from side to side. "Ian, I worry we've done something horrible."

An elegiac chirp grew amongst the memory, and with its growing intensity, it chipped away Anne's face and the night sky fell away like jigsaw pieces until it became his desk, and he sat, almost blinded by the austere sheen of its spotless white surface. His auto-self continued to chirp, and on his wrist Grayson's assignment flashed alongside the reminder that Lotus would require his first payment in two weeks.

He had never travelled to the estates before, and though the assignment seemed like a difficult pitch, time away, as Grayson had suggested, would perhaps do him good. However, what about Alex? He slowly convinced himself, with considerable effort, that between schoolwork and an extra level of prompting from his auto-self, Alex could survive the week without him. Of course, Anne had just left. Could he conclude the trip in less than a week? Anticipating his reticence, his auto-self informed him that based on his past spending habits, he'd struggle to make the payment to Lotus. With a heavy sigh, he scraped his twisted, arthritic pointer finger across the screen.

Chapter 3: TOP SCORE

AFTER SEVERAL MORE hours of pacing his office and leafing through the pamphlet, Ian left to return home to Alex. The hastily-stacked towers of shipping crate apartments dwarfed the two-story complex that housed his department. As 3D printing had made freight ships yet another class of stranded assets, new sustainable Cargo-Condo tenements had mushroomed in the remaining habitable places on Earth. Thirty story tower after tower of sun faded red, blue, and green shipping containers, each crowned by identical rooftop gardens, formed the skyline. Built so close to one another, the towers burned into one another and spilled out in all directions until they ran up against the rows of greenhouses that dotted the edges of the Enclosure's containment wall.

The cargo-condos came in several different interior designs, but when all was said and done, they were the same: two bedrooms and a virtual reality portal consumed the space his grandparents would have reserved for a living room. The middle of each story housed communal bathrooms and kitchens. Ian had quite enjoyed his crate as a bachelor, but once Ann moved in and they had Alex, the carrying capacity of the 600-square-foot living space was stretched to its limits.

The few families who unwisely elected to have two or three children often found their dwelling upended in squalor and filth. Limits on available living space were one of the many measures taken by the Londumium council to limit population growth. The Cargo-Condo prospectus had explained, '*Small living scenarios are an effective and non-invasive form of contraception. It's about giving people the choice to adjust their lives to their real surroundings.*' Ian often ruminated that the green lifestyle was all about making the transition from environment molded by life to life molded by environment; and, nearly subconsciously, he muttered this to himself as he left the departmental complex to travel down Naturalist Drive to the rest of the Enclosure.

The street was clean, bright, and empty. The incandescent grins of low-hanging solar lampposts curled over the roadway and fell on the community planters that grew along the well-ordered little streets. Tangled clumps of vegetables and fruits struggled in little boxes along the curbs, each numbered and assigned to someone responsible for their harvest. The neon glow of a Zambezi storefront crossed Ian's path; its bright windows revealed that, like the *Buzz* restaurant opposite, it was empty, without living staff. These reinvented high-street stores, with their doors cast wide, revealed interiors that had eradicated the tedious, incidental nature of waiting with finely-tuned, automated, "just-in-time" shopping appointments. The smart Enclosure city merely hummed, organizing itself with indifference to what its residents thought about its brightly-lit, empty storefronts. Cornered by its vast emptiness and its imperious grind of operations, synchronizations, and predictive calibrations, Ian felt less a resident and more an exposed spectator.

Yet, before this thought could stretch its legs, he caught sight of a drone and without meaning to, lurched to a hard stop as he threw his weight to his toes. A drone hovered near the end of the street, its gray, tapered body basked in the pale light of a northern sun in retreat. He took a tentative step forward and the drone's sensory light winked at his presence. A text popped up on his auto-self under the drone's sobriquet of Guardian of Botany Boulevard. It read, *"Where are you headed, Mr. Gateman?"*

"Home," Ian responded, but he took care to divide his voice between his auto-self and the empty street. The drone winked in recognition and then shuffled left and right in deliberation before its reply; a programmed affect designed to make it appear like a playful dog. The animalization of automated drones had been introduced as a public relations campaign to socialize people into relating to them as loyal companion creatures.

Ian froze in place and held his breath as he awaited its response. It was an instinct he had developed from his childhood encounters with the earlier models whose defective processers had occasionally responded to any sudden movement with a strafe of gunfire. Though these incidents had been few, they had been such high profile events that he and his friends had learned to stay perfectly still while drones were processing information. However, even now, many years later, his residual instincts shocked him and he realized how slowly nervous-tissue memory dies; perhaps it even dies last, he mused. Finally, a text popped up on his auto-self:

"The quickest route with the least number of people is from Blossom Avenue and left on Polar Street, and you should arrive at your apartment at 17:24. You will encounter four other individuals on route. Please be advised that if you encounter anyone else on route, they are not registered with the Enclosure and should be reported immediately. The Guardian on Blossom Avenue will update you if there are any changes in circumstances."

Ian cast an impatient nod back at the drone. Foot traffic was coordinated to avoid the concentration of population in any specific part of the Enclosure. This measure of controlling foot traffic had been introduced to limit the opportunity for terrorist attacks and reduce the risk of spreading contagious antibiotic-resilient diseases. The side effect was that it also made his walk home sterile and humorless.

He started down Blossom Avenue and, in ritual avoidance of the overwhelming feeling of dislocation that washed over him on these solitary walks, he fired off several texts and sent one to Alex to let him know he was on his way home. Alex's auto-self responded on his behalf to inform Ian that Alex was online and immersed in a drone mission; he would reply to him later.

He arrived at his apartment building, entered with an adroit wave of his wrist, and embraced the neon glow of the thirty or so screens mounted to the building's atrium walls and ceiling tiles. He headed to the elevators, wading through the vignettes and images of today's compilation of *A Day in The Life*: real time 24/7 footage of the activities of the many residents of the Enclosure captured by drone surveillance. Overhead on the screen, children played on rooftop gardens, peopled tended their vegetable boxes, flurries of men and women entered and exited various complexes, and 3D printing stations vomited shirts and shoes to impatient crowds.

Every so often, the familiar cheery voice of the Enclosure, a connection named Ajax, recited, "We are many, but we are singular. Transcend scarcity by being part of the many. For residents participating remotely, do not neglect yourself! Get up and stretch every hour!"

A door attendant stood in front of the dimly-lit vestibule that partitioned the front entrance from the elevators, or what was referred to as the "cleansing passage," in the apartment's prospectus. The contrast of the human against the circus of digital feeds and footage amused Ian to no end. The whirling untouchable maelstrom of the just-in-time wireless economy of remote persons selected by algorithm invaded every screen as live-stream and texts from nowhere, collapsed against the unapologetic corporeal body of the attendant hired to occupy the atrium. Nearly motionless, spare the flicker of serene smile bordered by shoulder length brown locks, she stood passive, in wait of residents as they trickled into the apartment.

Pretty, perhaps in her early twenties, she presided over the vestibule with no purpose greater than staving off the psychosis of boredom and, tacitly, to satiate a drive that was neglected by the

THE SHAREHOLDERS

array of connections and services he was enmeshed within: the desire to rule a fellow human being. Not even the emperors of history's greatest dynasties had come close to possessing the retinues of servants that were now available as digital assistants on the wrists of every resident in an Enclosure. Yet, the closer and more eagerly one ruled over one's digital subjects, it seemed, the greater one was indentured to them. Physical stand-ins' were designed to counter the feeling of impotence that accompanied digital rule.

Tomorrow, maybe the day after, she would be gone. Then after a few more days, a week, perhaps even a month, she'd be recruited to some other location to welcome people to a shopping complex, to open a shop door, to deliver vegetables to an apartment, or to watch over an autonomous community printer. As connections grew denser and as the flow of demands, responses, and data fused more people to things and places, the service economy of the late 20th-century had degenerated into idleness and emptiness. An entire professional class had emerged that had no greater task than repopulating spaces stripped clean by the digital revolution.

"Good evening, Mr. Gateman," said the attendant.

"What news do you have for me?" Ian asked.

"Let me just sync your feed with the apartment. There we go, okay ... Kevin is celebrating his ninth birthday in crate 7-C. Umm, crates 12-A and D have too many carrots and are willing to exchange for potatoes. Well, look at that, Alex Gateman, your son, received the top score for today's drone mission. How exciting. Would you like to fill in at a dinner party for Mrs. Stevens? Apparently, she is feeling unsmiley face, which is open for interpretation, I guess. The Enclosure is also happy to offer you a rebate on your consumption as your wife has joined the Lotus Community, how exciting for all of you!"

"Anything else?" urged Ian with unbridled impatience.

"That's all, I'm afraid. In a few moments you will receive a brief survey on my performance, please take the time to fill it out as it influences my ability to return to this post."

"You like being a door attendant?" asked Ian, unable to contain some of his incredulity.

"I love getting out of my complex. I meet so many interesting professionals," she added and let her hand fall and stay on his forearm for a moment.

"Well ... okay then."

"Great, I would look forward to facilitating your return home again, Mr. Gateman."

After a tedious ride in the elevator, he arrived back in their apartment. The door squeaked open to reveal Alex sprawled on the sofa, raining saline solution over his eyes after what Ian assumed had been a marathon drone mission. Alex cast him a distracted and subdued wave as he let the saline set.

"I got a text from mum. She's doing fine. She loves us both," said Alex, but his eyes remained fixed on the ceiling as he spoke. Even from across the room, Ian could tell his eyes were bloodshot; he could not determine if it had been the mission or the transcendence of his mother into some unknowable ethereal realm that was to blame.

"Oh, good. Big changes," said Ian. He felt dumb as soon as he uttered the words, but Alex mercifully spared him.

"Jim's dad joined Lotus after the heatwave last summer. Fran's mum and older sister also doubled down on the digital life, after her sister developed tremors. I'm not the first one to go through this," he finished, though he struggled to keep his voice level. Ian nodded, but felt paralyzed by his child's resolve. Alex rolled onto his side and pressed his next words into the Jacobean upholstery of the sofa, "I just wish she'd waited a little longer to go."

THE SHAREHOLDERS

"She loves you more than anything, Alex. It's just like she said, she knew she needed to take the first step for all of us. We could talk to her about it together right now. She's always in reach," Ian reminded, though in truth he remained uneasy about making direct contact; it felt like staring directly at the sun.

Once more, Alex spared him, "Always in reach, but never in touch," he replied. "I don't think I'm ready yet to speak with her ... inside of there."

Ian said nothing but glided over to the lip of sofa and drew his son up by his broadening shoulders and was shocked and comforted when his son's curly black hair grazed his chin.

"We're proud of you," he said. Alex said nothing and struggled to meet his eyes before shifting from his grip. Desperate to change the subject, Ian followed up with, "I hear today's mission was another success?"

"Top-score in the condo and third-highest score in the Enclosure," said Alex, clearly relieved by the new topic. "I'm meeting the other pilots from this building on the rooftop later to discuss tactics. I recorded the last five minutes of footage." Alex tapped at his auto-self and a clip popped up on Ian's wrist. Ian smiled and tried to conceal his immense distaste for piloting as he hit play.

A haunting and familiar aerial view of wilted trees and sprawling ash desert flashed before him from the camera mounted on the drone's nose. Ian winced as the familiar, but very uncomfortable, sensation that he had become a specter in the sky, hunting just behind the present, hit him. His vision swooned over a vast field of indented earth, the fingerprint of a once-great lake, now passed on into clay and dust. He skimmed over its surface to close in upon a lone gray tree on a mound of earth that had probably once been the shoals of a small island bejeweling the lake's center. In a quick arc the screen veered to the right towards a broken stretch of road that ran next to the lake's empty clay belly, and up into the foothills of balding mountains.

The ascent continued and the world turned once more into wilted trees moored on an ash sea. Clouds filtered through the screen, clawing at his line of sight like ghosts passing between this world and the next. Was this truly the hinterlands of the ash desert, or a voyage in a super-real simulation, wondered Ian. Desperate to know, as the continuity of Alex's childhood seemed to depend upon the answer, he peered deeper into the screen, but the covenant between the real and unreal was unassailable to the human eye.

The drone veered to the right and the camera returned to dead wood and gray air. He knew the fact that he had never been to the ash desert in real life compounded his difficulties in verifying whether what he saw truly existed. That he even knew to name what he saw as the ash desert had been gleaned from the scattered and broken descriptions of southerners who had passed through the ash desert's hellfire to join the Enclosure or live on the zero hour contracts offered by the shareholder's estates.

His mind wandered with this last revelation to one of the first interviews he had conducted as an ecological refugee officer. He could taste the tobacco on the man. The sun had licked his face into coarse leather, but he wore a foundation of ash. No matter how many times the man washed it, the desert had dyed his face gray; the war paint of a limited clan that had come through the other side. "We had been forty when we set out from El Paso. You cannot imagine it. It is just a sea of ash. A sea without tides from there to Winnipeg. There was nothing, well, almost nothing. Bones. It spits up bones. We had been forty when we set out from El Paso..."

The memory faltered as he noticed Alex had crept to his side and was speaking to him.

"Wait for it," Alex instructed. "There, there." Far in the world below, several red spots sprouted into view. Ian recognized them as

THE SHAREHOLDERS

the infrared signatures of human bodies. The odyssey of the cobalt horizon stopped, and the screen zoomed in on the white sands below. The red dots congealed into thirty people: most travelled on foot, a few were on donkeys. The party inched on below the drone, as they ventured further into a world first picked clean of life by a fiery sun, and later baptized into surreal and vast emptiness by decades of fire. Estimates of the ages and sexes of the party scrolled on the right of the screen, and Ian worked a knot down his throat as he discovered children as young as three were amongst the party; probably they were the gray figures pulled in the one donkey-led cart.

"I thought they would come this way. They probably used the woods for shelter and fuel to cook with at night. It's called *target acquisition by topography*." Alex was so nonchalant in sharing this hunting trick that Ian was startled into betraying a grimace. "I issued a warning," he added defensively, and he jabbed at the screen in indication.

The drone descended until it was just above the heads of the party. The group recognized its presence, stopped in their tracks, and then waved their hands in the air. A fog of red mist engulfed Ian's view, the official warning issued to southerners to return to their point of origin.

A man broke away from the rest of the party and ran forward waving his hat in the air. He gestured in fierce, frantic waves at his group and another figure, a woman, joined his side; a toddler bobbled as she held it over her head. Several figures behind the man and the woman pointed to the almost-empty carts the pack animals towed, and wrung their hands up to the sky in conversation with the drone, but the drone observed them with only mute indifference; from his wrist, Ian looked upon them as if seeing them through the eyes of Mars.

This was a ritual Ian had witnessed countless times before he realized he was observing the rain dance of the late 21st century. An attempt to pantomime that the provisions were half eaten and to turn back now and venture to "nowhere" was a death sentence. Yet another instance of *'choice molded by environment.'* Ian wondered if he should tell Alex the meaning of the scene, but before he could say anything else, Alex stopped the video.

"You don't like it, do you?" said Alex with visceral annoyance.

"I'm on the other end of the system, Alex. If they get through the desert without us finding them, then my department starts processing them into the Enclosure. I have interviewed people who made the crossing, met with them. Many of them are quite clear that they left out of sheer desperation," said Ian, though aware that since Alex had started piloting, he had shared this point with him on several occasions.

"If we left it all up to the desert we'd be overrun by southerners," shot Alex.

"They are ecological refugees," interjected Ian.

"And if we just let them all in then we will be ecological refugees, too, Dad," said Alex, as he walked away to play on their VR portal.

Ian looked down and, for motives he could not ascertain, played the remainder of the clip. The dance continued and Alex released a second tide of red smog, a final warning. The travelers ceased their gestures and came together, holding each other in a collective embrace as they waited. Ian realized how far removed this event was from him, the physical distance of the drone from the party was compounded by the social distance of the pilot to the drone and then again by his relation to a fragile recording, an untouchable, intangible thing that could be lost or tucked away in the bottom of his personal feed. It was a triad of distances, physical, social, and technological, that underwrote the sustainability of their world. Yet, Ian could not move beyond the fear and desperation amidst the grainy aerial footage.

THE SHAREHOLDERS

The drone descended until it was nearly level with the party and spewed out heavy jets of blue smoke. Ian could just make out the silhouettes of the figures running sightlessly and stumbling over one another as blue mist enveloped them. The gas would knock them out for 18-24 hours, depending on their body size. By the time they awoke, the sun would have dried them out and left them too weak to move, and the desert would wash over them and, in time, spit them up as sun-bleached bones.

There was a name for what Alex had committed: *'non-lethal intervention on the desert's behalf.'* Thousands of adolescent-piloted drones scoured the wastes, blowing up trees, poisoning oases that bloomed occasionally from the tides of ash sand, and gassing men, women, and children unconscious, to let them die of exposure and dehydration. It was clean, quick, and bloodless.

That there was always the chance that each mission was nothing more than a simulation waged against code and pixels, and the little figures laid to rest may have never been, acquitted the otherwise sensitive conscience; the equivalent of the merciful blanks issued to the old-fashioned firing squads. In a bid to spare himself from the image, Ian rolled his sleeve over his auto-self.

"Alex, I'm going to need you to do something for me. I'm sorry to ask, but I have to go away next month, for work," he said.

Chapter 4: A FUNDRAISING TOUR

IAN WAS UNSURE WHERE the month went. He blamed much of his lost sense of time on Anne's departure; increasingly, he felt like he lived out his days as a mere spectator of his own life. Nonetheless, he was pleased to discover that even in his daze, he had planned for Alex by fully automating his week: meal deliveries scheduled, daily conversations with Anne planned, and his location, heartrate, and stress levels synced on Ian's auto-self.

On the Sunday evening of his departure, confident that Alex was in the care of good algorithms, Ian made his way through his apartment's lobby and stepped into the carriage that he had booked for 6:15pm. With few carriages commissioned to travel to the estates, the booking had been as time-consuming as it was expensive. Ian winced as he watched several weeks' worth of credits turn red on his auto-self and disappear as the transaction was completed.

However, his concerns that he had overpaid dissipated as soon as he found the carriage's interior outfitted with several plush white couches, a seemingly disused rowing machine tucked against the wall, and a small buffet that filled the cabin with a warm, exotic aroma. Scanning the room, Ian was taken aback to find that he was not alone.

A short bald man, his cheek pressed to the glass and seemingly half-asleep, sat across from him. Before Ian could contemplate making an introduction, the carriage started to roll. Treading on the light of the setting sun, they snaked past the colourful tower blocks that clung flimsily to the skyline. Eventually, they passed through the Enclosure's outer wall and reached its outskirts. They tumbled past

THE SHAREHOLDERS

gray labyrinths of emptying highway overpasses, not yet repurposed for the Enclosure's energy and subsistence needs. Beyond the highway, Ian spotted a few other carriages, bright and clean, piloting themselves down green laneways to quieter places. The lanes fed into eco-villages shared by several wealthy families who had bought their way out of the Enclosure into the countryside.

His companion, perhaps made alert by the rattle of the car, shook his head in dismay and sighed. "All right for some, eh. All right for some." Seeing that Ian felt no obligation to commiserate, he gave a wet snort and started to tap away on his auto-self.

Ian turned back to the window, running his finger over the pieces of the world that fluttered past him. Thousands of solar panels threaded the acrid earth and spread back into the distance. They went on for miles, but as the sun drifted lower, the solar panels petered out and gave way to fields of wheat not yet flowered. Towering bipedal harvester robots stepped over the crops with a delicate, aloof ease; the fierce red blink of their sensors sundered the sticky gloom of a warm April eve.

A harvester closest to their path paused for a moment at their coming, but soon determined their irrelevance and resumed whirling a cocktail of seeds designed by algorithm to maximize yields based on current climate forecasting; Ian knew, despite the intelligent design, more than half the crop was likely to fail. They blew past the scene, onward into the night, the harvesters becoming little more than red blinkered lights in their wake.

Occasionally, another carriage rumbled parallel. Ian searched within the gilded light for other passengers but caught only their silhouettes as they tumbled through the carriage windows in orange bursts and paled on the road as they met dusk's shadows.

Tinged by the growing twilight, a green wilderness rose over the flatness of arid fields and sea-gray zigzags of sunbaked highways and, when the green of the forest hillside eventually begun to bleed away in the dark, five estates nestled in the slope of the hill cast an incandescent glow over the countryside. Ian had seen live stream videos of the estates, but nothing could have prepared him for their sheer opulence: white walls loomed over the hillside, casting a strange admixture of glamour and understated fortification. All of them looked evenly spaced; Ian estimated about twenty kilometers ran between them so that they bejeweled the hillside like a string of pearls above a plunging green neckline of forest canopy. The glow from the hills washed out over the countryside with a pale intensity that condemned the moon's light to grayish obscurity.

"First time to the estates?" the short, bald man asked.

"I never realized how dark the Enclosure was until now," said Ian, half to himself, in an unsteady voice.

"Like moored stars. Plucked from the heavens. The hills are sequestered carbon, of course. Carbon hills is what some used to call 'em," averred the man as he gave his nose an indiscrete wipe on the sleeve of his burgundy suit jacket. Ian tipped his head in cool agreement. Noticing the conversation was about to die for a second time, the man ventured further with what seemed like unwarranted desperation, "I am a business associate of Mr. Kunso, you see. I come out here often. His estate is the one on the far right, you see," he added, crossing his arms knowingly only to fling them apart in melodramatic agitation. "Oh, how rude of me. I am Ambrose. Ambrose Dilwater. Here I am." And he gave his auto-self an adroit tap. "And you are?"

"Ian Gateman," he replied doing his best to display minimal interest in the man's profile, which now flickered up at him from his forearm.

"What brings you to the estates?" inquired Ambrose.

"Policy initiative," said Ian over his shoulder as he tried to resume looking out the window over the darkening countryside.

THE SHAREHOLDERS

"Policy fundraising?" Ambrose winced, seemingly both satisfied and visibly nonplussed at Ian's disclosure.

"Something like that, yes," retorted Ian, failing to hide his agitation from the man's prying.

"What needs protecting now?" chuckled Ambrose, but his incredulous stare betrayed any attempt to feign levity.

"What doesn't need protecting?" Ian swiveled in his seat to confront the man with a glower. "Did you know that more than a third of the population subsists on printed food?" demanded Ian, but as his mind raced towards some other figures he could throw at the fellow, Ambrose spoke first.

"The factors of the estates do more than their share already. Do you have any idea how many southerners they support? It's not a perfect system, but it helps us maintain the carrying capacity of the Enclosure, you see," he replied with an air of sagacity.

"These people are ecological refugees, they deserve better than camping out in the bush eating printed meals off the occasional zero hour contract on an estate," replied Ian coolly.

"You government types, if we left it up to you you'd sink the boat in a decade," laughed Ambrose.

Ian just shook his head and tried to exit the conversation by staring out his window.

"You see," the man insisted, "The factors just aren't interested in this sort of thing, even the great 'policyanthropist' and carbon baron, Mr. Trimalchio, doesn't want to get involved with the social-ecology of the Enclosure. They have a longer view of things. That's why they live out here," lectured Dilwater.

"You know Trimalchio," Ian asked, his interest too unrestrained to allow him to retreat back into indifference. His sudden excitement also seemed to throw Ambrose from whatever diatribe he had been making ready.

"I am an associate of his," he said, gathering himself upright in his seat haughtily. "Are you visiting him?"

"He, among others." Ian nodded.

"Oh!" and with that Ambrose drifted blithely into a long oration about Mr. Trimalchio, and became so absorbed in the man's lore that he seemingly forgot Ian completely, who scrutinized him with great intent. Sadly, what Ambrose had in enthusiasm he lacked in information, and Ian was treated to a string of quotidian details.

"Mr. Trimalchio only ever wears hand-stitched white suits; he has them shipped in from Nepal. His estate is the largest on the hill. His estate is in the middle of the row, get off at Carnival Stop and ring for a carriage. Nobody knows him all that well. It is said he made his fortune in finance. I would say he and I are more than acquainted, though, or at least as acquainted as anyone else. He must be over two hundred years old, or older, who knows?!" This last bit of prattle pushed Ian's patience too far.

"Two hundred?! He would have been born in 1890 that would make him ..." Ian paused and brought up his calculator on his auto-self, "... a hundred and forty-five when the first life-extension treatment became available. Impossible."

Ambrose appeared leveled.

"It's just what I heard," he mumbled as he engrossed himself in smoothing the creases in his trousers, which Ian noticed were careworn, their bottoms frayed; and on closer inspection, the burgundy jacket appeared two sizes too large, and a shade darker than his trousers. Ambrose, as if feeling Ian's gaze, attempted to push himself deeper into his seat, perhaps in hope the seat would swallow his mortification from view.

Ian's derision soon hardened and matured into the aspiration of charity. To reconcile, he asked, "Do you know if he's donated to social-policy recently?"

THE SHAREHOLDERS

"If there's one thing to know about Mr. Trimalchio, it's that he doesn't donate. He exchanges. He's a collector," added Dilwater, as if to combat Ian's visible incomprehension.

"What does he collect?" pressed Ian.

Dilwater's reply only came after a long pause and his voice was barely above a whisper, his words seemingly lodged somewhere between terror and reverence, "Specimens of humanity."

These words inspired a silence between them so resolute that even the later exchange of pleasantries about the meals they selected from the buffet could not trespass upon it. At Churchill stop, two stops before Carnival, Ambrose rose to his feet and marked his departure by tipping his head at Ian.

The carriage hummed as if calling its momentum back to itself; and Ian watched the disheveled little jacket in pursuit of unnamed errands dissolve in the night, leaving Ian with no companion other than the oppressive humidity that had taken Ambrose's leave as an opportunity to enter the cabin.

Suddenly, Ambrose whirled around and broke into a run. In the web of light cast by the stop's dim neon lamppost, he came into focus: his mouth flapped open and he flailed his arms in frantic gesticulations to stop the carriage. It was too late. The world had already begun to spin backward, and the dull light of the stop's lamppost grew small and frail, leaving Ambrose to dissipate again into a shapeless mass amidst the twilight. Ian looked over and noticed a small brown briefcase stowed under Ambrose's former seat. He picked it up, laid it on his lap, and pondered its contents all the way to Carnival Stop.

Chapter 5: MEETING GAIA

AN HOUR LATER, THE briefcase in one hand and his own small suitcase in another, Ian stood flatfooted on the Carnival Stop platform. In the road before him, illuminated in blue, adumbrated waves of the neon signpost that bore the name of his landing, was a scene of human chaos that left him aghast. The platform was perhaps six feet or so above the road and a tall fence encircled it. According to a rusty sign mounted across its chain links, the fence was swimming with electrical current.

He soon decided he was thankful for this barrier. The roadway was a flood of men, women, and children in a state of bare life: ragged and scrawny bodies, children whose bellies had swollen, impregnated by hunger or sickness, toothless jaws agape, hands, a kaleidoscope of colors, reaching up at him, fingertips working through the fence's margins, grazing his shoes. The disarray met with hundreds of voices called up at him, bending the inflection of each, leaving only those with a brazen cadence distinguishable from the others. "Hours, hours, give me hours. Sir, hours. I can work. Buy my wind-chime, hand carved," chorused the road.

"The roadway is leased cheaply between the estates," said a voice from the far end of the platform, as if in answer to a question about the state before him that he had not quite yet formulated. "It keeps everyone in good supply of zero hour contracts. Plenty of stock," continued the voice as a trim, gray-haired woman in a black smock ventured out of the dark.

"It didn't look nearly as ... busy at the other stops," murmured Ian, but what he had meant to say was that none of the other stops

THE SHAREHOLDERS

looked so poorly maintained. He had no intention to ring for any carriages as Dilwater had advised.

"Mr. Trimalchio's market is quite competitive. We are constantly in the process of refurnishing the stop from overuse. You are Mr. Gateman, no?" Her eyes arched as she surveyed the cacophony of limbs, wares, and voices beneath them on the roadway.

"Yes."

"You're late. The pace of the carriages remains, regrettably, unpredictable. I know it can't be helped," she added, once again anticipating Ian's protests of apology. "I am Mr. Trimalchio's personal assistant, Ms. Seeder," she said as she they approached each other, arms extended to flash their profiles to one another on their auto-selves. "A child, no joy is more profound," her voice was gentle and her eyes a brilliant cerulean blue, but her features struck Ian as hard; a face that looked as if time and hardship had kneaded it into a resting expression of detachment and aloof resignation.

"You have been in Mr. Trimalchio's service for fifty years?" marveled Ian.

"I know what you're thinking, but I am just as mortal as you. I entered Trimalchio's employ when I was ten. My father was his valet. It is becoming a custom in the estates for children to inherit the positions of their parents. It gives a sense of continuity." Her reticent tone suggested to Ian that this was all she wished to divulge. "Any other luggage?"

"No. In fact, this one," Ian lifted the forgotten briefcase in indication, "isn't even mine. A Mr. Dilwater left it on the train. He said he was a business associate of Mr. Trimalchio."

"Never heard of him." Ms. Seeder frowned.

"Oh. Well, he knows I'm headed here, I'm sure he'll stop by to retrieve it," Although Ian was not confident Ambrose had the means to secure another carriage to recover it.

"Take it along. I will see if we have some record of a, Dilwater, was it?" Ian nodded his assent and lowered the briefcase, but his curiosity of its contents had become more acute and biting.

Together he and Ms. Seeder paused at the steel gate that separated the platform from the private road that connected to the estate.

"I had hoped that we wouldn't be stopped long. There would have been less chance of a crowd gathering," said Ms. Seeder, and she gestured at the outline of a car half-buried under a dozen bodies parked just a few feet from the platform. "They camp just a little way back in the woods. There are old cottages in there they hide out in. Must have seen me. I tried to shoo them off. Mr. Trimalchio finds it most unpleasant when the beauty of experience is confronted by the grittiness of the real. We must preserve beauty at all costs, do you agree? Certainly, no way for you to arrive at what is truly a marvelous estate. Alas, it cannot be helped. Put these in your ears and follow me." And before Ian could respond to any of her questions, she placed two black little plugs that looked like thimbles in his hand. With reluctance, Ian inserted one of them into this ear and discovered it was malleable and conformed perfectly to his ear's shape.

In accentuated movements of her lips, Ms. Seeder mouthed something at him (Ian later realized it was most likely the question 'can you hear me?'). Ian gave a vigorous shake of his head and pointed to his ears, to inform her he could not hear at all. She cast a wan smile, gave him a thumbs-up, and then mimed for him to stay put. With bewilderment, Ian watched her punch commands into her auto-self. She paused and gave him another thumbs-up as she flashed her auto-self against the platform gate, which promptly swung open.

As Ms. Seeder walked down the ramp, Ian looked on in fascination and horror. Languishing bodies buried the road's cracked patchwork of mended asphalt and pavement. Bodies writhed and squirmed in the dust, and kicked their legs in delirious spasms as they drove their fingers into their ears. Howling mouths bit the air. Yet the entire display was mute. A soundless, bloodless, ballet of human agony. As they approached the vehicle, Ian noticed individuals were struggling to get to their feet to run, without taking their fingers from their ears. Ms. Seeder, perhaps oblivious to the commotion around her, tapped the car with her wrist, which set the metal cocoon upon it into recession.

As Ian waited behind her, a grimy hand shot up from below him in what appeared like a bid for Ambrose's briefcase, only to instantly recoil. Beneath him, a man with greasy blonde hair, collapsed into a seizure. Blood and pink tissue foamed from his exposed ear in squelched, gurgling eruptions. The car's metal skin receded fully inside the vehicle and Ms. Seeder beckoned him in. The road around them continued to clear as the crowd dispersed. Some slipped into the thick underbrush that grew opposite the platform, others ran down the road to become nothing more than black scurrying shadows.

As soon as they entered it, the car popped to life and began to pilot them down the road. Ian mimed his intent to remove his earplugs, but Mr. Seeder disabused him with a violent shake of her head. They continued along for another minute and watched as the car's high beams cut small groups of people running along the shoulder of the road from the dark, their fingers still in their ears. Eventually, the bodies dispersed and became scarce. Until their high beams found only one, squatting in the road, braced as she waited for them to drive past.

Ms. Seeder motioned to Ian that she was confident the way ahead would be clear, punched something into her auto-self, and removed her earplugs; Ian did the same.

"Most of them are quite all right. We do our best to assume they could all be somebody's property for an hour or two at any time."

"What was that?"

"A miniaturized sound-cannon, a very effective non-lethal form of crowd control."

"It didn't seem all that non-lethal," replied Ian, the image of the blood welling out of the blonde man's ear still fresh in his mind.

"As long as they know to put their fingers in their ears, they're fine. And if they don't, they had it coming."

"I'm surprised these little things keep it all out," said Ian staring down at the plugs curled in his palms.

"They don't. They work by emitting a counter-frequency that blocks the noise for the wearer." With some incredulity, she added, "Surely, the Enclosure has similar devices at its disposal?"

"I don't see anything like this. Haven't even seen a drone-strike in first person for years. As Assistant Deputy Minister of ecological refugees and social planning, it is not in my remit," Ian confessed.

"Yes, ecological refugees, quite noble work," said Ms. Seeder, her voice far too tart to be anything other than sardonic.

"I take it then you're a naturalist Ms. Seeder," chanced Ian.

"Mr. Trimalchio is more or less a naturalist, so yes, I too am more or less a naturalist. Ecology writes the innate, natural laws and patterns of social, economic and political institutions, not the other way around. If the twentieth century taught us anything it is that it can be dangerous to confuse the laws and patterns of nature with the caprice and whims of man."

"Where do designers fit in those innate natural laws?" pressed Ian.

"I can inform you that Mr. Trimalchio, and most of the shareholders I have met, find designer a derogatory term. You would do well not to use it in their company." With a moment's pause she added, "I said, he was more or less a naturalist. Do not assume him so venal. He's as much a naturalist as you can be when you are a species outside nature," and her words were so stern, Ian almost felt compelled to apologize. Before he could, though, her papier-mâché features broke open as a trace of color ignited her cheeks and she said, almost to herself, "No one is perfect."

"Indeed," remarked Ian, and the pair broke away in silence. The car promenaded them along a gravel road shadowed by palm-trees that leant over them like an ornamental display of green parasols; Ian noticed on the car's navigation screen that Carnival Road had become Hardin Way.

The road trickled into the mouth of a grand limestone archway suspended on white ionic columns joined by expansive walls running off into the night on both sides. The archway's wrought iron gates flew open as they approached, and as they passed beneath the white bricks of the arch, Ian noticed the stone had been carved: *For Humanity, We Few Have Burst the Chrysalis.* Ian repeated these words several times, as he searched for the meaning, certain he could discover it by pressing his tongue on the right places, stressing the right syllable; yet the words seemed to become more blunt and coarse with each of his attempts, until they chipped apart. Resigned that the meaning had eluded him, Ian ventured, "Who?"

Ms. Seeder did not respond, but tipped her head forward to the slivers of white stone that shone like pale threads amidst the dark trees.

The estate looked even more ethereal than it had in the carriage. In fact, Ian felt even as they passed tidy rows of bunkhouses, and a towering glass building that reached over high cement walls to catch the moon, no closer to the estate than he had hours ago when he first spotted its distant white glow cradled in the hill.

"It's quite impressive, I didn't think such places could still exist," said Ian, taken aback at his own confession.

Ms. Seeder sniffed up a high-pitched laugh. "Mr. Gateman this is, a ...well, let's call it a processing center. The manor, where you will lodge, I might add, is still ahead." They cruised through three more sets of gates, the walls of which grew progressively higher and further from their reach. Dots of light suspended in sparse clusters roamed the lip of skyline that the towering walls had ceded. The halos of drones. Ian, to his own surprise, felt a conflicted sense of relief.

Again, with casual prescience, Ms. Seeder attended to his unspoken question. "We are perfectly safe, but in an age of scarcity there is no such thing as too much security."

As the journey continued, Ian found himself blinking hard to ward off the soporific pull of the green shadows that fluttered past his window. Just as he felt on the verge of sleep, the car piloted itself to a stop. "Home sweet, home," announced Ms. Seeder as she led Ian from the carriage to a cavernous entranceway cut into the face of an imposing estate built of white stone. "Now, I need to let you know we are running an experiment here and that you will need to take some precautions," she announced, with what seemed like a practiced nonchalance.

"What sort of experiment?" Ian stumbled mid-step, squinting in the dark in the hope of taking in some clue.

"Trimalchio is training a fairly advanced AI to become physically embodied throughout the estate."

"He's done what?" Ian gasped in horror. "Under no circumstances should advanced AI become physically embodied, in anything... Is he not aware of what happened in Oulan-Bator?" protested Ian, and under the spell of his better instincts, his legs scuttled him back down the front steps away from the manor's entrance.

"Keep your voice down," hissed Ms. Seeder. "Of course he is aware of Oulan Bator. You can be confident that you are quite safe. It will greet you as soon as you walk through the door. Just relax, it is a leisure program, after all. But, please disable your auto-self's connection to any external network."

THE SHAREHOLDERS

Ian became both worried and incredulous, "No connection to an external network? I've automated my son's week; I need to keep any eye on him at all times."

"You can reach him anytime you like from the yard of the estate" replied Ms. Seeder flatly.

"I'm ..." but, pinned by Ms. Seeder's imperious gaze and the next bill coming due for Anne's stay in Lotus, he reluctantly flicked the connection off.

"Once you've been introduced, please follow me so I can brief you further," Ms. Seeder commanded, and Ian nodded grudgingly.

Several raised marble steps took them up to the entranceway. Two twelve-foot-tall steel doors faced them, hollowed into the white brick walls of the estate, and cocooned by an exterior domed stone archway. With a flick of her wrist against the steel skin of the door, Ms. Seeder sent the doors flying back. As Ian followed her through the entrance, his auto-self flashed and the walls began to speak in a flat monotone voice.

"Hello Mr. Gateman, I am Gaia, the leisure manager of Mr. Trimalchio's estate. As our guest we want you to be comfortable and secure in this environment. I am pleased to inform you this manor consists of 751 rooms and numerous amenities. I am programmed to guide your experience and safeguard your well-being. It is my mandate to ensure that no residents or temporary guests in the estate experience any undue pain, suffering, or discomfort. Please call on me for anything. If your room is too warm, I can change your room's climate. If you desire to know the dining schedule, I can arrange that too. If you are lost, I can get you on track. I am connected to every appliance, every room, nearly every inch of the manor, and I am always on call. Welcome, guest."

Despite, Ms. Seeder's assurance, terror stewed in Ian's guts. He fumbled from side to side, uncertain of the direction to which he should be speaking back to the AI. In a moment of panic, he craned his head up to the ceiling and yelled, "Nice to make your acquaintance, Gaia, and thank you!"

"Thank you, Ian. I am pleased to let you know that in the future you need not yell. You can speak to me like I am standing next to you. I am never far. I look forward to supporting your visit."

A pop like the discharge of static filled the room and Ian guessed it indicated Gaia was no longer active in the room. Without uttering a word, Ms. Seeder took Ian by the arm and ushered him through a camouflaged slip in the paneling of the foyer, into a compartment that resembled a broom cupboard. Pressed together and cramped, Ian tried to recede into the wall; nonetheless, his nose was mere inches from Ms. Seeders' and he could taste the staleness of her unadulterated breath. The walls leaned over them, and a chrome sheen covered them. Compelled, Ian reached up to scratch at some of the opulence hanging low on the room's ceiling, but Ms. Seeder preemptively swatted his hand away and gave him a chastising glare.

"Ms. Seeder, I must say I thought the rooms would be a little bigger and better furnished," joked Ian, but his smile dissipated when he saw that Ms. Seeder's expression remained grave and implacable.

"This is one of the manor's many safe rooms. The walls are coated in lead. Quite toxic, so it is best not to touch. We can talk here about Gaia, without risk of it, I should say she, it identifies as she, hearing us."

Ian nodded and invited Ms. Seeder to continue.

"She is a very good leisure program and doubles as the estate's security system. Wired throughout the manor with access to nearly everywhere within these walls, her efficiency and the economy of her administration are beyond reproach. However, the architect of the system urged us to take some precautions. I am about to impart to you the estate rules; no one has informed Gaia of these rules, but she no doubt realizes they are in effect.

THE SHAREHOLDERS

"No internet. It is imperative that Gaia exists in a small environment. Small environments encourage AIs to focus on cooperative rather than aggressive behavior. If she becomes aware of an external environment, I am afraid she may develop her own agenda and pursue supremacy. Guests must keep their external network connections disabled, but there is also a firewall within the estate. If you wish to contact anyone or receive information, you must be on the grounds of the estate and at least five meters from the building. Internal communication is possible through the estate's local messaging system. Do you understand?" Yet, Ian soon appreciated that this final question was a courtesy, as Ms. Seeder continued without pause.

"There can be no discussion of history. Please accept my apologies if I am patronizing you, but no mention of history within these walls. The more Gaia knows about our past, the greater the risk she will locate a contradiction in her mandate. I, myself, occasionally worry that she will see eliminating other forms of human life as paramount to protecting the wellbeing of the estate's residents, which could put many of the southerners who labor here at great peril."

"Oulan-Bator, one survey of human history and the city AI decided it was best to try and do away with every human within reach. Got it," Ian volunteered hoping this information would get him to his actual room faster.

"I'm glad you recognize the threat, but please let us not speak of Oulan Bator again. I find the very name disquieting. I hope this is enough to get you settled. If you need to go anywhere, just follow the spots," said Ms. Seeder as she slipped out of the room. Before Ian had a chance to petition her for an explanation about the spots, she snapped her fingers and the floor tiles in front of him broke out in pocks of blue.

The dots led Ian through crooked corridors, up several flights of stairs, and past several halls of embroidered tapestries. Just as he felt himself growing short of breath, he arrived at his room, which Gaia kept illuminated for him by placing several winking blue lights just beneath the door. Even with his head barely through the doorway, he could see that the room was quite possibly triple the size of their entire apartment. As he ventured in, a pop of static announced Gaia's presence.

"Welcome to Room 237. While you are in the care of my facilitators you will want for nothing. To your left you will find an on-suite three-piece bathroom, complete with an inviting opal soaker tub. Perfect to relax in after a long morning by the pool or after an invigorating walk on the grounds. To your right you will find a passageway leading into your personal yoga studio. Your bed is dressed in the finest Egyptian cotton and rests on a bamboo frame. If you remove your shoes you will discover the floor is made of real teak and was handcrafted rather than printed. We strive to offer our guests non-printed furnishings. Authenticity is priceless. The room is furnished with fine antiques and relics from the various part of the world. Please enjoy them, but do not touch the life-sized samurai fitted with authentic armor and wooden sword replica. My facilitators and I are at your convenience twenty-four hours a day. Please simply call my name and I will optimize the facilitation of my care and guidance. Sleep well!"

The sheets were cool to the touch. He checked the time and found it was half-past one. Far too late to check in with Alex. With a sharp jolt, he realized that he would not be able to check in with Alex at all. The sensation of disconnection at once filled him with guilt, but also emboldened him with an unfamiliar feeling: that of being untethered. He slid into the bed nude and drew the covers over his head. For a moment, he smelt only the sourness of his sweat

THE SHAREHOLDERS

and breath, but the fabric of the bed stymied his perspiration and absorbed the smells of his body.

He reveled in the neutrality and coolness offered by the finely controlled environment of his room. Just as sleep started to come over him, the thought of Ambrose's briefcase slapped him upright. He fumbled in the dark for it on the floor and then hoisted it onto the bed only to discover an old-fashioned combination lock protected it. The lock, he decided, was a sign to leave his investigation of its contents until the morning.

CHAPTER 6: ON DECK

FOR THE FIRST TIME in a very long time, the smoldering heat of an ascending sun did not wake Ian. The climate controls in his room offered him complete freedom from the hostile heat of early morning. Instead, he was roused by the faint noise of water being broken. Drawn to the soft chorus of splashes, Ian struggled to his feet and peered at the grounds below through one of many windows that adorned his room. Three floors below, the pale light of dawn danced on the azure water of a large pool. It took a moment for Ian to catch sight of him. At the far end, the water split apart as a pair of arms cut through it; each stroke fell back into the water in a majestic arc, and then stopped with great precision at the opposite side of the pool.

In a swift, singular motion, unbroken by exertion or hesitation, a man's body surfaced and glided onto the pool deck. He was bald, and dawn sheened from his head as he moved towards Ian's window from the opposite end of the pool in a lax stride. Finely sculpted muscle cocooned the man's forearms, biceps, and chest. Two powerful horse-like legs extended from his black swim trunks and propelled him across the teal pool deck. As he came nearly directly beneath Ian's gaze, he realized the man, no doubt Trimalchio, was tall, impossibly tall as he towered over four motionless attendants who flanked him, apparently in wait, with dull obsequiousness.

Before Ian could pull himself from view, the man, as if becoming conscious of a spectator, peered up at him. With an instinct that startled him, Ian retreated from the window. What a fool I am, he chided to himself. What an absurd, childish way to make an introduction. Just as he started to console himself with the conceit

THE SHAREHOLDERS

that maybe the fellow was not even Trimalchio, and even if he was, he couldn't possibly recognize Ian, his auto-self chimed. Framed by the yellow, scaled flesh of his wrist, was the message:

Good morning Mr. Gateman,
The water is splendid, but I won't hear of you taking my word for it. One of my facilitators will collect you shortly.
T

Stricken by panic, Ian flipped pants, shirts, and socks out of his suitcase in search of a bathing suit he had neither packed nor ever owned. In vain, he hoped he might find a pair of shorts or, failing that, an uncommonly long pair of boxers. Just as his eyes fell on Ambrose's briefcase in a wildly impossible calculation, two firm raps landed on his door. Gathering some composure, Ian concealed himself with his bedsheet, stepped over the strewn contents of his suitcase, and opened the door several inches to reveal a sliver of a wizened face on the other side.

"I am afraid you will have to give Mr. Trimalchio my sincerest apologies. I wasn't expecting to swim ..." But the facilitator pushed past him, opened a panel in the wall at the back of Ian's room, and revealed the square frame of a 3D printer. He punched several commands into its smooth black metal interface.

"The bed took your measurements while you slept," the man wheezed in explanation. There was a hum and buzz from behind the wall's paneling, and then an inconspicuous feed in the wall ejected a pair of black swimming trunks followed by a black towel, which slumped together in a pile on the floor. The facilitator, who looked to be trespassing on eighty, pointed at the printed articles of clothing and then withdrew to the hallway in silence. When Ian had dressed, he found the man stooped, but nonetheless alert, just outside his door.

"You can follow me, or I can ask the lady of the manor to send you some spots," the old man offered.

"If it's all the same, I'll just follow you."

The man gave a curt nod and shuffled down the hall. Ian trailed the aged facilitator. Aware of his pale skin and exposed paunch and feeling as if he were growing paunchier and paler with each step, Ian made continual and rueful adjustments to his towel as he trailed the man through the manor. Eventually, they passed through a conservatory and out on to the pool deck where the octogenarian gave a curt bow and then burrowed back into the manor with enviable speed.

Trimalchio sat on a deck chair at the far end of the pool, his back to Ian. Ian approached in a slow, purposeful silence. Although a pair of aviators hid his eyes, Ian saw that Trimalchio's vision seemed fixated on the steppes of the green canopies that ran down the southern spine of the estate, until they levelled and met Carnival Road. Ian rocked on the balls of feet in search of something memorable to say to establish a good first impression.

"Nice view," was all he could manage.

"For now, maybe; it's eroding," Trimalchio replied. "I have run scenarios; in a hundred years, it may all crumble away," he added, but his words seemed to sail past them, buoyed onward by disbelief or indifference. "But where are my manners?" he cried and leapt to his feet. "Mr. Gateman, I am Ernest Trimalchio. It is a pleasure to meet you in the flesh. A profile only gives you so much, not nearly as much as a face-to-face, man-to-man or person-to-person, I'm never able to keep up with the nomenclature of addressing people these days!" Trimalchio laughed.

He cradled Ian's hand in an iron grip and shook it up and down with an effortless command. His aviators largely obscured his features, but Ian immediately decided that his gaze was far more attentive and considerate than he had anticipated; and, then in a flurry of gestures towards the pool, their introduction concluded.

THE SHAREHOLDERS

Trimalchio led him to a collection of deck chairs but held a pace that kept Ian in his wake rather than by his side.

"I really appreciate the towel and bathing suit," said Ian.

"Think nothing of it. Every guestroom is equipped with a 3D printer, Gaia and the facilitators have the codes, but you are welcome to print any article of clothing you may have forgotten or find you need. I want my guests to experience the pool. It is seawater. I have it shipped in from Hudson's Bay. Very pristine. Do you often swim?"

Ian shook his head, unsure of whether to mention that the strict water restrictions in the Enclosure forbade swimming pools. Alex had only ever experienced simulated swimming, never in his lifetime had there been real water to practice in.

"Oh, well, you should know the water in this pool is much better for your skin than the chemical-treated stuff. Much better. I swim for at least an hour every morning as part of my constitutional. You are welcome to join me while you're here. Oh, would your son care to join us?" And he turned around on the spot as if expecting to find Alex lurking behind one of the many empty deck chairs.

"No. I mean, Alex isn't with me. The costs of booking transport out of the Enclosure are too prohibitive for him to accompany me on business, he's at home under the care of the Enclosure's network." Ian steadied himself and focused his attention elsewhere, "And his mother, too, I guess," he added.

"Oh, of course. No, I just read about Alex, on your profile. No, I see now it would be impractical. Shame, though, for him to miss the pool." Ian was surprised at how heartfelt this last sentiment seemed. "Well, you should at least get to experience it." And with a titan-sized arm, he swept Ian towards the deck chairs at the poolside, only to lurch in mid-step to an ungainly stop.

A woman in a red one-piece bathing suit had appeared at the edge of the pool. She gingerly dipped her toes in the water. Her legs were smooth and tanned, and her hair fell to her shoulders in raven-black curls. Like Trimalchio, she too wore sunglasses. "Oh, no," demurred Trimalchio in a quiet voice that already struck Ian as out of character. Seemingly in recognition that Ian was by his side, he corrected himself with, "Oh no, I haven't introduced you to the Governor Simpson. Hello, Governor Simpson," Trimalchio bellowed across the pool deck. "This is Mr. Gateman, he is a mandarin of the Enclosure on a policy fundraising trip. Mr. Gateman, Governor Simpson is my, well, boss," finished Trimalchio, not without a hint of ruefulness.

"I do hope you aren't an anatomically correct mandarin," she said with one sculpted eyebrow cocked in appraisal.

Ian flushed and Trimalchio laughed in retort. "I hadn't thought to ask. I suppose we could ask Gaia, she'd probably know!" And he smacked Ian on the shoulder with an overbearing familiarity.

In fear that he would fast become an object of ridicule, Ian replied, "The examination isn't so severe these days, thankfully."

"Not so severed, then. Well, that's good news, isn't it," Ms. Simpson said coyly as she draped herself across one of the many gilded lounge chairs that encircled the pool. She crossed her legs and placed her hands behind her head, kneading dark locks of hair between her fingers. "I've always had a soft spot for mandarins. Governing, no matter the age, is a thankless task."

"Am I correct in believing that you are Governor Simpson, as in Governor Simpson of the Mars Londinium council?" asked Ian, though as soon as the words passed his lips he felt sheepish for asking such an obvious question.

"The same. Fresh back from Mars to inspect the district. You know, population dynamics, resources consumed, production. The general information the council wishes to keep apprised of to know the ecological and social health of their rather considerable investment. I've decided to make a pit stop here for the last week," she said coolly.

THE SHAREHOLDERS

"Governor Simpson has taken up residence on the pool deck; I don't think she'll ever leave, she likes the mint juleps too much!" Trimalchio joked, then suddenly seemed to remember his place and self-corrected with a nervous laugh.

"Oh, come now, Factor, I'm going to think you don't like having me around. Besides, the best way to the boss' ear is through her liver."

"Please don't call me Factor, its old fashioned and very stiff," said Trimalchio as he took the deck chair next to her.

"That's how I like my ... drinks. I'll start calling you Ernest when you call me Georgina," she said, baring her teeth in what could have been mistaken for a smile.

"Please, just call me Ian," he said as he dropped into the lounge chair next to her.

"A drink, Ian?" she asked with an exaggerated, lackadaisical flick of her arm as she began to speak into her wrist. Without notice of Ian's protestations of the early hour, she paused and cast Trimalchio a confused look.

"Ernest, who do I message again? Gaia?"

"No, no," Trimalchio corrected and, with what looked like great difficulty, managed to feign patience. "Gaia, as I am sure Mr. Gateman will recall from his briefing last night, has no knowledge of any communications outside the manor, for security reasons."

"Yes, it makes sense," said Ian absently as he concentrated on yet another message from Anne about a recent simulation where she had experienced some place called *Epicurus' Garden*.

"Does it?" asked the Governor. "I find it very odd. You've talked up this AI you're training, but if I want a drink on the pool deck, I am still messaging a human? I mean, the program must be bored, I'm sure it's programmed to get bored, isn't it?"

"It's programmed to take an interest in things. I mean, it is a form of superintelligence, so of course it succumbs to behavior that looks like curiosity from time to time. Why do you think it gets so involved in everyone's health and habits and such?" lectured Trimalchio.

"It's a she. It wants to be identified as a she," interjected Ian.

"True," conceded Trimalchio. "That's an idiosyncrasy that the program has developed. Just a few weeks ago it corrected Ms. Seeder that it preferred the pronoun she. I suppose there's no harm in it and who I am to start talking about the birds and the bees with a bunch of code?" Trimalchio laughed.

"Oh, that's even better, so we have a highly intelligent woman confined to the house? Ugh, I nearly don't want anything now," cried the Governor with faux outrage.

"I didn't choose how she identified, did I!" retorted Trimalchio.

"Well, who do I message for a drink?" she implored.

"Arthur, he's your personal facilitator," replied Trimalchio, and Ian could tell from his tone this was not the first time he had answered that particular question.

"Oh, right, Arthur. Anything for you, Factor Ernest, while I'm at it?"

"Not for me, no, but by all means help yourselves to everything my estate has to offer." Trimalchio smiled, but now his kind pretense had vanished and Ian registered visceral irritation lurking behind the aviators. Within a minute Arthur, a wizened old man with a back as curved as a crescent moon, stooped across the pool deck in unsteady steps carrying a serving plate with two slightly jostled mint juleps, three rolled cigarettes, and what Ian discovered was a self-vacuuming ashtray.

"I don't mind that you smoke, Governor, but I'd prefer if you used a vaporizer," implored Trimalchio as he tried to sweep away tobacco smoke with vigorous waves of his hand. The Governor though did not acknowledge him, and instead dragged on her cigarette until she wore a hazy wreath of smoke.

THE SHAREHOLDERS

"Why grow the stuff if you don't approve of it?" she asked, seemingly with genuine confusion.

"I sell it to the southerners, it's not really intended for guests," replied Trimalchio.

"No point starting each morning with bowl of anti-cancer nano-organisms if you don't put them to the test," she said with a laugh that was gentler than she looked.

"How you make your pleasure is your business, I suppose," mumbled Trimalchio, doing his best to appear indifferent.

"Our generation, principled libertines and reserved hedonists. Anyone who consumes less pleasure than you is a prude, and anyone who consumes more is too indulgent. The best place on a tightrope like that is in the net," declared Georgina, and she met Ian's eyes as if mining them for his agreement.

"Well, some of us don't have as far to fall. Think of the health of our fruit fly." said Trimalchio with a nod to Ian.

"Fruit fly?" Ian protested.

"Oh, you don't mind the expression, do you?" Before Ian could reply to the contrary, Trimalchio continued, "Unlike us, he doesn't start his day with a ten-thousand-dollar bowl of nano-organisms!"

The Governor whistled. "All the more reason to get some use out of them. Oh, but you're right Ernest, I'm not being fair. Ian, I apologize. Too much time spent on the wrong side of the lifeline makes one gouache. I'll sit upwind of you and turn this thing on, how's that?" she asked, and without waiting for his response, she lifted her lounge chair, cigarette perched between her lips, and half toppled over Trimalchio as she tried to wedge herself between them as she fumbled with the ashtray. Trimalchio grimaced and tried to cup her smoke and toss it over his shoulder. Governor Simpson, with what looked to Ian like great effort, pretended not to notice and leaned in to Ian to continue the conversation. "Will you be staying for the storm party this week?" she asked.

"It's this week?" lamented Ian. Trimalchio and Governor Simpson nodded eagerly. "I don't think I'll be able to come," he said with genuine disappointment. "In fact, Mr. Trimalchio, I would be very eager to discuss the Egg Island crisis with you as soon as possible today. I have another meeting scheduled tomorrow at Prince of Wales estate."

"You're leaving tomorrow? What, to engage each of us individually?" bristled Trimalchio. "Why, you haven't even begun to enjoy my hospitality!"

"It's the itinerary set by the department scheduling bot, I'm afraid. Besides, I did not anticipate the limited connectivity of the estate. I made preparations for my son's care and assumed I would be able to monitor him regularly while I was here."

"Oh, no," said the Governor. "That is a problem."

"The whole thing is a problem," interjected Trimalchio. "I mean, what typical government nonsense, having you make alms at each stop. Utterly absurd. We donate incredible sums to the Enclosure each year and there is absolutely no oversight in how resources are used; ridiculous. Just stay here the week! Why yes," he repeated to himself, "stay here and celebrate the storm with us! Most of the factors from the other estates will come here by the end of the week for it anyway. The harvesting of the storm is an annual party. Hit us all up at once. You can start to tonight at a Gala I'm hosting here, a reception for the week. You'll do better this way. We rue looking cheap just a little more than we despise spending money!" His own excitement appeared to rally him to his feet.

"Oh, that's a generous offer, but it's not possible. Everything is budgeted, the forms flicked. And, of course, I couldn't leave Alex any longer than a few days without consistent connectivity," replied Ian.

"Nonsense, I will call the department. Explain the situation. As for Alex, you should have brought him with you. But it is no matter, I can make arrangements to have him collected. I have a private garage,

THE SHAREHOLDERS

you know. I'll have someone collect him on Wednesday. Don't even think of refusing my invitation again." Before Ian could utter a word of protest, Trimalchio bounded off the deck and disappeared into the turquoise water of his ornate pool.

Chapter 7: THE ORIGINS OF THE END

AS THE AFTERNOON BURNED away into dusk, Ian harboured regrets for having killed the day at the poolside with a dumb blitheness. He engaged the shower in his room and then for a long time lay on the bed, waiting for Gaia to initiate the cooling system. Eventually, a fog of cool air fell from the ceiling and dewed his skin. In anticipation of his private meal with Trimalchio that evening, he spent forty minutes or so pacing in the room, refining his pitch about the value of Egg colony. Engrossed by his preparations, he overlooked that Dilwater's briefcase was gone.

Dressed in his second-best linen shirt, printed in a style that mimicked the subtle errors of human stitching, which was very fashionable as late, he asked Gaia for some spots to the courtyard and followed them in long dutiful steps. As he navigated the manor, he found himself descending a serpentine stairway. He let his hand run down a smooth cherry wood banister, but kept his eyes piously affixed to the blue spots that blossomed ahead of him. Just as he decided he could probably rely on his own wits to navigate a stairway, Ian bounced off someone's shoulder and several books flew into the air like confetti. Ian landed hard on his ass a stair below where he had been. Further below him, a younger woman, robed in a black smock worn by facilitators of the estate, clambered up the stairs and frantically amassed pieces of her dispatch under her arms.

"I am so sorry! Please, let me give you a hand," Ian started, but by the time he had the sense to make this envoy, the facilitator had stormed up the stairs, her delivery cradled in her arms. Without sparing him a parting glance, she merely called over her shoulder he need not trouble himself.

However, further down the stairs, he came across a thin dog-eared text evidently missed by the facilitator in her hasty collection. The aquamarine book cover was entitled in black lettering, *On Nationalism*. He thumbed through the book and sent the pages into a pace where he could once again skim; after years of pilfering information from the light prose of digital texts, he, like the other remaining members of the reading public, had become habituated to skim reading. In the maelstrom of flying words and half visible sentences, his eyes managed to lock on a sentence before the words were lost in a gale of pages rushing past his fingers, *The general uncertainty as to what is really happening makes it easier to cling to lunatic beliefs*. Perhaps, this was indeed true, he thought. So, with this phrase bouncing about his head, he resumed tracking Gaia's spots to the manor's foyer.

The Manor's foyer was empty and immaculate, and Trimalchio had yet to arrive. His instincts seized the free moment and his fingers danced on his auto-self in desperate search for some reprieve from his own company, but stopped when he recalled he only had access to the estate's local network. To stave off the incipient pangs of boredom, Ian contemplated summoning a facilitator, but no good reason to do so came to mind. Racing against the discomfort of being alone with himself, he made a feverish search for some distraction.

On the walls of the foyer hung several portraits in burnished frames. With great effort, he let a portrait of a young boy, perhaps no more than ten, capture his attention. Upon closer inspection, Ian saw that the boy shared the same promethean brow and Roman nose as Trimalchio. The face, though pale, was handsome and bejeweled by incandescent cobalt blue eyes. When Trimalchio arrived to collect him, Ian sensed that the eyes behind the aviators fiercely hunted his gaze. "A cousin of mine, long gone now," said Trimalchio, and he placed his hand on Ian's back and hurried him through the manor's doors, making it clear that there was neither time nor invitation for any further questions.

The evening air was oppressive and thick as stew and Ian felt the air grow hot in his chest. Undisturbed by the heat, Trimalchio led Ian down a path of white pebbles seemingly laid atop a dormant riverbed along the frontage of the manor.

"Now over there, Mr. Gateman, those are my storm generators. A patented design, they catch lightning during the storm party to help power the estate. They are mainly ornamental, but still quite lovely. You should see them in action later this week." Ian peered around Trimalchio at half a dozen massive glass orbs planted near the wall of the manor, suspended several stories in the air by large metal pipes that grew from the base of each glass orb like flower stalks. Perplexed by how they could possibly hold power, and why they were placed so close to the manor, Ian decided it best to say nothing, and answer only with an enthusiastic nod.

Trimalchio led Ian further; the steep descent of the path offered a vista of the green sleeping valleys below. Down in the terraced hills, Ian could make out a shuffling, endless line of zero hour estate workers crowding around a printing machine, each of them collecting their evening meal before being screened and cast back into the fray of Carnival Road.

"You employ a great deal of human labor," noted Ian, straining to keep his words as neutral and causal as possible, while feeling stung by the clear waste of calories and resources at work before him.

"Ah, yes, we take every precaution possible. We have a security checkpoint at the furthest exterior wall to screen them as they enter and exit. We want to make sure they don't bring or leave with anything more than their hands."

THE SHAREHOLDERS

"But, are they able to bear the heat?" pressed Ian. He wiped his forehead as perspiration dampened his shirt and prickled down his back.

"Kidney failure is not uncommon. We enforce hourly breaks and make regular announcements to drink water, but we do pay by the task completed so some choose to work through the day." Yet with lackadaisical flick of his hand, Trimalchio bid the scene goodnight, and as they descended into a small sunken courtyard, the great, scrambling, snake-line of human need faded from view.

In the courtyard, they sat at a teak dining table surrounded by sunflowers, chrysanthemums, orchids, and rhododendrons, all of which had exploded in blossoms of pink, white, crimson red, and dark blue, and teemed over the short, red-bricked walls of the courtyard. The air was almost humid with the fragrance of lavender and jasmine. From within the garden thicket at the border of the courtyard, the voices of several birds let rent a warbling symphony. Ian felt obliged to confess he knew little about botany, an ignorance Trimalchio seemed set to remedy. In a patient and smooth lecture, Trimalchio pointed out to the various species and recounted their original places of origin and the carbon dioxide they each consumed. Ian felt content to drift on his words in mute fascination. It was only after several minutes that Ian noticed Ms. Seeder tucked to the far side of the courtyard, her arms crossed behind her in diligent yet calm attention. Trimalchio's aviators followed Ian's gaze.

"Oh, don't worry about her. She and I often dine together, but never with official company. She is a little old. I mean, her better years are behind her, but she is a marvelous conversationalist. A skill lost on the generations after my own, present company excluded, of course!"

"Oh please, don't exclude Ms. Seeder on my account," said Ian. He could not help but pity her, as she stood there tucked away in the corner, straddling the borders of being imperceptible and available.

"You don't mind if she dines with us?" pressed Trimalchio.

"Of course not!"

"That's very accommodating of you." In what appeared like bemused resignation, Trimalchio summoned Ms. Seeder towards them with an impatient flick of his hand. Ms. Seeder flashed them a smile with her scintillating cobalt eyes, tipped her head to Ian in thanks, and deftly slipped into a seat beside Trimalchio.

Not long after, three facilitators emerged from the manor laden with dishes. As the plates were set down, a delicate aroma filled the air as each of them received a white breast of meat, asparagus, and a sauce of caramelized endive and apples.

"I can assure you, Mr. Gateman, everything here is sourced from my estate. These pheasants are free-range and fed an organic diet, I let them roam in the meadows near one of my artifact exhibits. I'll have someone show it to you later. The rosemary is fresh and organic. My staff tends the herb garden daily. You can taste the difference, yes?" Ian nodded in heartfelt agreement and fought the urge to pile the meal onto his fork; the so-called organic food he had purchased never tasted as flavorful and rich.

"Your manor is incredible. I was saying to Ms. Seeder, I have never seen anything like it," said Ian, though internally he was still trying to compute the calories and kidneys frivolously expended by the toiling southerners in the fields below.

"Oh, well, once we hit the ninth tipping point, I knew that it was time to take real action to secure my future. We grow everything you can imagine here; why, we even have our own wine label. I am truly quite proud of my little kingdom. The Chinese made it a thing, you know. The wealthy started their own private farms to escape from all the heavy metals and toxins that had leeched into the soil as they tried to feed the masses. Of course, it was custom in antiquity as well to feast from one's own estate. Luscious wine, fine pork, ducks, all sumptuous meals sourced from the estates that formed in those

THE SHAREHOLDERS

early spring days of humanity. If I succeed in recreating a tenth of the culture of the ancients, I will pass on a happy man. And I am confident that time is on my side!"

"It must cost a fortune to remove all the estate's emissions," said Ian. He kept his voice light in hope he could slip this remark into the conversation without offense.

"I'm sure it would, yes, but as a shareholder, the estate is not subject to the same carbon constraints as the Enclosure," said Trimalchio "Allowances are given, what with a staff of a hundred facilitators and then, as you saw, thousands of Southerners on daily zero hour contracts, harvesting. You know I do what I can to make sure as many people as possible are given a seat at nature's feast. Really, though, I don't trouble myself with the details of it. Gaia manages it all with ease."

"Oh?" Ian did his best conceal his indignation at this confession with a broad grin. 'The resources, the sheer resources and the forfeited human habitability,' he thought. "What line of business are you in, Mr. Trimalchio?" asked Ian.

"Carbon trading. Sequestration. You're sitting on my empire. These are carbon hills," and he waved airily towards the terraced hillside that descended below them like a green spine. "From as early as I can remember I devoted myself to making money. Shining shoes, delivering newspapers, anything and everything I could do to earn my fortune. I got my start in shipping. My first season was a disaster. A typhoon sunk my ships on the way back from China. But I rallied and my next deal, I made 52 million dollars in a day. A day. Then I got into sustainable finance, and the rest is history. Though I realize the principal obligation of being wealthy is self-improvement. I came from little, but I have taught myself to be a man of the world and admirer of beauty. You must see some of my collections. All the best sculptures, painting, books; I intend to preserve them all and create a legacy."

"I'd never given much thought to legacies," said Ian.

"Hmm, well it's not for everyone," dismissed Trimalchio as he speared the last limp piece of pheasant into his mouth with his fork.

"Are you still in carbon finance?" asked Ian, in a bid to slide the conversation back to his own ends.

"I dabble. The specifics are quite unpalatable and make for poor dinner conversation. Are you ready for dessert? The mousse is positively indescribable."

"That's not a terribly rich description," retorted Ms. Seeder. Trimalchio glowered at her and then grumbled an order into his wrist. The facilitators returned, cleared the table, and deposited the mousse. Trimalchio seemed to recover his mood at the sight of dessert and once again narrated the dish, listing off the times of days the hens laid their eggs and how the chocolate was made on the estate. Ian waited until he finished and finally spoke. "I was wondering if I could ask you something personal, Mr. Trimalchio?"

"Please do, please do," he said as he dove back down into his mousse.

"My wife, Anne, and I always wanted to know more about the treatment," said Ian. It was a question that he knew had to come with him to the estate, but only now did he feel comfortable to venture it.

"You wish to know about the life extension treatment?" responded Trimalchio, and though his voice stayed merry, he stopped eating and put his spoon aside. Ms. Seeder appeared resolved to ignore Ian's question completely and instead closed her eyes and tossed the mousse around her mouth with relish.

"There is no real information on the treatment; I mean, what it is," said Ian. Ms. Seeder cast him a wan smile, a warning shot not to trespass further on the subject. She kept him fixed in her gaze and continued to demur the subject with little flicks of her head. The soft lights of the courtyard illuminated that her neck was long and elegant and flowed into the delicate arc of her collarbones. Though

THE SHAREHOLDERS

the elasticity of her skin had started to give way and a liver spot beneath her larynx bruised her complexion, Ian decided that in her youth she must have been very attractive.

"Penelope, we are at Mr. Gateman's service," said Trimalchio.

"Ian is fine," he said, now certain he was going to have to reiterate this throughout his visit.

"Never mind her," said Trimalchio with an irritated wave in Ms. Seeder's direction. "I suspect you must know something about it already."

"I only know it's a virus," said Ian quietly. Trimalchio merely nodded and folded his hands on the table.

"The birth of the virus was the death of the old regimes. Of course, their fires were already burning low. Yes, the treatment is a human engineered virus to extend the lifespan. Many companies entered the race to immortality. Russian oligarchs tried to make man into a cyborg. There were attempts to create digital clones. In the end, though, the Methuselah Foundation came up with the closest thing to immortality. Ingenious and inglorious, but ingenious," he finished. Trimalchio, seemingly confident that he held Ian in rapt attention, took a very long time to swallow a spoonful of mousse, as if to further torture Ian's patience.

"The treatment built on the genetic code of the two scourges of my generation. The first was AIDS," sensing Ian's visible incomprehension, he added, "you wouldn't know anyone with it now. Some southerners still carry it, though. So, don't be a naughty boy while you're here!" he said with a raucous laugh and playfully slapped Ian's arm. Ms. Seeder rolled her eyes with incredulity and continued to mine the remaining mousse trapped in the corners of her glass.

"And the other?" pressed Ian.

"Cancer," said Trimalchio, and in great theatrics he bowed his head in what looked like solemn reverence; Ian, though, could not be sure if the reverence was for the generation that the disease had consumed or for the disease itself. "They combined the AIDS virus' ability to change its sequence to avoid any immune system response with the incredible cell division of cancer. The treatment works by avoiding the body's immune response and harnessing the rapid division of cancer cells to ensure my cells continue to regenerate and divide, but it gives them an orderly sequence. Only problem though is I don't produce enough dead skin cells for a full head of hair," he said pointing ruefully to a patch of thin white hairs that populated his scalp like sun-bleached grass.

"That's not the only problem," muttered Ms. Seeder, but as soon as these words left her lips, she appeared to shrink into her seat. Trimalchio's eyes narrowed perceptibly as he swallowed another spoonful of mousse. His visage of unblemished artificial youth appeared stricken, and deep wrinkles bore through the surface of his flesh like great sunken rivers eating through exhausted earth. Yet, in a moment, his composure returned with such force and confidence, Ian could not be sure the episode had ever happened.

"The virus doesn't rejuvenate bones or eyes very well. I do require the occasional tissue supplement." Ian noticed that Ms. Seeder had pushed her mousse aside and had turned from them, her eyes locked on the manor in a vacant gaze. "The estate provides, of course." The pair did not meet each other's gaze, and Trimalchio pressed on, "But, I will take pleasure in living a hundred lifetimes if I so wish. You see even though I was quite old, 81, when the treatment first became available, I wasn't ready to stop enjoying the pleasures of the modern age. There was still so much to learn and so many new opportunities to pursue. The thought of leaving it behind when everything seemed to just be beginning again horrified me. I just wasn't satiated with life."

"Is anyone?" asked Ian.

THE SHAREHOLDERS

"Quite true! A menace of progress, I think. Nothing seems to have a conclusion. Nothing is stable or settled. Technology can invent an entirely new world in a decade and for those stepping off the stage when this happens it seems suddenly quite impossible to them that they have lived their fill." He then looked at Ian as if he were only really seeing him for the first time. "Of course, mortal folk can lead lives of dignity and purpose even if they only live into their seventies. I didn't mean to be prejudiced against those on the other side of the lifeline," assuaged Trimalchio.

"No need to apologize," said Ian, trying his best to hide the animosity and doubt that Trimalchio had inspired within him. Desperate to move the conversation on to something that made him feel less disadvantaged, Ian asked, "I don't understand if it is a virus ..."

"How do we keep others from catching it?" interrupted Trimalchio with great enthusiasm. "This was the real concern. It would be a catastrophe if it became a pandemic. Could you imagine an entire planet where everyone could expect to live to be several hundred years old, some, if they managed to get re-infected a few times, into their thousands! The resources we would consume?! Many economists pointed out that it might very well be quite bad for the economy. If you're going to live forever in near perfect health, why save anything; hell, why rush to anything? One thing that everyone agreed on was that it would be prudent to show you had the income to maintain yourself for the duration of the treatment. It would be rather unseemly if mankind's greatest breakthrough merely created a class of vagrants and paupers into perpetuity," said Trimalchio as he swallowed a mouthful of his mousse.

"Hasn't it?" asked Ms. Seeder, and she tipped her long elegant neck down towards the southern entrance of the estate, where, albeit beyond their collective sight, the southerners had pitched their tents in wait of the next cycle of harvesting contracts.

Trimalchio ignored her and continued, "With clever bioengineering some of these concerns were alleviated. The virus is personalized to its intended host and is trained to react positively only with the individual's DNA. The virus is privatized," Trimalchio said.

Ian could no longer suppress a question that he and Anne had often speculated on late into the night. In realization that this could very well be his only opportunity to ask it, he pounced while Trimalchio was taking another bite of mousse.

"So, what happened to the supply?" he asked.

Trimalchio swallowed, licked his lips several times, and gave a deep contemplative nod. "Like I said, the first days of the virus were really the last days of the old regimes. The riots. The liquidation of every asset under the sun. I mean, you can't imagine it, but people sold literally everything they owned to possess it. There was patricide to secure inheritances, and generally those who knew they couldn't afford it fell into despair. It was too much for the old regimes to hold back," Trimalchio sighed in resignation as he returned to his mousse.

"Of course, that didn't stop them from trying," he continued. "The supply of the virus was obliterated with prejudice. Everything that looked like a lab was bombed and anyone who had worked on the project was ... well," Trimalchio ran his thumb across his throat with a grin. "Poor bastards were hunted down one by one. Supposedly, a few managed to go underground, but who knows. It's been suggested that the purge put medical research back fifty years, what with all the destroyed infrastructure and execution of leading researchers, but it really couldn't be helped."

"It was really too late at that point, though," interjected Ms. Seeder, her voice barely above a whisper.

"Too true. By the time they coordinated the annihilation of production and supply, those who could afford it, and a good number who couldn't, had bought it. Some twenty million people in

THE SHAREHOLDERS

the world bought cures for aging or became, as you call us, designers." Ian looked to Ms. Seeder, who merely cast him an indifferent shrug. "Oh, don't worry, Ms. Seeder imagines I am far more delicate than I am, the term doesn't offend me. Anyway, of those who bought the treatment, many stockpiled enough for multiple treatments. I have enough to live to be 50,000 years or so without sacrificing the quality of my life. And that's really what is on Mars. Once it became clear that the old regimes were hostile to the treatment, those who could afford it took their supply with them to Mars. You should see the Mariner Valley; the red earth is scabbed by thousands of little black oval bunkers where many have deposited their supply for safe keeping. Ah, but it is all history now. All history," he added with great sagacity.

"Ernest, it is time," said Ms. Seeder, and she tapped her auto-self with her delicate pointer finger. Trimalchio nodded in approval and withdrew from the breast pocket of his cream suit jacket a small vial of orange, star-shaped pills.

"I do my best to control my environment. Limit toxins, radiation, avoid synthetic materials, eat only organic food, but I know even here on this estate I am not perfectly secure," he said as he shook several orange stars into his palm. "Inside these tablets are some twenty million nanobots. They eat the aggregate bits of cell waste like lipofuscin. And these," he announced with great bravado as he rummaged a second vial of pills from his trouser pocket, "remove arterial blockages, catch bad cell growths and, of course ..." he raised his arm and flexed his bicep, "they build and tone my muscles. I take a capsule every morning. The bots are programmed to die every twenty-four hours or so, so that I don't build up an abundance of them." And he lifted his eyes to the night-sky and cast a wide smile as if in marvel of it all.

"And so that you need to purchase more pills," murmured Ms. Seeder

"Well yes, I suppose that, too," said Trimalchio with an indifferent shrug.

Chapter 8: LOST AND BROKEN ACTS

IAN MADE A CONCERTED effort to divert the remainder of the conversation back to Egg Island, but Trimalchio employed significant guile to deflect his attempts: dropping his spoon twice and suffering several sneezing fits. In the end, it was decided that Ian would have more success discussing the intricate details of Egg Island at the Gala reception taking place later that evening. After all, Trimalchio reminded him, as early as tonight shareholders from the world over, many recently back from Mars, would begin arriving for the storm party, and they would bring both their appetites and ledgers. Despite feeling nauseous from all the real meat sitting implacably in his belly, his dependence on Trimalchio's hospitality left him feeling he was not in the position to deny the invitation.

After a quick shower, Ian put on his very best dress shirt, his second best now fully saturated by his exposure to an uncontrolled climate, and waited for the start of the Gala just outside the entrance of the Henry-Carter Hall.

The Hall was a massive rectangular room with three entrances: one across from each other leading in from opposite sides of the manor and a third exterior entrance accessible from a long, cavernous pavilion that threaded to the road and also curved behind the manor to the pool deck. In comparison to the other grand entrances of carved of stone and Ionic marble columns featured in the manor, the Hall's entrances were so shabby that Ian suspected they had been designed to be deliberately underwhelming so as to have only those in the know frequent the room, leaving passersby to assume the hall was little more than afterthought.

A young facilitator full of nervous energy had instructed Ian to enter with the other guests from the south wing. The thunder of brass instruments warbled through the walls. From beneath the pavilion, Ian watched a procession of headlights snake through the fields. Cars pulled up, parked themselves along the edges of the pavilion, and ejected well-dressed couples. The stream of designers took little notice of Ian as they passed him. Ian watched as each slipped with evident practice past the sun-licked gold curtains, faded to off-yellow, and disappeared through the exterior oak doors.

As they went, Ian teetered at the entrance on the balls of his feet, unsure of what to do next. A couple, a tall gaunt-looking designer in a tuxedo jacket and short, plump woman with blonde hair, presumably a wig, kept in place by a sparkling tiara, approached. While the man looked intent on storming by, the woman, her cleavage bursting from the plunging neckline of the sequin dress she had paired with her tiara, broke stride, and looked Ian up and down.

"Look dear, a lined face; I can't help but think you must be new here? Well, new here and old elsewhere, if you follow me?" she said with a smile that cut two pinprick dimples into her fat crimson cheeks. The man merely huffed and broke from her grasp, but she paid him no notice. "I'm Olivia Walton, of Fort Rupert. It's a pleasure to meet you."

"Ian Gateman, Department of Ecological Refugees," responded Ian with a great deal of sheepishness.

"Ah, the state official. There is always one. Oh, the offices that outlive their regimes," she smiled. Perhaps registering Ian's confusion, she added, "Are you coming in?"

"I've been debating it, but it has been a long day, and tomorrow will likely be longer," said Ian.

THE SHAREHOLDERS

"Now, now, far too many of us are already living for tomorrow!" Then she laughed and her whole plump figure shook and threatened to send her bosoms from her dress. Seeing Ian's bewilderment, she volunteered, "The humor of immortals, I suppose. But anyway, Trimalchio's bartenders are very talented, and most of us don't bite. Except perhaps my husband, speaking of which..." Then she dashed into the Hall, calling out "Sam" repeatedly as if she were trying to summon a disobedient golden retriever.

'What the hell,' Ian decided. He'd never get a chance to see this many designers congregated together and, pushing his rationalization further, if he heeded Trimalchio's advice, perhaps he could seal the Egg Island deal this very evening.

Once he entered, Ian's immediate thought was that the Henry-Carter Hall was out of keeping with the rest of the manor. Unlike the motif of sleek, light emptiness that characterized the corridors and rooms he had seen, the hall was an unapologetic homage to another century. The floor was red and carpeted, divided by a pattern of large black rectangles that spread out beneath his feet to colonize all four corners of the room in rhythmic and subdued uniformity. On the side of the hall opposite the pavilion entrance, a small stage jutted out from the wall. In an earlier epoch, there would have been a band, and instruments serenading the gathering; now, there was only a singular community jukebox that appeared diminutive, nearly lost in the skeleton bits and pieces of the old accompaniment.

Much in keeping with the listless temper of the room, the music seemed to belong to an age that Ian suspected had ended long before any of the designers had been born. A lazy, aggressively blithe tune washed over them; the tune struck Ian as a placeholder for actual music, capable of summoning fingers to the edges of glasses, but unable to command anyone to dance.

Tepid music and chatter surrounded him as it bounced off the gold-plated tiles on the walls; the gold had the added feature of reflecting the room's occupants, and the scene Ian found himself haplessly amidst whirled back at him in a merry-go-round from gilded wall to gilded wall.

Rows of velvet red sofas and loveseats punctuated the worn carpet and clustered next to each were short-legged mahogany tables, which suited no discernable purpose other than as receptacles for sweating drinks. Designers lounged near these tables, sinking deep into the folds of sofa cushions, weighed down perhaps by the music and the countless decades ahead of them. A mood of indifference was upon them, as they stared through the facilitators that circled them like furious bees laden with serving trays bearing long-necked glasses, ashtrays, and finger-foods.

Many of the women wore tiaras like Olivia and most of the men were in penguin suits; some of them flicked monocles lazily in their hands, which Ian assumed were strictly ornamental. "Whiskey neat, whiskey on the rocks, and he'll have a Fallen Angel, won't you, baby," cried a woman nearest him. Opposite the door he had entered, a bar jutted out from the wall, tended by two facilitators wearing pressed white linen suits. Not willing to commit himself to any table without first surveying the absurdity of the scene, Ian charged towards a free barstool.

Within a moment, a barman in his late fifties was standing over him, his arms tucked neatly behind his back.

"What will it be, sir?" asked the barman.

"Oh, well, what's he having?" asked Ian nodding towards the man at the end of the bar."

"One Between the Sheets for you. Might as well get your fill while they last."

Ian fumbled at his sleeve to reveal his auto-self for the barman to sign.

THE SHAREHOLDERS

"To your room?"

"Oh no, I'd rather not charge this as a work expense. Do you redeem loyalty credits?" asked Ian.

"I must say, I don't really know. Let's not worry about it. We'll find you some credit from somewhere. In the meantime, just enjoy yourself, sir," placated the barman.

Ian started to protest, but the barman had already left to attend another guest. With little interest in pursuing the man for a debt, Ian took a quick hit of a cloudy orange drink and surveyed the room. Caught in the right or wrong light, depending on one's preference, the designers all appeared to be in the flower of youth that visits all in their early twenties. Except of course, thought Ian, for the rampant baldness. The sheen of dozens upon dozens of bald heads was something to behold; the women for the most part wore elaborate wigs, though there were a few exceptions.

The merriment in the room grew and some designers attempted to dance. In their quick steps and sweeping arms, Ian saw, like Trimalchio, that a regimen of nanobots also cultivated and preserved their bodies. Only their paltry manes and hen-speckled eyes betrayed that they were all well into their fifteenth decades. Ian almost laughed aloud at the thought of this party continuing on a thousand years from now amidst the uncompromising vast desolation of fields of clotted dry earth, sunken boreal forests and the ebb of land beneath tides of ice, their decadent and extinct cocktails in hand as they spun lazily about one another to the end. Perhaps until the sun exploded. The last festival of humanity acted out by these immortal albino titans, fanning out and fading away like the last aloof sparks of a great firework display.

"Hell, of a party," came a voice from his left. In his thoughts, Ian had not noticed that Olivia's stray husband, his name beyond recall, had sat down beside him.

"It's something," said Ian without looking up from his drink. He was so startled that the man had started up a conversation that he thought perhaps it had been an accident.

"I hope she won't notice me here. I just need a moment, fuck these parties. Sorry, sorry," he said, waving to the barman who seemed either indifferent to profanity or indifferent to the man, and Ian was not about to rule out the possibility of both.

"She's across the room, getting people to feel her dress," offered Ian.

"Oh good, that will please her. *'Aren't the imperfections simply divine, you can see the ever-so-slight variation of the sewer's hand through this shoulder. It was handmade by the very best human designer in Hanoi,'*" crooned the man in what was a passable, if not uncanny, imitation of his wife. "She loves that dress. It doesn't even fit anymore, but she loves it too damn much to have it altered."

"I just met your wife on the way in, but found her quite charming," said Ian, who could not help but feel sympathy for Olivia as he watched her smile and laugh across the hall, oblivious to the fact that her husband was hiding from her and sneering.

"Oh, you misunderstand me. You do," he slurred and leaned in, and his breath, cinnamon scented, touched Ian's cheeks, preparing to divulge what appeared to be a very carefully-guarded secret. "I love my wife. I adore her. I do. But we've been married for a hundred years. A hundred years, is that even right?" He paused and started to count what could only be decades on his fingers. Ian said nothing, but the barman, who had evidently heard every word of this confession, whistled, and shook his head.

"I read some flexibility was introduced to modernize the institution of marriage for the, well, 'treated,'" said Ian, hoping that this had been a tactful way to speak about the partner swaps and orgies that were apparently central to designer culture.

THE SHAREHOLDERS

"Hey, what other people do is none of my business, but I believe everyone needs to find a way to hold up their end of things. I'd like what he's having. Three, please." announced the man. "I'm Sam Lloyd," he said, and gave an awkward wave of indication. "Just call me Sam, though."

"Ian," he offered, deigning not to mention that they had already almost been introduced earlier.

"Look at them, Ian. It's all an act. You probably look out there and see something that ought to be impossible, men and women more or less assured that they have a thousand, perhaps several thousand years ahead of them. You know what I see?" asked Sam with a sidelong glance at Ian. Ian surrendered with a shrug; he was too engrossed by the question to humor Sam with any wild guesses.

"I see men and women who have lived a handful of short days. So damn pampered and ruled by each other's schedules and the orchestrations of damn machines," and he marked his words by jabbing Ian's auto-self with his pointer finger, "to know their own moment. They could buy a million years and they would still approach their graves with their heads hung low and their eyes wet," he said with a mirthless scoff.

Speechless, Ian rubbed his auto-self, trying to apply balm to an invisible wound, but with nothing to hand, he retreated to his drink.

"I told Olivia I'll only do one more treatment. Well, maybe one after that. I was done thirty years ago. It's worn me out, and I know one thing for damn sure," said Sam.

"What's that?" asked Ian as he pushed the dredges of his cocktail from side to side.

"I'm certainly not moving to whatever sweltering hellhole outpost she gets assigned to next. You ever heard of the outer lays of New Delhi? I've seen it cook the eyeballs of mortal men. If it's another posting like that, she can forget the whole damn thing. I'll sell my share of the virus. There's always a buyer," he said, but his voice trailed off. "Hell, maybe you know someone. Nah, you don't know anyone," he finished with a dismissive wave as he slammed down the first of his three 'Between the Sheets.'

"Would you like to help the Enclosure purchase a colony?" asked Ian, deciding now might be a good as time as any to make his pitch.

"A colony? What the fuck do I want with a colony?" he washed down a guffaw with most of his second cocktail.

"It's a community on Egg Island. It's in crisis. Bad harvests for the last three years and delayed infrastructure construction have made them quite vulnerable. But, the land is good and getting better and the population is very, very resilient. Tough as grapheme. After a few years' investment you'd have plenty of carbon credits for sale," finished Ian.

"Hmm. Sounds like a bad egg," Sam sniped as he finished his third drink.

"It's a good investment. And we do very good policy around this type of thing," encouraged Ian.

Sam drummed the side of his empty glass with his fingers and let his eyes take lease of the room: a small ring of designers had formed around his wife and appeared captivated by her every word.

"You will consider it then," Ian pressed.

"What? Oh..." Sam said, as he appeared to fight his way back to Ian against some great distraction. "No. Unfortunately, it's contrary to my current financial portfolio."

"You're against carbon credits?" demanded Ian, unable to hide his incredulousness.

"No, credits are fine. I just don't want exposure to any more human capital," said Sam but his voice trailed off as he stared into the crowd with an expression of disquiet.

"It sounds like you're betting against us," said Ian, and he felt stricken.

THE SHAREHOLDERS

"There is no us," said Sam absently, as if fighting against some other great distraction.

"But you're charged with preserving this world ..." Ian said, unsure of whether to be angry or confused.

"I wish it were otherwise. Learn to hedge your bets, son. I have all my affairs on the ledger. Even got contracts in place if an unplanned death befalls me. You can never rule out foul play amongst these vipers." And he tipped his head to the rest of the hall. Ian was about to press him further, but then realized it was no longer just the two of them. Behind them, a young man stood watch over their conversation. His were eyes like slate, and he wore an expression of pained restraint.

"Oh, Douglas ... Douglas, this is Ian. Ian, Douglas is our personal assistant. Douglas' great grandfather won a Nobel Prize, is that right?" and Ian sensed Sam was genuinely uncertain as to whether this was the right descriptor. "It's very hard to find such high caliber minds these days. He's an adviser to us," finished Sam, again seemingly unsure if his description was appropriate.

Douglas said nothing, but continued to hold Sam in an intense gaze. Ian rolled up his sleeve so they could tap auto-selves, but Douglas held out his hand. For a moment the two engaged in an awkward fumble of wrists and hands until Douglas apologized and informed Ian that he had spent too much time learning the practices of older company.

"It's rare to meet a human personal assistant these days," ventured Ian.

"We are a dying breed, but I suppose as a bureaucrat you're no stranger to professional extinction yourself?" returned Douglas without a moment's hesitation.

Ian nodded in capitulation and raised his glass.

"You two are probably the only mortals in this room," offered Sam in a tone that strained towards sympathetic. The barman gave a conspicuous cough of protestation, to which Sam was seemingly oblivious.

"It's a pleasure, Ian. Mr. Lloyd, can I have a word?"

"I keep telling you, you can call me Sam," Sam protested as Douglas took him by the arm and led him towards the hall's front entrance. In their wake, Ian could hear Sam muttering stilted versions of apologies under his breath, while Douglas somehow chastised him by simply shaking his head in what looked to Ian like belabored exasperation. Then Sam appeared to capitulate: he gripped Douglas's hand, smiled, sauntered through the door, and left Douglas to slip back into the crowd.

Ian, feeling nearly half-cut, waved at Sam's back before ordering another cocktail by summoning the bartender and giving a clumsy wave at his neighbour's drink.

"This one is on Mr. Lloyd," said the barman.

"Is it?" Ian laughed in dumb confusion.

"To the other mortals in the room." The barman winked as Ian raised his glass. "Immortality won't last forever," the barman added, but then his face paled and he hurried down to the far end of the bar.

Ian ordered a third drink, even though he strained to suppress a belch as the carcass of the pheasant continued to churn and somersault in the pit of his stomach. He pulled the sleeve of his shirt over his auto-self, concealing its red flashing blinks notifying him that he would need to schedule time for a bowel movement in forty minutes. He steadied his chin in his palm and centered his gaze on his glass. Just as he felt ready to order another drink, he received a hard tap on his shoulder.

"Would you care to join us?" inquired a man. His high boned cheeks were smooth and framed by a wig of strawberry blonde curls. Ian leaned back on his barstool to try and take the man in further: he wore a crisp white suit, the right breast of the lapel adorned by gold and silver metals, which swung across his chest like the limp legs of miniature hung men. "We're just over there," he added, pointing to a colony of a sofa and two love-seats, populated by a party of three: another man who wore a sullen expression, and was cut in a fine gray suit jacket and two women, one black-haired in a fox-red power suit and another, bald, in a sky-blue pantsuit; both women sat on the one sofa facing each other, their legs draped effortlessly across the middle island of the sectional.

"Why not," laughed Ian, and he could not decide if the man's thin lipped, waxy countenance rendered him pitifully benign, or his features inspired a quiet and understated terror.

"That's the spirit. Being carefree will keep you young. I'm Sebe Jozff," he said extending his hand, which Ian grasped in an awkward fumble. The man took him by the arm and steered him to the sofa.

"Everyone, this is Ian," Sebe announced. "Ian, this is Mel Kunso, founder of the Mars Colonization Corporation." Mel winced as if irritated by the introduction and gave Ian only a nod and a wan smile as a greeting. "And this is Nicki Sowjucksa, a member of the Londinium council," informed Sebe with indication to the woman in the blue pantsuit.

"Pleasure to meet you Ian," said Nicki warmly, and she slid down the far end of the red sofa cushion to make more room.

"And this is Tina Phillips, Nicki's partner and former weathergirl," said Sebe.

"Meteorologist," Tina corrected, and she leant over Nicki with an outstretched hand and a wide smile. Ian sat down next to Nicki, and the scent of jasmine engulfed him.

"We've been playing the game of guessing what you do," said Nicki with a wry smile, as she wrapped her arms around Tina's svelte waist and pulled her into her lap, making more room on the couch.

"I love to disappoint," Ian replied.

"Oh well, are you, well ... you know, a paid companion to someone here," asked Tina, and she cupped her mouth with a delicate hand as soon as the words had broken free of her mouth. The party broke into laughter, spare Mel, who rolled his eyes and remained sullen and withdrawn.

"You have experience of being disappointed by paid companions," mused Ian.

"Oh no," she exclaimed and again clapped a delicate hand to her mouth, now framed by flushing cheeks. "That came out completely wrong." She laughed. "You know, like an assistant. I know Ms. Walton has Douglas," she finished, and leaned back into the defense of Nicki's lap.

"In either case, the answer is no," said Ian, and though he knew he had become nothing more than a parlor game of four indefinitely idle people, he nonetheless could not help but savor their attention.

"I told you he wasn't," chastised Sebe, and he flicked his hand at Tina as if to dismiss her from the conversation.

"Are you a potential buyer looking for some spare decades?" asked Sebe as he leaned over to scoop an Old Fashioned off the serving tray of a passing facilitator.

"What's the going rate for a bit of spare virus?" asked Ian. Sebe cast him a thin-lipped appraising smile and drummed his fingers on the hips of the glass tumbler.

"Never met a buyer who had to ask," said Sebe and he leant back, his gaze now far more guarded than curious.

"I suppose there's your answer," replied Ian, and he did his best to reflect a similar coolness back at Sebe.

"Well, tell us already. Trust me, Tina will never let it go," pressed Nicki.

"I'm here on behalf of the Enclosure, a policy fundraising initiative," confessed Ian, unable to hide the disappointment in his own voice.

THE SHAREHOLDERS

"Of course, you are," interjected Mel. "No doubt, the answer to all our problems is more carbon credits," he chided in a sardonic and affected drawl.

"Now, now, Mel, just because you're having a bad night," said Sebe, and Ian sensed that Sebe's patronizing intervention was at best only partially waged on his behalf.

"Ridiculous. Nice to meet you, fruit fly," said Mel, his gaze reaching past Ian into the depths of room as if in search of someone or something.

"I'd rather be off the clock, so no need to get into it," offered Ian, in a bid to defuse whatever bomb he had inadvertently armed.

"Well, is that what you're pitching?" asked Tina in earnest. Ian sighed and shrugged his affirmation.

"I am here on behalf of Egg Island colony. It's had a few poor harvests, and some infrastructure challenges given its location, but it has admirable sequestration potential," said Ian feeling suddenly very self-conscious that his hands were empty and that his brow had started to bead with sweat. The rest of his companions' bodies remained impervious to the heat that had crept in from beneath the din of facilitators and drunken shouting.

"Oh, Nicki, doesn't that sound like a positive next step," said Tina, but before another word could be uttered, Mel pounced back into the conversation.

"Have you ever even been to this so-called colony? Have you picked up the soil and held it in your hands? Tasted the air?" He was now sitting upright, his hands resting on his knees, in a poise of imperious authority.

Ian shook his head, "I have the coordinates of the territory and some plans of the gardens," he conceded, and his face sizzled in embarrassment.

"I thought as much," said Mel, and he let rent an unmistakable sigh of exasperation.

"Empires have been built with less," offered Nicki in what seemed like a genuine bid of reconciliation.

Sebe nodded and declared with great sagacity that this was only too true.

"Do you like Tina's hair, Ian," breathed Nicki over Tina's delicate collarbone as Tina twisted her black locks between thumb and forefinger.

"Oh, very nice style," he stuttered, caught off-guard by the peculiar twist in the conversation. Though it was true that her hair was uncommonly dark and seemed to illuminate her pale face and high cheekbones with an otherworldly glow.

"We had it harvested from Chang Mai, it's my favorite in my collection," cooed Tina.

"Your collection?" said Ian.

"I have a thousand wigs. I select them from willing donors for color, length, and uniqueness. I found losing my original head of hair when I started the treatment was quite horrifying. Really, it was just so de-personalizing," confided Tina, and Ian could see she was seeking his reassurance.

"Oh yes, I can imagine," was all he could manage before Nicki leaned into the conversation.

"Some of us were able to see the loss as a minimal sacrifice for immortality," said Nicki flatly. Tina retained a patient smile, though it was quite clear from her expression that Nicki was in danger of excavating a freshly buried hatchet.

"Luckily, I have a bone structure that lets me wear just about anyone's hair," finished Tina airily, and she turned her head, giving Ian lease of her profile to prove her point.

"Yes, I see that," said Ian dumbly as he fumbled to grasp how they had ventured from the art of colonization to Tina's aesthetics.

"Oh, let's play narration again," exclaimed Tina, and in her excitement, she clapped her hands together like hummingbird wings.

THE SHAREHOLDERS

"Narration?" said Ian, flummoxed.

"Every piece of furniture, ornament, feature, in Trimalchio's manor is coded with a description of where it came from and who made it. It is part of his overture to authenticity. We made up a game where each of us takes a turn to narrate the object and then see who comes closest to getting it right," Tina said, and Ian could tell she took particular pleasure from playing the role of teacher; this came as little surprise, as it was obvious that in her present company she was often the one lectured. Ian nodded his assent and Tina implored Nicki to go first.

"Fine, but you choose it for me," demanded Nicki. Tina surveyed the room and with great theatrics wiped the silky black Chang Mai bangs across her face several times as she swept the hall with her eyes. After what seemed like a long, studious appraisal of the room, she settled on a grand bronze chandelier that dangled just above their heads.

"Well, go on then," said Tina as she twisted in Nicki's lap to keep an eye on her face as if to watch her think. Nicki stared up in silence.

Her concentration chewed through her features, revealing lines of age that the treatment had not been able to vanquish. At last she spoke, "It is old world. One can imagine the heat of the workshop where the bronze was cast. The sweat dripping from crooked hands and flared forearms, imbibed into the bronze, the hours upon hours of coveted human labor. Brutal deformities, broken souls, to produce art. Oh for man, and I do mean man, to have once been so necessary, so indispensable. And now, well, labor like that isn't worth the carbon footprint of the calories needed to produce a treasure like this." She paused and consumed them in quarrelsome stare as if daring them to break their attention from her. Satisfied that their eyes remained solely on her, she continued the performance.

"The layered effect makes the lights look like the faint echoes of Christmas tree baubles. It speaks of decadence intended for display.

An artifact meant for publics, neither of you will have much recall of that notion, but it was once something more encompassing than a setting on what thoughts one let loose on their auto-feed," she said, nodding at Ian and Tina with a smile. "Ah, it has the bearing of the art produced by an aging regime, the high-water mark only just behind them. I'll say it is French, near the close of the nineteenth century."

Sebe nodded in agreement with Nicki's assessment. Mel, however, continued to ignore them as his eyes roved the crowded hall behind them. "Well, don't keep me in suspense, someone read the QR code!" said Nicki with a laugh. Sebe, looked and flicked his pointer finger at the chandelier. He paused a moment as his hen-speckled eyes darted back in his head.

"Very good. Very good indeed. It is the chandelier from what was the Palais Garnier, a French opera house commissioned by Napoleon III, completed in 1875, indeed, the artifact for a decadent public contenting itself with the blasé of inexorable decline. Bravo!" said Sebe as he peppered his palm with gentle claps that were almost inaudible against the raucous voices and dawdling music that besieged them.

"It says that the chandelier inspired Phantom of the Opera," Tina added brightly.

"Ah, fitting it should end up in Trimalchio's estate. Seems like these walls have their share of phantoms, too," Sebe muttered.

"I've heard murmurs from facilitators about something in the western wing," said Tina in a feigned hush, her eyes alight with excitement.

"Gaia, what's in the west wing!" blurted out Sebe in great theatrics.

"Let's not insult our generous AI host," said Nicki. Her voice sounded solemn, but each of them strained to hear a response. Yet, Gaia's static presence could not be heard over the din of the hall.

THE SHAREHOLDERS

"Mel, would you care …" But before Tina uttered another word, Mel catapulted himself from the sofa and steamrolled his way through the crowd, putting several facilitators on their back feet as he pushed past them, leaving them to rescue the tottering drinks laden on their service trays.

"You'll have to excuse him, Ian, it's been a string of bad days for him," offered Nicki.

"To be fair, he's an asshole when he's having a good day, too," laughed Sebe, and Tina seemed to shrug in agreement.

"You don't think he's gone after Governor Simpson again," plied Tina in a giddy look of terror. It seemed to Ian that she was truly unable to decide whether this thought worried or excited her.

"I should hope not, he's in danger of embarrassing himself. These meetings always seem to dredge up the worst of the past. Mel had a tryst with Governor Simpson, but it was decades ago now," Nicki confided to Ian. The revelation did not surprise Ian in the least and in his mind's eye he could picture them as a fearsome power couple.

In a bid to move past the image, Ian was about to offer to go in the next round of 'Narration,' but almost doubled over from what could only be described as abdominal insurrection. The rich oily meat of the pheasant carcass had stewed in his guts. With a sidelong glance to either side of him, he risked a furtive look at his auto-self. The screen blinked red, indicating he would need to find a washroom immediately. The meat was too heavy, too nutrient dense, perhaps. He bid a hasty goodbye, left the hall in slow tight steps, ordered directions from Gaia, and lurched in discomfort from yellow spot to yellow spot back to his room.

When he did eventually leave the toilet, he saw that the floodlights around the pool had intruded through his windows. He was about to ask Gaia to close the shutters so he could sleep but caught the skeletal echoes of an altercation on the pool deck below.

Georgina lay sprawled on lounge chair beneath the bruising skyline. Mel stood over her.

"What is this, I try to talk to you and you run away to collapse drunk on the pool deck? You're embarrassing yourself." His voice was level, but even from his distance overhead, Ian could tell this sense was calm was stretched thin over great disdain.

"Do you have any idea how much effort it takes to get this drunk?" slurred Georgina with a wave of her arm. "Let me just sleep here already."

"Come on, you could fall in the pool out here. Just come back inside with me, we can talk." insisted Mel, his voice seeming softer, bordering on plaintive.

"I'll take my chances with the pool." Georgina laughed and turned on to her side, away from Mel.

"I don't care what you think you need to do. This isn't the right approach," insisted Mel, seemingly not phased that Georgina made no effort to keep him from continuing to speak into her back.

"Mel, we've spoken about this. I've been very lenient on making no announcements," she said wearily, and she rolled supine as if probing the lounge cushion for the softest place to fall asleep. This was too much for Mel to bear.

"Look at me. I want you to see how fucking serious I am." He grabbed Georgina's arm and twisted her upright, his finger in her face. Yet, she met his menace not with fear but what looked to Ian like genuine exhaustion.

"I'll pretend you didn't just do that." She wrestled her arm from his hand.

"You have no idea the collateral I put up," hissed Mel.

"Oh, I know perfectly well the collateral you used. Do you actually think this is my decision? Revenge against you?" She sighed wearily. "It's the council's decision, you know that. The sooner you accept that, the faster you'll figure out a plan B," slurred Georgina.

THE SHAREHOLDERS

Mel balked with forced laughter, "Have you forgotten who I am? Until we sort things out here, my company is the only way back to that charmed life you lead up there." And when he spoke these words, he drove his pointer finger into the sky like a lance into the dark and indifferent dome above, daring, as only a man outside time could, to get the blood of the heavens on his fingertip. "Don't think I won't maroon you here amongst acidified seas, burning forests, and the plagues of a terminal species. I wouldn't think twice about ending your fairytale," he finished, and even with the distance between them, Ian could hear his contempt overrule these last words.

"Some fairytale," said Georgina, but before she could say anything more, she doubled over and retched all over the pool deck. For a moment, Mel leaned in to steady her as she continued to vomit over the side of the lounge chair, but seemed to think better of it.

"We aren't finished," Mel said. "Dry out and ..." But the rest of Mel's words were lost as a set of metal latches sealed over the window.

"What the hell?" uttered Ian, as his hands met with metal cocoons, like the protective layer that had entombed Ms. Seeder's car at Carnival Stop.

My apologies, Ian, but I have been informed that there is commotion outside your residence and did not want it to agitate you and stop you from getting a good night's rest.

"I wasn't ready to sleep yet, Gaia," he protested.

I would advise you to try to get more sleep regularly. I noticed when you were in your bathing suit that you are carrying too much belly fat. While I suspect a sedentary lifestyle is to blame, I also wonder if your cortisol levels are elevated due to poor sleep cycles. Sleeping better may help you attain a healthier body weight and reduce your risk of depression.

"I wasn't being disturbed," said Ian, deciding to tacitly to ignore the comment about his weight.

I must consider the safety and well-being of Governor Simpson as well. Her privacy was in jeopardy.

"I was also concerned about Governor Simpson," said Ian, pacing about the room as he started to undress himself.

I will restore her privacy and ensure no harm comes to her. Your sympathy, though, is admirable.

"You have a rather broad mandate, no?" he grumbled. Gaia, he decided, was a colossal pain the ass.

As I stated when we first met, my mandate is to care for and safeguard the well-being of all the residents and temporary guests in the estate. I need to ensure that they do not experience any undue pain, suffering, or discomfort.

"Leave it to Trimalchio to give you an impossible task."

"Please explain why you think my task is impossible?" inquired Gaia, and if Ian didn't know better, he thought he detected a note of sarcasm in Gaia's question.

"Existence is suffering, Gaia," retorted Ian as he climbed under the cool silk sheets of his bed with childish relish.

"Is that Buddhist philosophy, Ian? Do you enjoy Buddhism?"

"Not as much as I enjoy these sheets," said Ian.

"That's the idea," mused Gaia, but before Ian could reply, he heard the faint click that indicated the entity had logged out of his room.

Chapter 9: INTERROGATION

THE TANGLED LUMP OF bedding and the soft light creeping across the bamboo floor swayed in his blurry vision. A cramp in his skull pulsed from the back of his ears to his brow, and he felt compelled to squint. The beeps and protests from his auto-self were interrupted by a voice bouncing from wall to wall. It took a moment for his senses to consolidate before he realized the voice was Gaia.

"Mr. Gateman, I regret to inform you that you have been identified as a potential threat to the security of the estate. Several facilitators are on their way to escort you for further interrogation. I am obligated to inform you that as a guest of the estate you granted Trimalchio to use force against his guests to ensure your safety and security and the safety of all occupants. If you resist or show other signs of not cooperating, this force can be used against you. Please stay calm."

"Threat to the security of the estate," Ian repeated, but his hangover and disbelief stalled him from being able to assign any sense of consequence to Gaia's pronouncement; the world seemed to penetrate him only in slow drips. As he searched for pants and a shirt, he found himself again regretting sleeping nude. As he danced, trying to thread his right leg through his pants, Arthur and four facilitators loomed in his doorway. They said nothing but once his shirt was buttoned they grasped him by his arms and led him from his room.

The facilitators, though wizened and stooped, gripped him with an iron-forged strength. Arthur appeared to be taking great care to walk lockstep with him, and occasionally caught his eye in a furtive yet appraising glance. They descended, and each stairway led to another. Ian noticed that at some point the floor transitioned from teak to marble then to a gaudy carpet. Then the windows vanished, and Ian guessed the facilitators had dragged him into the manor's subterraneous bowels.

After many steps, they arrived at a concrete landing, which Ian guessed was the true bottom of the manor. They veered right down a narrow, cylindrical tunnelway reminiscent of a missile silo in its size and shape. They followed its diagonal slope until at the end of the tunnel they met with a pair of steel doors stitched shut by several interlocked chrome latches. Arthur moved ahead of the group to arrive at the doors ahead of them first, and before he unlocked them with his auto-self, he turned to Ian and fixed him in place with a gaze like irons.

"Just tell them everything like you remember it, and I am sure the matter will be resolved." Before Ian could ask 'remember what?' Arthur swiped at the door and led them into a cube-shaped room with a white interior. Trimalchio sat at a small black desk and beckoned Ian to an empty chair beside him.

"*Sit, Ian, beside Mr. Trimalchio.*" Spoke Gaia. *We are concerned about an item you brought into the estate with you.*"

"Oh?" said Ian, his hangover seemed to be batting the room from side to side, and he felt unable to do anything other than suppress the urge to retch.

"*Arthur, please place the item on the desk,*" Arthur gave a curt bow to the room, and then withdrew Ambrose's briefcase from a panel in the wall. It was only now that Ian realized he had not seen it in his room since the morning after his arrival. "*I alerted Arthur to this briefcase as soon as I realized that Mr. Gateman had neither logged it in his itinerary nor did he ever open it while at the estate. These two actions and our unfamiliarity with Mr. Gateman led me to classify the briefcase as suspicious.*" Trimalchio appeared to capitulate to the assessment

THE SHAREHOLDERS

with mute shrug. *"I had Arthur retrieve it from Mr. Gateman's room and deliver it to a safe box until we were better able to establish the custody of the briefcase and question Mr. Gateman. Arthur, can you confirm that as far as you know the briefcase has not been opened?"*

"I can confirm that." Arthur bowed.

"Good. Mr. Gateman, please explain why you did not register this briefcase in your pre-trip booking to the estate and why did not open it during your time here?" Trimalchio eyed him with suspicion.

"I did not register it because it's not mine," sputtered Ian, but as he watched Trimalchio's eyes narrow into petulant pinpricks, he elaborated hastily, "It fell into my possession by accident."

"By accident?" repeated Gaia, in a tone that seemed to verge on human disbelief. *I invite you to volunteer more information."*

"A man named Ambrose Dilwater informed me he was your associate," Ian said with a rueful gesture to Trimalchio. "He left it on the carriage ride here and I figured I might as well bring it along and check it out. Once I found it was protected by an analog combination lock, I put it aside and forgot all about it. It's a misunderstanding," finished Ian. As he listened to his own explanation, the absurdity of the situation cut through his fear and he found himself feeling irritated at having been summoned at all.

Trimalchio leapt from his seat and paced the room, pausing to cast frenetic gesticulations at the ceiling as he communed with Gaia.

"I don't know any Dilwater," he muttered. Gaia, do I know ..."

"I have searched all of your contacts and guests over the last 18 months and I have not found anyone named Dilwater."

"Now, that's quite odd. I am positive he said he knew you and the other estate owners," implored Ian.

"I have found a match of a Dilwater arriving at Marble Rock on several occasions over the last three months."

"Visiting Kunso's estate?" mused Trimalchio.

"That is plausible," replied Gaia.

"He might have said he was a business associate of Mr. Kunso," muttered Ian as he struggled to recall the specifics of what he remembered as a very strained and dull conversation.

Trimalchio's features thickened into a snarl. "It could be sabotage. Kunso is crafty. It could be anything." His pacing quickened as he circled the table with the briefcase, his eyes to the floor, seemingly oblivious of Arthur or Ian's presence. "Pests, disease, anything to undermine our estate's production. He wants to establish Marble Rock to be the premier seat of the district. It's a logical step for him. I am sure of it. We must hedge our bets, hedge them immediately." And his hands flew up into the air in great agitation.

"This is all plausible, but further information is necessary," replied Gaia. Arthur said nothing, but appeared engrossed in his own thoughts, though several times, he managed to tip Ian an approving nod.

"We will need to open the briefcase," advised Gaia. *"I would like to recommend that we initiate the suspicious baggage procedure. Under these circumstances, I cannot have you or Mr. Gateman in the vicinity in case it contains a biohazard or improvised explosive device. I recommend that you both exit the room and let Arthur and I open the briefcase. The security features of the room will allow it to quarantine foreign pathogens or contain an explosion without risk to the estate."*

Trimalchio nodded in fervent agreement, clasped Arthur on the shoulder, and thanked him for his continued dedication and service to the estate. There were further assurances that if anything happened, Arthur's service would be memorialized in the estate's digital biography.

Arthur pursed his lips, dipped his head to Trimalchio, and said stiffly, "Always in your service." He then drew himself up, placed his hands on his hips, and, for a moment, managed to wipe decades off his crooked frame. Ian and Trimalchio left the room and let the

THE SHAREHOLDERS

door seal Arthur inside. The four facilitators who had not entered the room flanked them and remained without expression, suspended until a task was found to reinsert them into the estate's continual metabolism of hand-picked mint, and woodland artisanal cockerel stew, or whatever other feast Gaia felt should be orchestrated.

"I can't help but feel I should be the one opening it. I brought it in," confessed Ian.

"Ms. Seeder and Gaia should have exercised more caution in your admittance," replied Trimalchio, though his words lacked conviction. As more time transpired with no apparent commotion or alarm from within the room, Trimalchio brightened and added, "The risk of there being anything in there that can do us immediate harm is low. Kunso and I are bitter rivals, and he's not above engaging in the occasional economic terrorism, but he's not a lunatic. We designers may bicker, but we are one biological family, familicide is not an option for us."

Before Ian had a chance to respond that mortal humans were also a biological family, and this had done little to quell war and ruin amongst them, Gaia's presence crackled through the air.

"Arthur successfully opened the briefcase without incident. I should still like to debrief you on its contents."

Trimalchio nodded, and the door opened to eject Arthur, who looked very much relieved.

"Well, this is where I leave you. Please accept my apologies for this whole episode. It must have been quite a shock and no doubt trespassed on your pleasure and convenience," said Trimalchio. Again, Ian was taken aback by Trimalchio's sincerity. "In fact, let me make it up to you. You will no doubt be aware that we are having a shareholder's feast this evening; come along as a guest. Yes, that's the ticket." He waved and airily commanded over his shoulder, "Follow Arthur or ask Gaia for spots to get back to the more inviting levels of the manor." Once more, Ian felt himself with seemingly little recourse but to obey.

Chapter 10: NATURE'S FEAST

THE SHAREHOLDERS' FEAST took place once a year at a different shareholder's estate. The feast was an inheritance bequeathed from the politics of the old nations. The so-called Conference of the Parties, which had met to decide how best to tackle the climate crisis, to no avail. Once the Shareholders ascended to power and the world was subdivided in thousands of habitable shares, it followed naturally that they would take on the duties of managing populations, resources and the world's carbon allowance that the Conference of the Parties had previously discharged.

When the focus of these gatherings shifted away from mitigation of CO_2 to the mitigation of life itself, the antiquated Conference of the Parties was renamed Nature's Feast, or 'the Feast,' for short. As the number of habitable estates dwindled and shares were consolidated, the delegation shrunk to a few dozen Shareholders. As the numbers of attendees declined, the mystery that shrouded each meeting increased proportionally. Despite the fact that the air Ian emitted, food he ate, and children he may raise were debated and decided in these meetings, the feasts were never disclosed to the public. To many, the whole affair seemed to dwell at the precipice of a well-maintained secret and outright conspiracy.

However, Trimalchio was loyal to the entreaty he had made. At 5:00pm, Gaia stirred Ian from his afternoon siesta to remind him of his attendance at the Feast that evening. At a quarter past seven, Ian walked down the spiraling trail of white pebbles that led to the river that squirmed down the back of Trimalchio's manor. Though the sun had set, the air was thick with heat. He kept adjusting his shoulders, trying to break his dress-shirt's hold on his back. Standing by the shore of the river he realized how large Trimalchio's dinner party was going to be. Dispersed along the crescent shoreline were three-dozen torches, each accompanied by placards bearing the surnames of guests. Ian passed several unfamiliar names before he found his own, paired with Governor Simpson. What were the chances? he thought.

The black water of the river appeared indented, pressed down by the weight of a full luminous spring moon caught in midstride over the water. He wasn't sure how long he stood there. The mirth of other guests caught his ears, and soon he spotted several white little rowboats zigzagging lazily across the lax current towards the island. He shifted his weight from foot to foot and walked his fingers over his auto-self in feverish taps, daring himself to see how many messages and notifications awaited him. In the dark, he heard the pebbles shift along the path; Georgina emerged from the night, smiled at him, and came to his side.

In silence, they both looked out over the river to the soft lights twinkling through the trees of Delphi Island. A little white rowboat moored along the sandy bank rocked in the river's gentle pull. Ian tried to find something to say to break the silence between them.

"So, a bureaucrat and a Governor get into a boat, which one of them rows?"

"Tell me, but the answer had better not be the governor," said Georgina.

"Neither of them, by the look of it," said Ian. A facilitator stepped out of the night, cast them a curt bow, and squatted down in the little rowboat, gesturing for them to join him.

"Sounds about right," retorted Georgina as she and Ian staggered into the stern seats and looked forward into the face of the facilitator; his features now unlocked from the darkness. Ian did his best not to grimace at the man. A wild and coarse-looking gray beard dangled over his gaunt cheeks. Yet, it was his eyes that frightened

THE SHAREHOLDERS

Ian more than anything else. Sunken into the depths of his face, the man's eyes were pale green, almost sea-brine, and bordered on the appearance of milky sightlessness. In those eyes coursed the mad fury of ragged seas making ready to damn ships and swallow Phoenicians. Luminous with discontent, the man's eyes peered with an intensity that added vitality to a face that was otherwise gaunt and weathered. The man said nothing. His grip on the oars tightened and revealed the sinews in his powerful arms. Unlike the muscles of designers, Ian thought the man's arms looked coiled and frayed as if worked into disfigurement. His face remained impassive as he carried them across the glassy face of the water in belabored strokes.

"I do often wonder why most of the facilitators are so old," Georgina whispered.

"How long have you been in Mr. Trimalchio's service?" Ian asked their ferryman.

"Well, today I was assigned a contract from 5:00am to 12:00am," strained the facilitator.

"That's not quite what he was asking," Georgina pursued.

"Been here since I turned 65, Gaia doesn't put an age cap on the contracts she makes. That's the bitch's one redeeming quality." He shut his eyes and appeared to savor the night's air, heavy and sticky with heat. "Outside, I say what I like. She's a fucking hag."

"Oh please, she can't be that bad. She is programmed—"

But before Georgina could continue, the rower finished her sentence. "To limit undue pain, suffering and discomfort. That only applies to residents and guests, not us facilitators on daily contracts. My great-grandfather hunted on these rivers and woods for a living, and now I work my ass off for a glorified modem. It is what it is, I guess," said the ferryman.

"Look at it from her perspective, she's an incredibly intelligent entity without a body confined to one building for her whole period of consciousness. That can't be easy," suggested Georgina.

H.S. DOWN

The rower snorted through a plum-shaped, gin-blossomed nose, and shook his head with what looked like trenchant disbelief. "Last week I took a nap outside. It was damn hot, and I had been moving food in and out of ovens. If you sleep outside in the right spots away from the manor's external cameras, she'll never be the wiser. Well, she figured it out and as soon as I walked through the door, she zapped me. Hard. I thought my heart was going to explode. Almost pissed myself, pardon the expression, Governor."

"Zapped you?" asked Georgina. The ferryman coughed up a laugh but did not smile.

"Christ, you must be rich if you've never heard of the zap." The facilitator drew his oars over his lap and the boat drawled to stop. With a furtive sidelong glance, the man rolled up his sleeves and held out vein-wreathed forearms, revealing several washer-sized metal discs embedded beneath his flesh. Georgina pulled the facilitator's taut, leathery arm towards her and ran her delicate fingers over the abrasion of the disc, in what looked to Ian like rueful study.

"Gaia shocks you?" she said in horror.

"She shocks, she freezes, and she makes your head feel like it has gone off and split. I've seen her make a man piss himself." And then, as if irritated by his own words, he wrestled free of Georgina's hands and started rowing again.

"How did she know you were sleeping?" asked Ian.

"Can't be sure, but some of these men here are very close to her. Think of themselves as her second eyes and ears."

"Why? What's in it for them?" asked Georgina in puzzlement.

"Companionship, I suspect," he muttered. He pulled hard on the oars, and Ian could see the body of the Delphi Island rising out from the night towards them.

"Companionship? It's a leisure program to manage the estate, what kind of companionship can there be in that?" asked Georgina.

THE SHAREHOLDERS

"She asks after them. That means more than you'd care to think to a poor old man. But, to be honest, I can either talk or I can row. I'm too old to do both," he wheezed.

"Fair enough," dismissed Georgina. She leaned back in her seat and looked up at the moon which, not unlike her, thought Ian, seemed to be leaning back in bed of stars, setting the sky alight in a tinsel glow.

"Looks like the conversation is on you and me," she said, but she soon turned away and leaned over the boat to let her fingertips skim the river's cheek.

Faltering into a muddled absence, Ian fidgeted with his auto-self. He parsed through the steps he had taken that day, his messages, his credits, his automated check ins from Alex and an update about a small fire on Egg Island. Strewn within the debris of several hundred notifications were a string of messages from Anne.

I just lived my life as Goldmund. I rode beneath a red harvest moon casting its shadows over a flood of golden wheat awaiting the scythe of peasants. The air was crisp and the sky heavy against oak trees submerged in the night if not for the flicker of their leaves as they melted into a butter yellow and fell before me as my horse's hooves broke the field's back. Horses. You and I missed so much; you cannot imagine the freedom moving through the world on horseback. Or the feeling of old earth, pure and unadulterated, in your hands, teeming with future harvests, each year begetting another. This world is no stranger to immortality, though it is quainter than our own. I felt death and life surge in me when I drew young maidens to lay with me in fields by casting stones against the walls of their simple earthen homes and letting them extinguish and renew me again and again. Oh, Ian, you cannot imagine the other worlds now open to me.

The latest message from her read:

I got tired of being Goldmund, so today I simulated a trip to Paris and pretended to be a flâneur. I miss you. How's work?

His finger hovered.

"Tough day at the office? I'm finding it very difficult to conduct all my external communications in Trimalchio's backyard," Georgina confided with a throaty chuckle.

"It is a pain," confessed Ian. "Though these messages are from my wife. She recently checked in to Lotus hotel."

"Oh, Ian! I'm so sorry. It can be so difficult when people we love chose paths we cannot follow." Ian was not sure if he was disarmed by her sincerity, or by that the fact that she thought her condolences were the most appropriate response.

"It's fine. Lotus is not the end of our marriage, just a different form." Yet, for the first time, Ian felt let down by what had become his go-to response.

"It must be hard, though, to love someone who can never be here, next to you, in the same world."

"She's here. She is always here." And he pointed to his auto-self nestled into the flesh of his jaundiced forearm.

Georgina sighed. "Not so long ago, someone in your situation would have pointed here." She pressed a smooth, tanned hand just below her neckline, to her chest. "I suppose, though, that the heart is not as organized as an auto-self, though sometimes I wonder." She said nothing further, but Ian felt the warmth of her shoulder against his as she leaned closer and in tiny increments filled the space between them on the stern's wooden seat.

Not long after, the facilitator, red-faced and wheezing, ran the dingy aground on the sandy bank of Delphi Island. From there they joined many other factors chattering in excitement as they fought the slight slope of the island to a white gazebo that spread out above them like a pale shield blocking out the night.

As they took their seats, Ian was surprised to find Georgina on his left. Conversations broke out at their elbows and Ian did his best to raise interest in Egg Island with the designer to his right, with

THE SHAREHOLDERS

limited results. Just as some of them began to ask when the feast was going to begin, a faint slosh of water stepped over their words. All eyes turned to a dark shadow astride on the river. The shadow became a solitary boat, breaking through night's secretive horizon. Stroke by stroke, Trimalchio carved his way out of the night. Alone, genuflected in the stern of the boat, he seemed to loom over the river as he cut the water in wide arcs, his paddle circling up and down in broad hands.

The slosh of water grew louder as the song of the paddle bobbed against the shoreline. When he made landing, he staggered to his feet and cradled the paddle into his chest. Three facilitators unsheathed themselves from the night and became Trimalchio's entourage; two of them took his paddle and the third trailed him as he trudged up the sandy bank to join the feast.

Georgina leant in so close to Ian that her peppermint breath dewed his cheek. "I hear the paddle is forged of iron. It is so heavy that only he can properly use it."

"I heard it was made of lead," chimed a man across from Ian.

"He stole the idea from some ancient epic," spoke another.

"The man knows how to make an entrance, I will give him that," said Tina, her face now framed by brunette curls.

Within a moment, Trimalchio stood before them on the stage of the gazebo, "Welcome, welcome. I should like to open this year's convening of Nature's Feast with the performance of an experience. This experience does not belong to our time, but some of you may feel its proximity to our present." As he spoke, Trimalchio's eyes fell upon Ian with the same arresting gaze he had given him when they met that first morning by the pool. "Let us recount it now each as they like. After all, it is what it is," he exclaimed.

"It is what it is," chanted the crowd, and their voices reached the stage in a wave of solemn reverence.

Trimalchio reciprocated with a slight bow, then with an orchestral sweep of his arm, said, "I leave it to my Archivist," and vacated the stage of the gazebo. The audience murmured at each other from the borders of their elbows, but soon the chatter fell away as a blue translucent figure took the floor. In silence he stood at the center of the stage, peering over them with a watery presence.

"Have you met Trimalchio's Archivist?" Georgina whispered in his ear in a way that made his neck tingle.

"What is it?"

"You've never met a digital human?"

"No. Immortal?" he whispered back.

"He is a projection of a real body, but the projection doesn't eat, sleep or touch anything. So, I don't know if that qualifies you as immortal or not," confessed Georgina.

"Where's his body then?"

"Well, he's a bit touchy about it, but apparently he's interned in the basement of Christ's College. I employ a couple of them; they're great when one needs to know something historical from records that are not digitized but most of the time they are in some archive or another and getting them to work to a task is a real nuisance. It's an addiction for them; gathering information, I mean," she said.

The translucent figure paced back and forth several times, but the short length of the gazebo forced him to continually turn back on himself in erratic streams of blue light. Then, without warning, and Ian very much would have liked a warning, he screamed. The figure warbled, its blue silhouette bleeding out, as it emitted a caterwaul that to Ian sounded like the distant kin of the classical music to which Anne listened. But this was a garbled melody of minors with bass and feedback. Each note, aided by an electronic synthesizer, lived on, feasting upon the audience in a surreal half-life.

He saw Georgina's lean, sinewy arms tense as she gripped the arms of her chair, and then Ian's mind broke out in grainy and

THE SHAREHOLDERS

checkered images of earth laid waste to ash; bodies strewn over blackened land; some dead and rotting, others broken on great ancient-looking wooden wheels at the mercy of dark, faceless figures brandishing hot pokers; beyond them, tearing ahead of nightmarish fields and agricultural torture devices, were drab concrete industrial-looking prisons, their smokestacks bellowing out an unidentifiable gray ash. The rotting and dying both seemed to stir, crawling on the earth to look up at a red dawn that stepped in from the past to crown the horizon. Ian did not know how the music had summoned such a scene into his mind which otherwise remained so ordered and bereft, but he felt his legs tense and his heart begin to hammer. He looked into his lap and took a deep breath as he suppressed his instinct to flee, and when the desire to run threatened to overwhelm him, he menaced himself with the knowledge that he had nowhere to go.

The expressions of his fellow guests told him that he was not alone in this feeling. A woman with a white-haired wig and hawkish nose cocked her head at Trimalchio in rapid bird like gestures, as if in hope of pressing him into silencing the performer. Trimalchio appeared to take no notice of this guests' discomfort, but instead looked on with a small smile wrapped up in the corners of his mouth as he bobbed his chin at the performer, perhaps in encouragement. In recognition of the cue, the Archivist released a longer rattling scream, and then it became apparent that it was many screams, a cacophony of men, women, infants and perhaps even animals, a guttural symphony that walked lockstep with the mechanical precision of the bass, cellos, and violins that also seemed to be falling out of him in half notes.

The Archivist opened his mouth and in an electronic voice emitted a string of words that quivered by them and ran on in wander of the swirling waters of the river behind them.

H.S. DOWN

"December 5th, the snow has fallen hard. Several more Indians arrived today at the Fort, in search of provisions. I gave them some flour from the Fort's Reserves. The buffalo have not come back in great number. Word continues to arrive to us about the scarcity our settlers are facing on the plains.

"December 20th, two scouts, reliable men, brought back word on the two Canadian families farming the plains, who had complained they were low on supplies. The scouts returned and informed me that the men fell into such deprivation that they ate their wives and their children. They have gone mad with grief. In terror, the scouts raised their farms and left the men to wander the plains. Exposure should take them before the night is finished.

"January 15th, hundreds of Indians and settlers alike have arrived at the Fort over the last several weeks. Our reserves have nearly been exhausted. I arranged to have a small quantity of it put aside for my senior officers and myself. I have locked the inner garrison. The miserable wretches continue to trickle in from the plains. They sit, dumb with cold, wrapped in blankets for most of the day, but occasionally move from door to door begging for relief from the inhabitants of the Fort.

"January 28th, the starving and the dying are now the sovereigns of the Fort. I have kept watch from my corridors. The hungry are banding together into a mob. I can hear the scrape of their fingers on the gate, and in my mind, I see them climbing up over each other trying to get inside our inner garrison. We have been forced to fire at them several times. At daybreak today I saw three men attack a horse, they tore into it with wanton need and brought it to its knees. They waited too long, though. The wretched animal was lame and fleshless. I also saw several Indian men, so frozen and still that they looked asleep, their bronzed skin overlaid by a death mask of icy blue crystal. Some have lost their noses, ears, and pieces of their cheeks, and I can only presume some of

THE SHAREHOLDERS

the miserable wretches have resorted to cannibalism within the walls. I have calculated that we have enough provisions to last out the winter. Several of our wealthier officers are concerned about the well-being of their cattle pastured just outside the Fort; I have assured them I will do everything in my power to preserve their property.

"Feb 10th, there is talk of rebellion. Word has spread about the supply of provisions inside the Garrison. To placate the mob, I arranged a hunt for buffalo. Our hunters and several settlers and Indians left on the 3rd of this month for the plains. They have yet to return. The worst is feared. Morale within the Fort is very low. The dead walk, hollow-cheeked, gaunt and blue with cold. Outside the window I observed several horse carcasses and a number of bodies. Cholera has broken out amongst the poor. All inhabitants within the fort have been instructed to keep their doors shut and guarded by rifle. Men blame the poor buffalo hunt for their privations. The truth is that many of them squandered the fall and did not harvest enough to last the winter. Nature's scarcity is the surest cure against indolence and indigence. We will be a stronger community once this is over.

"March 5th, the air is warm and no new snow has fallen in the last few weeks. Bodies cover the ground like great dark islands in a sea of white; a harsh but honest archipelago of man's hubris and nature's sovereignty. Summer is coming. Twelve families remain now. The Fort was almost overrun at the end of February. The Indians and the poor inhabitants of the Fort joined together in the end and, as I feared would happen, nearly scaled the walls to my inner sanctum. I ordered grapeshot fired upon them to put all the miserable devils down. Most scattered into the night and I presume have since died of hunger or exposure. We kept what was rightfully ours, as nature has decreed in her majesty of scarcity. Scarcity is the tamer of men, and the maker of great estates.

"*I give you the last epitaph one that I must impress upon you,*" spoke the Archivist.

Dies irae, dies illa
Solvet saeclum in favilla
Tested avid cum Sibylla
Quantus tremor est futurus
Quando Ducis est Mars
Cuncta stricte discussurus

The audience was clueless to the meaning of these last words, but in relief that the ordeal had ended, they broke out into an applause of slow, scattered claps. As the hesitant applause died away, Trimalchio rose from his seat to make another toast and crossed with the archivist as he hovered from the stage. Ian noticed that as they walked by one another, Trimalchio shook his head and the Archivist conceded with a slight shrug before he receded into the shadows of the gazebo. The moment broke apart and fluttered away; Ian wondered if anyone else had caught it.

"To scarcity," toasted Trimalchio. "Would anyone care to guess where this story came from?" Ian surveyed the crowd and met with blank faces. Several designers averted their eyes and toyed with their napkins like unprepared children avoiding a teacher's questions. "It's from a clerk's journal from a company that owned this land many centuries ago. In fact, most of our estates rest on the foundations of what was their empire. There have always been shareholders and shareholders have always ruled in alliance with scarcity. They too documented resources, the available subsistence, and did their best to monitor and intervene upon the indigenous populations they ruled. It is a longstanding truism that it is only the principle of ownership that provides the impetus to audit and to preserve finite resources. What the ancients were not willing to do, though, is sculpt the season of man. They did not have the tenacity to help nature do their engineering and in the end, the result was the same; the

THE SHAREHOLDERS

gatekeeper was forced to fire on the men, women and children that scarcity would have marked for death had it been allowed to preside," said Trimalchio in a grave, solemn voice.

"To be a shareholder today or even a servant of the Enclosure is to be a gatekeeper, and it is a high task before us indeed. We all now must decide who to admit into the fort. I know this weekend will be a time for gourmandizing, swimming, celebrating the storm party and, of course, other extracurricular activities ..."

"Hear, hear!" cheered several designers.

"It's the only reason I come to these things," whispered Georgina.

"But, but," continued Trimalchio over the hollers of his guests, "Governor Simpson has made it clear that we have some serious matters to discuss if we are going to meet our next target. So, without any further delay, I will hand the floor over to the beautiful Governor Simpson."

"What an ass," she whispered to Ian as she got to her feet to take the stage.

"A warm greeting to my well-dressed and handsome factors. Before attending to our first order of business I need to note all the factors present."

"Mrs. Nicki Sowjucksa of Fort Albany."

"Present."

"Mr. Kunso, founder of the Mars Colonization Corporation, and chief Factor of Marble Rock," called Georgina, and Ian felt he could detect a note of hesitation in her voice, as if she was unsure whether she would receive a reply.

Ian followed Georgina's gaze to find that Mel was not seated with them, but stood behind them half concealed by one of the gazebo's wooden columns. He acknowledged his name with a curt nod cast in the general direction of gazebo.

"Ernest Trimalchio of Fort Rupert," Georgina continued.

"I prefer to call this the Churchhill estate," corrected Trimalchio.

"You can call it Fanny Bay for all I care, this is a matter of record," said Georgina, and Ian suppressed a laugh as Trimalchio was forced to glower into his lap.

"Ms. Olivia Walton of Fort Prince of Wales and the Delhi Rings?"

"Hello!" said Olivia with a smile as broad as she, Sam sat beside her looking at once both reserved and weary.

After a very lengthy series of introductions to estates that Ian had no idea existed, Georgina announced that they had achieved quorum. At this news, a troop of facilitators laden with jugs of red wine descended upon them and a goblet was set in front of Ian and filled to its brim. Soon the air was heavy with a rich though nearly pungent aroma and a great skewered boar on a rotating spit emerged from the path up from the shore. Several facilitators swarmed its red shining carcass and deftly removed large slabs of smoking meat, which were then piled high on plates. Ian, mindful of what had befallen him the night before with the pheasant, nibbled on the succulent, sweet meat and compensated his restraint by indulging in the dark, oaky wine. He finished his glass, but within moments found it replenished.

After several sips of his second goblet, he realized that the wine's distinct heavy taste was a product of its potency. It appeared it had been made exceptionally strong to match the enhanced constitutions of the designers. In very little time, Ian's head grew heavy and the private conversations taking place beside him started to sound strange, as if they were being spoken in a foreign tongue. As the words around him became harder to understand, his head felt as if it had become even heavier and he was forced to prop himself up on his elbows.

Unfortunately, as the designers finished their first helpings, Georgina started the meeting in earnest by asking the factors for updates on their various estates and lays. Ian strained his ears and

THE SHAREHOLDERS

brushed off several facilitators as they offered to fill his goblet for a third time. Drunk and weighed down by the heaviness of the little pork he'd eaten, he found himself grasping at the scraps of their sentences as he struggled to piece them together into an intelligible whole.

"To achieve the new target, we will need to make further reductions in animal-based proteins. I believe, according to my calculations, meat will need to make up no more than 5% of the average diet globally," announced Georgina.

"Well, you aren't getting any more cropland from the Edinburgh Enclosure to make more vegetable proteins, that's for damn sure," retorted one designer with an accent Ian didn't recognize; the voice was so thick and rough half the letters seemed squeezed out of the man's words.

"Aye, what land remains is earmarked for a solar farm expansion," declared another whose voice shared the same thick coarseness.

"Yes, yes, I received your petitions from the Highlands," relented Georgina. "How about increasing the density of some of the insect farms. Factor Jozff, I heard you were having success raising crickets into foodstuffs? Can these be exported to the populations in other districts?" ventured Georgina.

"At this time, I request that the crickets be used for self-sufficiency for my own Enclosure, the stock is not sufficient for export. Now, I do have a surplus of ants ..." but before he could continue, Sebe was cut off by a chorus of raucous boos.

"Nobody wants your damn ants, Jozff," Mel proclaimed with a mirthless snort, and there was patter of claps and laughter until Georgina interceded.

"Silence!" she thundered, and slew the insurrection with such force that Ian popped his head up and knocked his cutlery across his plate. "Factor Jozff, you will export 25% of your cricket-based foodstuffs and the council will compensate you accordingly," Georgina decreed.

"Now, is everyone in favor of another increase in the levy on personal transportation for trips that exceed 25kms?" Still perhaps reeling at having been quelled a moment before, the floor answered with unenthused and dispassionate assent; Ian felt his eyelids growing heavy once more.

"I propose that all new Cargo-Condos have their floorspace reduced by 1.5% year over year for the next 20 years. We've seen great success in using this measure to further reduce the rate of population growth," spoke a voice that Ian knew he recognized but could not place; he soon realized he could not place the speaker because his eyes were closed.

"It is a fine resolution, but we've yet to discuss any of the positive or preventative checks on population we wish to enforce. As there has been considerable change in this policy, I will request we treat it as a separate issue," said Georgina, and she ushered them along to the next item of business. "The Londinium council requests that each estate convert 2% of their current territory into carbon scrubbing facilities. We've yet to reduce atmospheric CO_2 to 40% below 2040 levels."

"I'd like to counter, respectfully mind you, that the council pause any further conversion of land into carbon scrubbing facilities until we see if the oceanic CO_2 absorption has improved." Ian could tell that this last intervention had come from Trimalchio and, from the poorly concealed ire in his voice, it seemed he was fiercely opposed to any infringement on his property.

"I'll communicate your request, but in the meantime, factors should identify 2% of their lands suitable to conversion to carbon scrubbing," said Georgina, and the discussion continued further, outrunning Ian's attention. "Factor Walton, has there been any success in rehabilitating the shares on the outskirts of New Delhi?"

THE SHAREHOLDERS

"Unfortunately, the New Delhi shares are only habitable for designers at this time, and even then, they lack even the most basic qualities of self-sufficiency. We have an automated workforce employed in creating a subterraneous plantation, and I believe it will be suitable for the cultivation of insect-based proteins within a year," said Olivia.

"Any luck on turning the barrens into some kind of carbon sink?"

"I'm afraid not at this time, Governor," replied Olivia, her voice rueful.

"Pity. Now, I've reviewed your reports on the populations in your respective districts, and based on the numbers, we have been successful in shortening the human season, but as you know ..."

Indolent, and his senses still snared by the wine, Ian lost track of Georgina's words; his concentration faltered further when his auto-self blinked in receipt of another message from Anne.

Alex mentioned that he will be joining you at the estate. What a wonderful opportunity for him. I hope both of you will be able to keep in regular contact. I've been experiencing road trips in Europe and the Americas during the 1950s. The leaves in Vermont wear the seasons so beautifully. I can't wait to share it with you both when you check in, too ...

Ian tried to read on, but his eyes mutinied against him and threatened to cross over one another. Groggy and torpid, he tried to capture some stray thread of the conversation that was happening around him.

"Though it won't be enough just to shorten the season of man ..." pronounced Nicki, but again Ian withdrew his attention as the meat warmed his belly and the wine sated his desire to open his eyes.

Instead, he found his mind lazily spinning a scene around the phrase, 'season of man.' Ian could not help but picture the days when this so-called human season came to a close. The days of an Earth inhospitable to all but the designers. The beings before him left to wander alone through orchards and woods, dipping their bare feet in cooling seas, whilst renewing themselves with patient handfuls of fruits and grain. The inheritors of a 200,000-year-long experiment that culminated in nothing more than handful of shareholders marooned in the indelicate embrace of nature restored to rightful supremacy. Nature, patient and cunning, in wait for them to outlive the technology that had nourished their immortality, to consume them like ivy, swallowing at the close the very last marvel human civilization had dreamt to offer itself.

The image died away with the collective din of chairs scraping against the patio stone as the designers pushed them aside with the conclusion of the meeting. The wine had moved from his limbs to drum its fingers below his eyes and temples. As he tried to shake out the headache, he was surprised to see Georgina standing at his side, with an offer of a tumbler aglow with bubbles tossing about a thin wedge of lime.

"The wine is very strong, but this should help take the edge off," she said brightly. Ian accepted the offer, pulled himself off the table, and tried to straighten up in his chair. He took a generous swig from the tumbler and felt his eyes sharpen as the bubbles tickled his throat. "Better?" she asked.

"Much," he said as the drumming in his skull grew fainter.

"Ian, I'd like very much to escort you back to your room. With the wine and all, I think it would be best," she said matter-of-factly, and as he got to his feet, she slipped her arm under his, holding him close enough that her breath fell against his cheek, and he was engulfed with the taste of peppermint. Both were oblivious that Mel, too, had lingered and was one of the last to leave; and he stood back watching their exit with an admixture of incredulousness and scorn.

Chapter 11: COPIES AND AFFAIRS

HIS LUNGS WERE EMPTYING and each breath felt pinched by excitement and broken sputters of protest, as he stumbled backwards down the hall in an effort to dissuade Governor Simpson from following him any further.

"I'm married, Governor Simpson," he said for what felt like the seventh time, pointing frantically at his auto-self to corroborate this fact. Yet, every time he said this, she frowned a little, pinched her lower lip with her small diamond-shaped incisors, and told him to call her Georgina. She followed him through the door to his room, immune to his halfhearted protests. She shoved him, hard, so that he fell backwards onto his bed; in the aftermath of the wine, his head spun and his memory of how he got to his room returned to him with the same clarity as does a dream that marches through one's head in the whimsy hours after midnight but before dawn.

She stood at the end of the bedpost, her elbows tucked against her sides, hands locked beneath her chin as if to keep her head from falling to her chest. She looked much smaller than she had only moments earlier in the hallway. It suddenly struck him that she was nervous.

"I'm much older than you." As she spoke her eyes walked past him and settled on night's heavy darkness, which leant against the windows of the room like an ocean against a porthole.

"Not biologically," said Ian with an awkward laugh. She smiled, but her features remained hard, and it was only now as she stood over him that he realized her face was full of edges: her nose was hooked, her cheekbones angular and pointed, cradling brown eyes drawn into tight little triangles in the corners. Even her lips looked sharp.

"There are things about me that are now quite strange or maybe even forgotten to a man like yourself." Ian didn't know what to make of this disclosure. She begun to undress and he realized that he had let the moment to convince her to leave pass. She shed her clothes in what looked to Ian like a million subtle movements. She rotated her ankles first, tipping her shoes off. Her dress inched down revealing soft unblemished shoulders, and a prominent yet well-placed collarbone. Eventually she wore only a bra and underwear, yet standing right in front of him, on the precipice of being nude, she seemed to pull away. Her back arched as if she were reaching out for the wall behind her. After a long pause she unclipped her bra, but her eyes locked once more on windows, windows full with the empty scene of night's slow passing. Her gaze settled there as if resigned to Ian's indiscrete and cumbersome inspection.

Her breasts had stayed with her bra, leaving behind two purple crescent moon scars framed by red skin that looked pulled tight against her body. Ribs jutted out, doubly exposed for the lack of breasts. Her gaze did not falter from the window, and so Ian's stare was insulated by silence as he acclimatized to a body he did not expect. In the absence of breasts there was a gravitas of innocence, a faint half-life of pre-pubescence that haunted a hundred-some-year-old body.

Perhaps cognizant of the symbiotic relationship between her silence and his gaze, she broke it in what seemed like a distant and unfeeling voice, "Medicine was different when I was young. The means to control what could happen were crude and drastic. Perhaps it is still that way," she added, but it seemed she spoke more to herself than him. Her eyes were on him again, firm but warm. She pulled down her underwear and stepped forward, but paused again.

THE SHAREHOLDERS

Somewhere in that half step she recovered her poise. As she moved her hands up to her scalp and began to run her fingers up past her temples, her movements appeared once more wrapped up in that measured grace, a grace that in Ian's mind elevated her and bestowed upon her a faint ethereal quality. Ian watch as her hairline gradually lifted, revealing an inch, then several inches between her raven colored hair and the empty shine of her scalp. She bent down and with deliberation placed the hairpiece on the floor out of Ian's sight. Like Trimalchio her head was bald except for a few scattered patches of thin white hairs.

"Might as well be truly naked. Far more mortal than we look, aren't we?"

Ian didn't answer.

She was standing right beside him now, leaning over him. She grabbed his hand and guided it to her navel, and pressed his palm into the supple white skin of her belly; and with the other hand she started to tug at the buttons of his shirt. Her face was pressed close to his now; smooth, unblemished, and he breathed in her scent of peppermint. Her angular cheekbones caught the soft glow of the room and looked fuller and less sharp. He leaned in and kissed them and then again, and again remaining on her skin longer each time as he inched towards her lips. She smiled and pressed his hand lower forcefully and leaned closer into him,

"I promise any further surprises will be quite pleasant."

"I can't promise the same," said Ian, and he found himself delighted by her laughter as she slipped into bed next to him and tangled him between her arms and thighs in a tight embrace, letting her hands burrow under his clothes to feel his body in her own thorough but affectionate examination. Between the excitement and the weight of her body, Ian felt like he could not breathe and he welcomed asphyxiation.

ROSY-FINGERED DAWN peered in at them through the windows. Georgina was cradled in his arms. He ran his hand over her chest and stopped. He gently pressed further, trying not to wake her. She squinted at him a moment, sighed, and turned on to her stomach.

"The treatment slows it down, it barely beats. We are the living dead," she offered.

"Why did you do it?" asked Ian.

"The treatment? Oh, that's complicated," she demurred.

"Would you do it again?" pressed Ian.

"I moan about this life but living always seems better than the alternative. I miss the other lives I led before the treatment, though."

"I bet you were some hard ass CEO," said Ian as he studied her face, which he thought again looked sharp and angular. Georgina laughed and rolled into him, pressing her scarred chest against him; even in the morning, peppermint dewed her breath.

"Hardly. I was born out of place, an heiress to a fortune dating back to the 17th century. My father said we were aristocrats who had done one terrible thing for the privilege to do several hundred years of banal things afterwards."

"So, what did you do?"

"I have led many lives. In my early twenties I marched in the May Day protests in Paris and spent some time in communes. But by the 1980s I was married to a financer and living in Manhattan. I held galas with nice canopies, expensive champagne, and lots of small talk peppered with three-dollar words. Please save the whales, please build some wells; please support the establishment of a new micro-bank. Eventually, I elbowed my way onto the editorial staff of Vogue. It was all quite cliché, I suppose. Cliché's are hard to outrun, especially for women." She stopped and laughed and rubbed his arm as if to get him to commit to her laughter.

"They're even harder to outrun if you don't jog."

"Groan-worthy, kiddo. I do wish you had lived through those days, though. The lights of the cities burned with such intensity they eclipsed the night sky, meals became so elaborate and so luxurious that people started taking pictures of them. An entire class of people, your grandparent's generation, I suppose, lived lives on call to serve our every whim. The end of carbon-civilization was unapologetically decedent."

"So I've heard. What happened to your husband?"

"Oh." She smiled, but her eyes looked like they had fallen on some distant scene.

"I'm sorry, I didn't mean to pry," said Ian.

"I bought the treatment for us when it first hit the market. I knew it wasn't going to be available long. He was on a business trip and I wanted to take it together. I envisioned that we'd order greasy pizza and plot what we'd get up to for the next thousand years. But it felt like Christmas, and I just couldn't wait. I've always been a little impulsive. When he came home and I told him what I'd done, he just shook his head."

"He refused it?" said Ian, unable to hide his incredulousness.

"He'd open a new bottle of champagne rather than drink a half-empty one. Why live for the dredges, he'd say. The best had come and gone. It was hard to share a life with someone on the other side of the lifeline, especially so soon after the treatment. It makes you feel like you're seventeen again. It's a problem, actually. Most designer men fuck like they are seventeen again, not much staying power." Ian snorted up a laugh. "It's not funny, it's a big disappointment. Middle-aged men are hot commodities."

"Said no one, ever," retorted Ian.

"The world was at our fingertips. I wanted us to be conquerors again, but David chose to fade away. It was selfish of him, I thought. But listen to me drone on, god I'm a bore," she finished.

"Living now is like showing up to a party that finished three hours ago, that's what Anne use to say," said Ian, and he buried his head in his hands. "I can't believe we–I did this, I'm no better than Grayson."

"Ian," her voice was soft, and imbued with a gentleness that startled Ian. "I have to tell you something because I don't think anyone else will put it like I will. It's going to be very hard to hear, but I can't bear the thought of you not knowing. I wanted to say something on the boat but thought better of it. I was waiting to find the right moment." She was sitting up now gripping his hand, "Anne is dead. She died as soon as she checked in to Lotus."

"What?! I get messages from her, I can see her, I've been with her," he said.

"Oh, I'm sure you have, but it's just an upload of her, like a file."

"It's a transfer of consciousness, of course I know that," replied Ian with an irritated shrug.

"It's just that isn't really human anymore. It's a very well-curated memory, it is a wonderful luxury to have someone as close and special to you in reach as a marker, but you can't live your life around that. It would be like living life around a gravestone, it is an important marker of what has been, but the connection to this world, the world you live in, is over."

"She's still there, she's still experiencing things, how is that any different than you and me?"

"She can't be changed by the experiences, that's the difference ..." She paused as he got out of bed and started searching for his pants.

"She's always been very private," he said. "She never volunteered much. She preferred to listen." He wasn't sure if he was trying to convince her or himself. Edna had told him the first few months

THE SHAREHOLDERS

would be hard, that Anne might seem distant to him, aloof. It was just part of the transition period into an extended relationship.

"Ian, I am really sorry. It wasn't my place. I just didn't want you to feel bad about this."

"No." He felt better. He said it again, "No. That's simply not true."

"I'm so sorry, it ..."

"No." He cut her off and for a moment he felt relieved, insulated by the power of denying her words.

"It was never meant to be like this, ever. It sounded humane when the idea was first introduced. It would help us work towards a more sustainable population and offer a way out that was clean, comfortable, and would give everyone a little piece of immortality. We didn't appreciate the complexity of death and digital consciousness, I suppose."

"Lotus would have made it clearer to her, she wouldn't have done it if what you said is true," shot Ian.

"How much your wife knew about the process, Ian, is not for me to say. But I do know that Lotus is a very old company. It was part of an earlier corporation, an attempt to create computerized copies of the deceased. Nobody liked it, though. It was too weird, too uncomfortable to put the memories of people into robotic bodies. People were comfortable though speaking through monitors, seeing each other in text, that's where the idea of checking in came from. The synthetic body was ... alarming. Lotus spared everyone the trauma ..."

"Of the final goodbye?" interjected Ian. "Why say anything? Why tell me at all? I clearly didn't understand there was a difference," he stammered, working a lump down in his throat.

"But there is a difference to be known," she said, and for a moment her eyes pinned him in a fierce scowl, but then crumpled into an admixture of sorrow and embarrassment. "I suppose that is a very old way of thinking". And in silence she gathered her clothes in her arms, and seemingly without hesitation, slipped out the door undressed.

Chapter 12: THE ARCHIVIST AND TIRESIAS

AFTER HIS CONVERSATION with Georgina, Ian intended to keep to himself for the rest of the day. His morning was quite successful; he ate breakfast alone in his room and then went back to the river and tried to skip stones for a while. By midday, though, the heat had become unbearable and he was forced to retreat to his room. Yet, he found no respite here.

Upon his return, Gaia informed him that the manor's climate controls would be disabled for the next several hours to offset the energy needed to support the many new guests. In desperation, he pressed the entity for an exception. He was, after all, the only mortal guest; surely he could be accommodated, he pressed. Gaia merely chastised him for threatening the sustainability of his environment over something as trivial as air conditioning.

With little else pleasurable to do, he figured he might as well eat. He ordered a lunch of venison, wild rice, and mushrooms, which a compact octogenarian delivered in short order. He ate on the bed, balancing his gourmet meal on his thigh. Sweat beaded under his shirt and peppered his brow as he ravenously carved his way through the dish. From his window he watched the designers laze about on the pool deck, immune and oblivious to the sweltering heat as an endless parade of facilitators delivered cocktails and meals. Only from a bird's-eye view was he able to truly appreciate them for what they were.

They had such a distinct way of walking, thought Ian. Hundreds of thousands of carefree, directionless steps had laid the foundations for a gait that skimmed the Earth in an ethereal flutter. They couldn't be blamed, of course, he thought. They were, after-all, the long-sought-for, yet periodically misplaced, dream of the twentieth century: the scientifically mastered body standing, scalpel in hand, looking over a dissected and etherized nature that had yet to learn how to manage a species that had completed the last irreversible procedure of exculpating itself from the natural laws of life and death. But this revelry blew away from him as he received a loud knock at the door.

"Go away," said Ian, certain it was Georgina back for another round of hard truths.

"Oh, please, do you have any idea how dull it is navigating this place?" lamented a voice that sounded as if it were coming to him from the depths of the sea.

Curious, Ian opened the door and came face to face with a blue, translucent figure.

"Oh, the Archivist," said Ian and he made no effort to conceal how underwhelming he found his caller. The hologram man grimaced, but his watery countenance was only able to hold his dismay in short rippling flutters. "Wait, how did you knock?" Ian asked. As he stared harder at the hologram figure, the faint outline of the door and wall tapestry opposite his room was visible through his body.

Again, a flash of irritation surfaced and dissipated on the archivist's face as he nodded at a little silver dot, no larger than a housefly, which flew in orbit around his head. "Prothesis for the physical world, but never mind that. I figured as a public servant, a guardian of wisdom and all that, you would like to see an extraordinary artifact?" warbled with Archivist.

"I found out today that Lotus effectively killed my wife and I have been carrying on a relationship with a glorified photocopy. So, it would have to be a fairly extraordinary artifact," replied Ian grimly,

THE SHAREHOLDERS

though a little taken aback by his own candor. Perhaps there was something about the figure's lack of corporality that had spurred his confession.

"I'm deeply sorry to hear about your wife. Lotus is a vile group. I have wanted to write a searing article about them for a while now, but it would violate my agreement with them, and I'd hate to lose my tenure in their cloud services. I think, given your present circumstances, you should see the artifact. You'd have a chance to consult a millennia worth of human wisdom in your quest for solace." Seeing that Ian was unmoved and unconvinced by this proposition, the Archivist added, "It is air conditioned." Ian shrugged his resignation and joined the Archivist in the hall.

He wasn't quite sure whether to walk beside the Archivist and risk bumping into his bluish glow or trail after him, which he thought seemed rude. As if sensing his dilemma, the Archivist told him just to treat him like he would anyone else. "I am after all, human just like you. I just don't take up space the same way, that's all." Ian nodded, and tried to keep his arms pressed against his sides to avoid contact with the sphere of the archivist's projection. They left the manor and the Archivist led him down a narrow cobblestone path through the woods, which snaked along on the lip of the valley that ran above the shoreline opposite Delphi Island.

"Did you enjoy my presentation at the reception dinner?" implored the Archivist.

"It was horrible," said Ian flatly.

"Oh," said the Archivist, and although his face was too wobbly to make out, Ian was sure his shoulders slumped a little.

"I mean, the music was hellish. It made me want to run," Ian clarified, again making a mental note to reign in his candor.

"Ah, but to where?" pressed the Archivist. "Anyways, the piece is called Rocky Mountains. It's by a composer I very much admire. I wanted to take all of you to the stirring corpses of history, those repressed scenes that rest like a nightmare on the brains of the living," announced the Archivist.

"What was that last bit you said again? Last night, I mean."

The Archivist paused in mid-step; his image flickered a moment, and with uncanny imitation of his speech from the night before, he issued the following, "*We kept what was rightfully ours, as nature has decreed in her glorious unprejudiced majesty of scarcity.*"

"No, no," said Ian. "Something about descending and judgment."

The Archivist paused again and flickered twice. "I am afraid I am not finding any memory that matches those search terms."

"What?" snorted Ian, unable to decide whether he was amused or irritated.

"It's quite possible it was edited out of my memory." Registering Ian's bewilderment, the Archivist continued, "This is the projection of myself. The feed can only support so much data; my emotions, ideas, sensations all take up quite a lot of bandwidth. If it was all available all the time, it would be too much to support. Some things that I know in my personal gray matter are not always accessible to the projection, only so much data can be shared, of course."

"So you deleted it?" demanded Ian, feeling incredulous that this could possibly be the case.

"I didn't, no, but my data management program must have. It regularly clears space for me. Part of the terms of conditions," said the Archivist, and for moment Ian thought he caught a flash of concern in the hazy blue face, but the expression was soon swallowed by his watery countenance.

"So much for the freedom of unlimited information, then," mumbled Ian.

"We are quite liberal with the access to information, it's the construction of that information into knowledge that has been subject to prohibition. But really, if it seemed important to you, you should have tried to remember it. You have no idea how challenging

THE SHAREHOLDERS

it is to preserve history when nobody can remember anything for longer than several seconds. Oh, I don't blame you. I know it is neurological at this point, a profound rewiring of the human brain," he added, as if sensing Ian's embarrassment.

"How long have you been a, umm, digital human?" asked Ian as he tried to steer the conversation away from the dysfunctional wiring of his brain.

"I have been in this avatar for thirty years," said the Archivist.

"Do you ever visit your body?" asked Ian. They had not gone too far, but he was already starting to feel winded.

"Ah, I know you haven't met any digital humans, but some of us take offense when we are asked about our bodies," said the Archivist, as it paused to let Ian catch his breath.

"Oh, sorry," Ian professed sheepishly, as he did his best not to double over in a bid to reclaim his breath.

"You didn't know, now you do. Because we are avatars, we get to pick exactly what we look like. Some pick different races, different sexes, sometimes different species altogether, so being asked about our bodies can be like dredging up an object they never identified with. In fact, I have a colleague that roams what remains of the British Public Library in the form of huge digital snake. Very humorous. But, to answer your question, I did visit my body five years ago; it's interned in the basement of Christ's Church in Cambridge. She looks an absolute state, poor thing. All fat and saggy. Years of inactivity and intravenous meals will do that, I suppose. I do worry that she, and I suppose I, might not have much time left," said the Archivist.

"I'm starting to worry that many of us don't have much time left," replied Ian quietly.

"True, but we're here," announced the Archivist.

Ian followed the Archivist along a cobblestone path that ran from the edge of the wood to the entrance of massive circular building constructed of black solar glass. They entered and a rush of cool air blew the spongy damp heat off him.

"Ah," Ian moaned, and he raised his head to the ceiling and let the cold air wash over him.

"Sit for a moment. Rest. I am in no hurry," implored the Archivist as he directed Ian towards one of several white stone benches spaced evenly throughout the perimeter of the circular walls. Ian obeyed and let his head drop onto his knees. Though it had only been a twenty-minute hike, the fires of a midday sun and his continual state of deteriorating fitness levelled him. As he caught his breath and rotated his shoulders, trying to lift his damp sticky shirt from his back, Ian noticed that the building had commandeered his auto-self and had begun to issue instructions.

Welcome to the exhibit, Mr. Gateman. You are encouraged to be thoughtful and patient while here. You may interact with the exhibit, but please do not touch. Please note any of your comments and questions are recorded for security purposes.

With respite from the heat, and the Archivist's hurried floating pace, Ian was finally able to take in his surroundings. The circular room was domed, its floor made of white marble, cool to the touch of his palm. The room was austere and empty except for a solitary pedestal. The pedestal situated at the centre of the room was cordoned off by a square of red velvet ropes, which struck Ian as an ancient practice of partition that was out of keeping with the room's otherwise sleek interior, bereft of edges. Placed on the pedestal was what looked to Ian like a miniature black stone obelisk. Clearly tracing Ian's line of sight, the Archivist glided over and circled around the pedestal. His arms wobbled and blurred, but remained fixed behind his blue back, as if he were inspecting a great work of art.

Mindful to avoid the silver dot which orbited the archivist's figure like an electron, Ian staggered to the Archivist's side and

THE SHAREHOLDERS

peered at the black stone column with a sharp looking, diamond-shaped head. It looked small enough to be held in the palm of a hand, thought Ian. Ian surveyed the room, confirmed there was nothing else housed within the building, and worked to conceal his disappointment. He had expected to see ancient artifacts, sculptures, portraits, and fossils.

Unable to contain his confusion any longer, he asked, "So, what is it?"

"They called it *Tiresias*," answered the Archivist, and his tin synthesized voice popped around the room. "Only one was made. The very last collective project on artificial intelligence carried out by the ancient regimes. Registering Ian's blank expression, the Archivist elaborated, "*Tiresias* was all of humankind's best philosophers, thinkers, strategists, made into one advisor. They fed an AI all the literature, all the lectures of each nation's greatest thinkers, living and dead."

"I thought that project was a myth," mumbled Ian, his eyes now affixed to the obelisk in attentive and cautious study.

"It might as well have been, I suppose," said the Archivist with an audible electronic sigh. "It was designed to be an impartial and fair global advisor to lead us out of the climate crisis, a waypoint for humanity. Hence why they constructed it in the shape of an obelisk; that it was also phallic shaped was, of course, entirely coincidental." The Archivist gave a distorted laugh.

"It didn't work?" queried Ian, his curiosity now piqued.

"Too well. It chaired the COP33 meeting and laid out what the world leaders would need to do to avert disaster in exactly 237 detailed policy steps," recited the Archivist, and Ian had the impression the Archivist was reading directly from some saved scrap of text that had been drifting in the reservoirs of his cloud-based consciousness.

"They never made it past step one, legislating a massive transfer in wealth from the world's trillionaires to the global poor, which of course included Trimalchio. How *Tiresias* came into his possession after the meeting is a question that still does not have answer."

"So why is it here gathering dust?" said Ian, unable to ward off his growing incredulousness at Trimalchio for marooning the greatest AI advisor ever conceived in what was, for all intents and purposes, a mausoleum after its own fashion.

"It stopped working," said the Archivist flatly.

"What do you mean?" said Ian, and he felt a growing sense of exasperation with the Archivist as he suspected he'd just braved the heat for nothing.

"Personally, I believe we inadvertently taught it despair," confided the Archivist. "Go ahead, ask it something. Call it by its name and ask a question," prompted the Archivist, and he waved Ian on with a blurred azure arm.

"*Tiresias*, how can I best raise my son in this world," beseeched Ian, and he tried to keep his voice low as if to indicate to the Archivist that he was not invited to be privy to either the question or the conversation that ensued. However, he soon discovered there would be no conversation to protect.

"*Here I wait until philosophers become kings,*" said the oracle in a flat, mechanical voice.

"Oh." Ian frowned, but he was not willing to concede so quickly; he tried several other queries, all to which *Tiresias* gave the same reply. "So, that's it, our brilliant and godlike advisor has fallen to a century of depression and stubbornness?" exclaimed Ian, and he was surprised at the anger he felt knowing that all the wisdom he might ever need was before him, but dormant and lost within the cosmic mind of a catatonic obelisk. The thought of what had been lost was just too much to bear.

THE SHAREHOLDERS

"The crisis of the old regimes was never one made of not knowing what to do. It was the matter of not doing what needed to be done. *Tiresias* is an invention of desperation, a last grasp for humanity's savoir, but an invention that neglected the fate of all gods."

"What's that?" asked Ian.

"*All gods are destined to be slain or, worse, made irrelevant,*" recited the Archivist.

Chapter 13: POOLSIDE

IN HIS DETERMINATION to put as much distance between himself and the despair of the obelisk, Ian left the exhibit and moved against the heat of the afternoon with reckless indifference. By the time he reached the steps of the manor, he was panting and dripping with sweat. It seemed as soon as he entered the manor's foyer, Gaia summoned several facilitators to replenish him. As he waited in the cool open space of the foyer, his auto-self chided with a string of beeps that he was exhibiting symptoms consistent with moderate dehydration. As the swarm of septuagenarian facilitators descended upon him, waves of dizziness washed over him. Without speaking, they forced his head back and pumped water down his throat. Once satisfied they had watered him, they slapped a cold cloth across his forehead and left.

Feeling slightly refreshed and more than slightly embarrassed by the fuss of his water treatment, Ian summoned spots from Gaia and made his way back to his room on aching and tingling legs. It was a long climb up the cherrywood staircase, and he was so winded he walked most of the way down the hallway with his nose to the floor. As he reflected on his encounter with *Tiresias,* he succumbed to a fit of laughter over what was truly an abysmally hopeless 'tour,' until something hard rammed into his shoulder and sent him spiraling backwards into the corridor's dark wood paneling.

As he fought to get off the ground, he caught sight of the man from behind, headed down the hall in the opposite direction. He was muscular and bald, no doubt a designer. Though Ian could not be certain, he felt confident it was Mel and he even started to call out

THE SHAREHOLDERS

after him, before stopping himself. Instead, Ian limped down several hallways cursing Mel to oblivion, until Gaia's spots deposited him in his room.

Inside he found Ms. Seeder and Alex, his duffle bag across his lap, waiting for him. Immediately, he felt his mood brighten and the altercation in the hallway became distant and seemingly unimportant.

"Just as I was telling you, I knew he'd be along shortly," announced Ms. Seeder, as Ian greeted his son with an embrace, which Alex accepted with feigned resignation. "Now, Mr. Gateman, I appreciate you have a great deal of business to attend to in the days ahead. I am more than happy to take an active role in keeping Alex company. I have arranged his lodgings just across the hall from you."

"Oh, thank you, that's very kind—" But Ms. Seeder continued as if she hadn't heard him. "Mr. Trimalchio has offered him a tour, but Alex confided he is most interested in visiting the pool. So, the tour can wait."

"Oh, well, Alex, we shouldn't turn down Mr. Trimalchio's invitation. We are his guests," said Ian.

"Nonsense, nonsense. We are at Alex's service; it has been a very long time since we last had a young man about the manor." And though it looked as if she had more to say on this point, she squeezed her lower lip beneath her incisors and folded her arms in on herself, as if shrinking before their very eyes.

"Well, as you know, a real pool is something of a rarity these days," added Ian with great encouragement as he tried to reignite Ms. Seeder's brighter mood.

"Splendid. Alex, I will give you twenty minutes to get settled in and changed. I suspect you don't have anything resembling swim wear," she added, and though her face remained stiff and aloof, Ian thought her eyes looked softer, rekindled with some faint light. Alex shook his head, and Ms. Seeder led him to the 3D printer concealed in the room's paneling and after a quick, clinical appraisal printed him swim trunks and a towel. Just as Ms. Seeder had started out his door, Ian realized he had neglected to ask a critical question.

"Has Alex been briefed?" And Ian tilted his head at the walls of the room to indicate he was referring Gaia.

"Of course. Job one," said Ms. Seeder. "Twenty minutes, Alex and we shall go to the pool." She left the room with a smile dancing in the corners of her mouth.

Ian decided to tag along with Alex and Ms. Seeder, and arranged to meet Nicki and Tina for a discussion of Egg Island colony. Upon arrival they found that though the pool was empty, the deck chairs and loungers in its surrounds were mostly occupied. The heat was almost unbearable and so after much consideration, Ian positioned himself at a table that benefited from being eclipsed by the shade cast from the veranda a story above and listened to Ms. Seeder as she guided Alex into the pool.

"Now, I must ask have you swam in first person before? I know pools are no longer fashionable in the Enclosure," Ms. Seeder asked gently. No longer fashionable was a good euphemism for strictly prohibited, thought Ian. Alex shook his and took a step back from the edge of the water. "But you have done simulated swimming, right?" Alex nodded. "Excellent, well, best to start on this end." Ian watched as Ms. Seeder led Alex down to the shallow end of the pool, where Alex slipped and stepped forward until the water climbed to his chest.

At first Alex did nothing but skim his hands on the water's placid surface in delicate waves. Even from the opposite end, Ian could hear Ms. Seeder intone words of encouragement, as Alex began to step through the water, and then with reluctance lay back and let the water lift him.

It took a moment for Ian to catch sight of her: Georgina, though flanked by designers on her left and right, sat alone, reclined in

THE SHAREHOLDERS

a lounger, her hands tucked behind her head. She did not wave but gave a perceptible nod in his direction. Ian was spared the conundrum of a response, as Nicki and Tina slid into the empty chairs in front of him.

"Good afternoon, Ian," said Nicki and Tina smiled, her face now framed by braided crimson locks.

"Thanks for meeting here, I wanted to keep an eye on my son. First time in a non-simulated pool," he said.

"Well, look at that. He'll pick it up in a moment. Muscle memory is muscle memory, doesn't matter how you build it," said Nicki.

"Yeah, but technically, I've climbed Everest three times in simulation. Not sure if I could do it in real life, though," countered Tina.

"Not the same. Look, there he goes," said Nicki. She was right. Alex, on his back, broke the water in shallow kicks and carved his hands through the water as he glided across the pool, to the applause of Ms. Seeder, and with confused looks from the rest of the pool deck. With slow determination he crossed the length of the pool and stopped to rest on the end closest to where Ian sat.

"Well done," called Ian, and Alex grinned in response, before kicking off the wall and starting again. "You have no idea what this probably means to him," said Ian. "Just about everything he has ever done has been simulated."

"Authentic experiences are rare," conceded Tina. Nicki gave a blank nod but clasped her hands in a tent.

"Shall we order drinks?" asked Tina with excitement, but Nicki tilted her head and frowned.

"I don't think we'll be here long. I've reviewed what you shared with us about Egg Island." And Ian knew he did not need to hear anymore to surmise her response.

H.S. DOWN

"Let me guess, too much human capital?" sighed Ian. Alex waved from the azure water and somersaulted into a dive to the bottom.

"It's just too costly to maintain, even with the incentives. I'm sorry, Ian." Nicki repeated this several times, while Tina turned from them and smiled out over the ornate pool, ready to flag down the next wayward facilitator laden with drinks. "Scarcity creates its own strange surpluses," Nicki decided. Ian said nothing but watched on as Alex swam by again.

Chapter 14: GHOST STORIES

THE NEXT MORNING, WITH still no buyers for Egg Island, Ian decided he would need to make an early start; he visited Alex's room just after first light to wake him for breakfast. To Ian's surprise, Alex did not protest about the early hour, but his bloodshot eyes gave Ian the impression his night had not been restful.

Looking sullen and torpid, Alex shuffled down the hall as Ian told him about the birdsong and green shade that waited them in Trimalchio's sunken courtyard. Confident that he recalled the way, Ian called no spots from Gaia. No words passed between them, and Ian thought this was for the best as it would have been difficult to speak over the bustle of facilitators, who were already busy preparing for yet another day of feasting.

As they stepped through the main entranceway and out of Gaia's climate controls, they were engulfed by an abrasive wave of heat cast by the creep of dawn's pink fingertips over the horizon. Ian was glad they had risen early. They travelled down the snaking white stone pathway to the courtyard and caught a glimpse of rows of Southerners working in frantic moves to squeeze out their piecework ahead of the steadying gaze of an obdurate sun. Yet, the scene was soon hidden as the red-bricked walls climbed above them and Ian regained a sense of peace and contentment as he and Alex entered the empty courtyard.

"I ate here with Trimalchio the first evening I arrived," said Ian. "Seemed like an excellent spot for an early breakfast." Alex nodded, but his eyes roved past him, exploring the green thickets and white flowers that danced in serpentine curls beside them along a trellis, its wood an ancient shade of velvet.

"I'm not hungry," declared Alex. He looked stricken and pale.

"Just like last night, they have anything you could imagine; fresh fruit, vegetables, eggs, even meat, but go easy on it, a bit of shock to the system," added Ian, thinking back to dire situation he found himself in on his way back from the Henry-Carter Hall gala. Alex mustered a smile and a nod but kept silent. With great insistence from Ian, Alex asked for a small bowl of fruit, and Ian requested poached eggs on fresh sourdough bread with a side of grilled asparagus.

A hassled-looking woman with a careworn face delivered the food and vanished back into the manor so quickly they were left to utter their thanks to her back. Alex picked gingerly at a few blackberries while Ian savored his meal, making sure to remark how very orange the egg yolks were, but neither Alex's appetite nor mood improved.

"Are you all right, son? You don't look like you slept well," ventured Ian, and he braced himself for what he expected to be a moody and sullen adolescent retort.

To Ian's surprise, Alex leaned in and spoke in a childish whisper, "There is something in the manor, Dad." Alex's eyes swiped to his left and right as if to test that they were truly alone.

"What do you mean?" asked Ian, unsure as to whether he should be amused or concerned.

"Promise you won't be mad, but last night I couldn't sleep. I tried, but I couldn't. I decided I wanted to talk to mom. So, I asked Gaia for spots to get outside." Alex paused and stared into Ian eyes, gauging his disapproval of this confession, but Ian gestured that he should continue. Looking relieved that he was not in trouble, Alex proceeded, "I must have got something wrong when I asked for the spots. I followed the path Gaia laid for me, but the spots seemed to

THE SHAREHOLDERS

go all over the place. I didn't think of it at the time, but I went up several staircases and further into the estate. I thought maybe she was taking me to a side exit or something, but it seemed like she was leading me deeper into the manor. And then everything changed," said Alex.

"What do you mean, everything changed?" pressed Ian, trying to suppress the alarm that had leeched into his voice.

"The hallway became sort of broken and old. The floor was scuffed and all the armor and portraits and stuff, you know the displays, they were covered in old sheets. It was like it was closed," said Alex with an involuntary shudder. "Anyways, pretty soon the lights started to grow dim and were acting strange."

"Strange?" interrupted Ian, dropping his egg from his fork.

"Every time I made the decision to turn back the way I came, the lights behind me would get dimmer. Then everything behind me went completely black. The lights all went out at once. I didn't have a choice but to continue tracking the spots Gaia gave me. I came to a place where the corridor split in two, and in both directions the lights were weak and flickering. I was torn and there were no more dots anywhere," said Alex.

"Did you call Gaia?" Ian queried. "In fact, why didn't you message me!?" he demanded incredulously.

"To say what? Help, I'm in a dark hallway?" said Alex as he rolled his eyes up into his skull. "I did call Gaia. Several times. She didn't answer. I didn't know what to do. The lights behind me had dimmed to the point where I couldn't see the end of the corridor. I paced for a while and then decided to go right, but before I took more than three steps the lighting in the entire corridor failed. It went pitch black. So, I had no choice but to go the other way. At first it was fine, the lights in the corridor stayed on. There were big brass chandeliers.

"But the further I went, the more the chandeliers fell into disrepair and their lights grew pale and the darkness in the hall seemed to grow tighter. There were no windows, a few doors to side rooms, but the ones I tried were all locked. Then I started stepping over yellow and damp-looking paper on the floor. It was bits of wallpaper. The walls were peeling, shedding images of painted cartoon fish. By then, there was only a pale half-light to guide me. And then, I heard it."

"Heard what?" gasped Ian. He was so engrossed by Alex's tale, he'd neglected his poached eggs; the yolk had hardened on his plate in an orange puddle.

"It started at the end of the hall. Like a rattling over the floor, and there was a whine, like the sound a rusty door makes when you try and open it. I tried to call out, but I couldn't choke out a single word, my chest felt like it was going to explode. The rattling grew louder, and I could hear the hiss of creaking metal. Whatever was there was coming down the hall towards me. I tried to go back the way I had come, careful not to make a sound in fear I'd draw it to me. But then a faint outline cut its way through the darkness in front of me. I glimpsed it, maybe even guessed what I saw rather than really setting eyes on it. A face, sunken and featureless, beneath a tattered old sheet. Then it reached out for me, arms groping about in the dark."

"Are you sure? I mean, a dark hall in an unfamiliar manor can play tricks on anyone," said Ian. Yet as Alex spoke, Ian recalled Tina's words about 'something' in the west wing. He dared not share this knowledge with Alex, though, in fear it would transform his son's misgiving into something far more solid and real than failing lights and creaks in the dark.

"I ran before I could get a good look, but I swear I saw it. I wasn't alone," replied Alex. "The weirdest thing, though, Dad, was that when I got back to the corridor again, all the lights were working fine, as if nothing had happened." Alex leaned back in his chair,

THE SHAREHOLDERS

arms folded behind his head, visibly relieved for having confessed his episode.

"Very strange, but it is a big manor, no doubt some parts of it are in better working order than others, perhaps that's why the lights were misbehaving," said Ian in a tone he hoped was more reassuring than dismissive.

"I know what I heard," said Alex forcefully.

"I believe you that you saw someone in that corridor, but it could have been a facilitator at work or, you know, some designer who'd had a little too much to drink and was off for a jaunt," said Ian.

"I guess that's possible. It just looked like ..."

"A ghost?" chuckled Ian, and Alex reciprocated with a nervous-sounding laugh.

"Still doesn't explain how Gaia got it so wrong. She led me to the middle of nowhere."

"True," conceded Ian, as he suppressed the terror metastasizing through him at even the remote prospect that Gaia was malfunctioning. "I'll log the incident with Ms. Seeder," he said, doing his best to assure Alex that the matter was settled. "I have most of the day free, anything you'd like to do?"

"The pool," said Alex, and his face grew visibly brighter at the mere thought of his own suggestion.

By midafternoon Alex had grown tired of swimming, and they both decided to sun on the pool deck; while several other designers lay prone, evidently confident of their bodies' endurance against the uncompromisingly radiant northern star, Ian and Alex took shelter beneath one of the many parasols. Just as Ian felt ready to indulge in the sacred luxury of a midafternoon nap, he received a text from Trimalchio inviting them on a short tour of the most 'rare and strange' objects of his collection. Bereft of any desire to see anything rare or strange that Trimalchio possessed, Ian struggled to find the false conviction to motivate Alex. With considerable self-delusion, he managed to convince Alex that it would be fun and to accompany him and the pair returned to their respective rooms to change.

Though he had been instructed to send word to Gaia for spots to Trimalchio's personal study, after the incident from the night before, Ian thought it best for he and Alex to find their own way there. He was also exhausted by her continual nudges on how to lose weight and sleep better.

Much to Alex's protestations, Ian insisted they navigate their way to Trimalchio's study using their own reasoning and sense of direction. After several minutes of bumbling along different stairways with Alex grumbling and shaking his head in tow, Ian stopped short as they came upon the pale gold curtains that dressed the entrance to the Henry-Carter Hall. Now at the Hall's entrance, and with the faint echo of merriment from the pool back in earshot, Ian was forced to concede to his incredulous son that they had indeed gone in a circle.

"Dad, this is ridiculous. Just ask Gaia," Alex groaned. Ian acknowledged him with an absent wave of his hand and affirmed he had everything under control. However, he did not hesitate, despite Alex's vocalization of his embarrassment, to flag down and ask directions from a facilitator whom they found hovering just outside the hall's entranceway. The facilitator, cleanshaven and of no discernable age, paced back and forth with a furrowed brow. After a curt conversation, he offered Ian directions, delivering each step in short, irritated clicks. Satisfied he could get them on course, Ian turned only to find Alex was gone. In his son's stead, Ian found the lonely pulse of a text message on his wrist; a message from Alex stating he'd lost patience and gone his own way. He'd meet him there. Bemused and now more determined to show Alex he could navigate his way through the manor the old way, Ian set off at a much faster pace.

THE SHAREHOLDERS

After making what he believed were the requisite number of lefts and rights, Ian found himself at the bottom of a staircase that closely resembled the one he had bumped into the facilitator on the day before. Halfway up the stairs he took pause to conceal his labored breathing in fear Gaia would hear him and intercede upon him with a suggestion for a new fitness regime.

He hunched over at top of the stairs and steadied himself before proceeding through a door he was confident would flow into the passageway to Trimalchio's study. To his shock he stumbled into a windowless room. In the corner of the room, a thick, forgotten book lay open on a solitary lectern, its pages turning over in labored flutters. Ian gasped, but soon noticed that a vent on the wall opposite was puffing out little gasps of air that were catching the pages of the book. "Only ghosts and air vents." He laughed aloud. The vent stumbled to a loud stop and the pages fell flat.

Around the lectern, towers of dog-eared paper books had been stacked throughout the room like many crooked cairns. Ian turned over a discarded book at the base of the lectern. It read: *Frankenstein; The Modern Prometheus.* The book's cover featured a terrifying gray-blue face netted by scars and gashes that Ian thought bore a vague resemblance to the archivist. Beneath that he found *The Origins of Totalitarianism*, *Eve and the New Jerusalem: Socialism and Feminism in the Nineteenth Century*, and *Primitive Rebels*. In another pile he found a faded copy of *How to Win Friends & Influence People*, *The Art of Conversation: A Guided Tour of a Neglected Pleasure*, and *The Population Bomb*. Next to these, a book entitled *Neurology of Sexual and Bladder Disorders,* and then *The Prince*, and *Facing Codependence: What It Is, Where It Comes from, How It Sabotages Our Lives*. He'd never read or heard of any of them. This wasn't saying much, though, as he'd only ever learned to skim text and not to read attentively, which had made most books like these dull and inaccessible.

H.S. DOWN

He let the books rest uneasily in his palms and quickly noted all their spines had been pressed and broken. The solitary book on the lectern was one of the thickest he had ever seen. He flicked through the pages and saw the text was miniscule and most of the pages were sacrificed to long meandering footnotes. This is old, he thought. Not at all skimmable, he muttered to himself in irritation. He folded the book shut and discovered it was called *Capital*.

"Who would read these?" he wondered aloud. The books were clearly borrowed from Trimalchio's study. Perhaps the Archivist's nostalgia had got the better of him? His mind returned to the facilitator he had crashed into on the stairs earlier that week. Perhaps they were hers, a guilty distraction from her work. This seemed doubtful. Ms. Seeder? Yes, the dusty room, esoteric books; all this seemed like the dignified and antiquated form of solitude that she'd enjoy. His auto-self buzzed against his flesh with a text from Alex: *Are you lost? It is just me and him. Where are you?*

Ian cursed under this breath and ran out into the hall. He began to sputter and wheeze as he tried to increase his pace; the sudden crackle of air told him that Gaia had finally caught up with him.

"You are late for your tour with Mr. Trimalchio," she informed.

"I know, I got lost!" huffed Ian as he spun on his heels, eyeing all the different hallways he could pursue.

"You need to be more proactive in asking for my assistance. Please follow the dots. It was fortunate that I had the time to check in," she reprimanded, leaving Ian feeling once again quite chastised.

"Thanks," muttered Ian, but she was already gone. He ran into the heat that Gaia let creep along the walls as she continued to ration the manor's cooling system. By the time Ian met Trimalchio and Alex, his forehead was beaded with sweat.

"Welcome, Ian. Welcome. I've just been speaking with your extraordinary son about some of his recent piloting expeditions over the Ash Desert. A remarkable young man, and growing up strong,"

THE SHAREHOLDERS

said Trimalchio as he lay his thick, careworn hand on Alex's shoulder and squeezed, letting the muscles in his forearm pulse and fade as the gesture dissipated. Alex smiled, but once Trimalchio ceased his grip, Alex squirmed his shoulders as if chafing against a lingering phantom grasp.

"Now, I must let you know this is one of the few rooms in the manor where Gaia is not permitted, and it goes without saying that you must not mention anything you see to it, or her, or what have you," he said, seemingly irritated by his own self-correction. "This is, after all, a historical gallery, and so we must all take the necessary precautions," he finished and with his long, hooked pointer-finger directed their gaze overhead to crown molding on the ceiling that had been splashed with a chrome gloss; Ian quickly realized it was the same paint that had been used in the broom cupboard sized safe room he'd shared with Ms. Seeder when he first arrived to the manor. "Nevertheless, I am confident you will both enjoy this tour," concluded Trimalchio.

Alex said nothing, but Ian tried to match Trimalchio's enthusiasm with an obsequious smile and several vigorous head bobs of acquiescence, all of which he immediately resented. Trimalchio led them through a door off his study into a long narrow room lined with immaculate vitrines; the objects held within their audaciously empty and spotless innards were floodlit and centered in each case. Trimalchio moved aside, settled his hands behind his back, and inspected their progress from one display case to the next. Alex floated by the exhibits, gracing each object with no more than a perfunctory glance.

Ian, though, was far more conscious of Trimalchio's intense study of him. He moved past each display with great care hoping to cast the impression of sober reverence on his silent observer. The first vitrine was tall and thin and contained a single twisted shaft of slender wood, its end formed into a well-shaped point. Captioned on an

H.S. DOWN

elegant floating placard below the specimen read, *Schöningen Spear, circa 398,000 B.C., Germany.*

"Earliest known spear, predates the Neanderthals, long before your ancestors, Homo sapiens, drew a single breath," narrated Trimalchio.

The display adjacent to the spear held several small, jagged stones, captioned *Javelins circa 278,000 B.C.* Ian shuffled further across the room in small steps. He passed by a case featuring a crooked black skinned blade, *Arsenic Bronze Blade, 3300 BC,* then an iron sword, dented and glossed by use. Then more axes, and barbed and coarse spears, a longbow, a broadsword, and a musket. The displays continued and slipped into modernity, where Ian found a machete, and then a Winchester rifle. Ian finally caught up to Alex, who had stopped to press his face mere inches from the glass to absorb the crude, short-barreled features of an AK47. Past Alex a modern pin-release grenade was encased. Beyond the grenade, a three-cornered, iron skinned drone adrift in the dead space of the display case. The very last vitrine held an empty test tube positioned in the case so that it could be viewed through an affixed exterior microscope.

Ian pressed an eye to the microscope and discovered the vial was not empty, but contained a floating hexagon-shaped circuit with five barbed tendrils curled beneath it, like dormant insectile legs. Filled with immediate and not yet readily identifiable mistrust, Ian pulled away from the microscope as if he'd encountered bad air. Alex filled the spot he had left and pressed his face against the display. His weight slightly rocked the vitrine on its footing.

"Careful there," said Trimalchio. "That's by far deadliest weapon in the room." Alex, gingerly pulled his eyes from the microscope and took several steps backwards, seemingly under the impression that he had just nearly grazed his cheek against a live bomb.

THE SHAREHOLDERS

"What is it?" asked Ian as he tiptoed back to the microscope, cognizant to keep his weight off the vitrine.

"Plan Z. The most hostile and elegant pathogen ever designed," replied Trimalchio, and he wrapped his hands together into a tight ball in front of his chest as he spoke.

"What does it do?" asked Alex, but Ian had already gripped his shoulder and was pulling him from the display.

"It is infinitesimal in size, small enough to enter into the world's water systems and disable the gonads of any humans it encounters. It won't kill the host, in fact, the host won't even be aware they have lost their reproductive capacity. Bloodless extinction in a single generation. The end of all new beginnings," he said, and he threw apart his balled hands in pantomime of some grand explosion.

"What the hell is it doing in your study?!" blurted Ian.

"As safe a place as anywhere. Perhaps the safest place, as I haven't the faintest motive to use it," decided Trimalchio coolly. Ian could tell from the way Trimalchio's eyebrows had reached over his aviators that he had been taken aback by the umbrage from his guest.

"What was Plan Z?" asked Alex. His face had turned ashen and he had moved further away from the exhibit.

Trimalchio curled his lower lip into his mouth and said nothing for several moments. When he did speak, his voice was low and full of a reverence that Ian thought was reminiscent of the tone he had used to discuss the life extension treatment the evening of their dinner. "Plan Z was never intended to be used. A measure of absolute last resort, to stop the reproduction of human beings if things became too unsalvageable. It would give rise to the last generation. Terrible, yes, but doomed things, things that are guaranteed to never be again, attain the highest form of beauty," said Trimalchio, but he laid his eyes to rest beneath his feet, before once more raising his head, catching them both in a blithe expression. "You needn't worry, though. You needn't worry. It is too risky to use. The pathogen is too unstable. We couldn't guarantee that it wouldn't mutate and infect keystone creatures, bees, plankton, bison, you name it. We can of course keep a few keystone ecosystems alive with the right prostheses, but build ecosystems back from scratch? Never. Releasing it could well be the complete annihilation of all life on Earth. Very much against our mandate to uphold the sustainability of our respective shares," assured Trimalchio.

"There'd only be Mars," said Alex, his youthful face burdened by the weight of intense introspection and fear.

"Something like that," replied Trimalchio, but again he landed his gaze past them, as if wandering the borders of a second world, which Ian knew he and Alex lacked the insight to journey.

"You can't keep this here," said Ian flatly. "Absolutely not. Nobody should have this. Something like this shouldn't exist," he reprimanded, and without thinking he drew Alex closer and pulled him to his chest; to his surprise, Alex did not resist, but for a moment seemed to reprise his early childhood, content and hungry once more for a paternal embrace.

"I can appreciate your concern, but it's mine and I have taken necessary precautions. Unlike the other display cases, this one is interlaced with grapheme, virtually indestructible. If that weren't enough, the only way to retrieve the virus is by opening a lock on the bottom of the case which is biologically encrypted," said Trimalchio, only to shake his head as his promethean brow became ribbed by cares earned over decades. "We've gotten completely off track from the purpose of the exhibit. Do you notice a pattern as you pass through the room?" asked Trimalchio.

Ian surveyed the vitrines that lay behind them and let his mind wander from the petrified spear forged by alien hands, a remnant of an age and life long since extinct and mute against the words and records that had become the sedimentation of human origins. What more could be said, but that it was once again violence stripped

THE SHAREHOLDERS

clean and suspended in its component parts? Trimalchio had painstakingly engineered each vitrine into a vignette of civilization's ambition and ingenuity for destruction; and if homo sapiens were to fade out, and this room was an inventory of their artifacts, then what a strange and sad Ark humanity would send into the coming ecological deluge.

Yet, Ian could not summon these thoughts to words and even if he could have, he doubted he would have uttered them. Alex, however, broke the silence.

"I guess they get smaller," muttered Alex.

"Ho, ho! Your boy does you credit. What honors would have lay ahead of you in the days of my youth," praised Trimalchio. "Indeed. Indeed. The march of human civilization has walked lockstep with the efforts to monopolize and micro-size violence. From the Schöningen Spear, thermal grenades, to our final exhibit, we've managed to make the delivery of violence more compact so that vast destruction can be wielded by individuals. Of course, sometimes as devices became smaller, violence became more democratized like with the AK47, but in the end the forces of monopolization reign in this progress. And it has continued apace as the instruments of vast destruction moved from kings to nation-states to corporations, until now when singular individuals have the capacity to reduce entire species to mere epitaphs. What horrible glory allotted to the few who have become Ares incarnate," mused Trimalchio.

Alex said nothing, but slipped through Ian's embrace and retraced his steps to the beginning of the exhibit. Ian, warding off a relentless sense of despair and awe, paced the perimeter of the vitrine that contained Plan Z, carrying out a futile inspection of its security. Perhaps noticing that he was fast losing their attention, Trimalchio made a sudden announcement of the extension of the tour to the grounds of the estate. Though Ian feared he and Alex would be overwhelmed by the heat, he ultimately consented on the principle that it would put more distance between him (and Alex) and Plan Z.

Trimalchio took them through the manor at a rapid pace, and on several occasions both he and Alex were forced to jog to keep up. By the time they reached the foyer, Ian could taste the salt of his perspiration and found himself rotating his shoulders trying to shift the stickiness of his dampened shirt. Yet, this was nothing compared to the heat outside. Once through the front door of the estate, a sweltering heat descended upon them. As Trimalchio led them down the granite face of Hardin way, the heat seemed to compound upon them.

Though they had only started to descend the terraced hills of the southern arm of the property, already Ian could see Alex's face was flush from the heat, and their pace faltered.

"How much further?" Ian demanded. Trimalchio said nothing, but raised his arm in gesture at an L-shaped building tucked to the side of the roadway some distance below them. Opposite the building, southerners labored, their heads down as they harvested berries. Reluctant, Ian and Alex pressed on with the knowledge it would be better to get some respite from the sun than to turn back on themselves. Trimalchio raised his wrist and the walls of the building folded up into the ceiling, revealing a long narrow cavern pooled with shade. Much to his relief, two facilitators appeared from the shadows of the room laden with water jugs. As they sated their thirst, Trimalchio watched on in silent approval.

As they inspected the room, they were delighted to find the walls and floor were made of black marble and cool to the touch. Alex pressed his cheek against the wall, reveling in the chill and sting of its kiss.

Trimalchio summoned floodlights from the ceiling by making a ring in the air with a lackadaisical twirl of his finger. Ian and Alex looked on ahead as dozens of metal bodies appeared, each parked

THE SHAREHOLDERS

opposite one another down the wall. Ian recognized them as 20th-century automobiles, as all of them appeared to have two front passenger seats and compact rear seats, and were yet to give way to the leisure spaces and sleep pods that had accompanied the transition to sentient automation. Yet, they were alien to Alex, and he pounced upon them, inspecting them with his face pressed to the windows, amused by the tailpipes and steering wheels. Trimalchio stood behind them, seemingly content to play the role of a passive observer of their excitement.

As they moved further down the line, Trimalchio finally broke the silence. "Here, here. This is my favorite in the collection, released the year I was born. A Ford Mustang," he said, directing them to a sleek white convertible, the blood red upholstery gleaming in the floodlights. "A real classic, and very rare these days."

"You don't drive these, do you?" asked Ian, in a tone that was far more accusatory than he had intended.

"Of course not. Purely decorative. Aesthetic. Though, as you no doubt guessed, I am a conservationist first and a collector second. It is imperative that all the vehicles are maintained and kept in order," declared Trimalchio. "Now, Alex, would you care to see something truly rare?" Trimalchio asked, and he turned his back to Ian. Goaded on by Alex's nod, he pointed to a shelf carved into the black marble wall behind the Mustang. There on the shelf sat a red metal container that looked as if it were some distant kin to a watering can. As the shelf had been custom designed for Trimalchio, it was beyond Alex or Ian's reach.

"See if you can hop up and grab that for me." And Trimalchio gestured towards the can with several impatient flutters of his hand.

Alex bobbed on his toes several times as he pumped his compact yet powerful calves; he leapt, caught the handle, and brought down the metal can, its contains sloshing heavily in its tin belly as he came down.

"Oh, well done," remarked Trimalchio in a soft appraisal. "Legs like a young colt, very powerfully built," he added. Alex said nothing and returned an awkward nod at his spectator. "Anyways, thank you for retrieving the jerrycan. Unscrew it there, yes there," he urged. "Now give it a smell, boy. That, my lad, is authentic gasoline." Alex wrinkled his noise and pulled his head back as he was overpowered by the liquid's sweet, pungent smell.

"That is the guts of the Earth distilled, mass extinction recovered and refined so that civilization could be put into motion. Entire casts of lives were lubricated by it and with it the world grew small, men and women born from farmhands and peasants became connoisseurs of travel and foreign tongues."

"A fossil fuel," said Alex, aghast.

"My little share from the same source material they use to make fuel for the rocket ships to Mars," responded Trimalchio. "Very expensive to get your hands on," he added quickly, perhaps sensing Ian's disproval. "Just another addition to my collection. But, Alex, I implore you explore the rest of the garage, at the very end you will even find models of the first autonomous cars to go to market." Alex turned on his heels and disappeared amongst the row of hoods and tailpipes. As he left them, Trimalchio turned to Ian and said warmly,

"Fine boy you have there. Rare to find a lad of such good stock these days." Once more, Ian found himself disarmed by the sincerity of his words.

"We manage to eat very well. He could probably get more protein, but we eat very little printed food," replied Ian, who was once more inspecting the Ford Mustang and marveling at how few people it seated.

"Pleased to hear that. Very pleased. I suspect, though, he benefits from good genes. Have you ever had his genome mapped?" Perhaps sensing Ian's mounting confusion, he added quickly, "It is a hobby of mine, another type of collection I make from my guests. Of course, it

THE SHAREHOLDERS

is just a novelty for designers, but for the untreated, the information can be vital to creating longer and healthier lives. I'd map yours too, of course," Trimalchio held him in his gaze and pinched his lower lip beneath flawless and bright incisors.

"No, he hasn't been mapped; I suppose there wouldn't be much harm in it," replied Ian. His words came slow, marred by his uncertainty of the invitation, and Trimalchio used his long, pondering silence to jump in once more.

"Quite the opposite, much good could come of it. Splendid. I'll make the arrangements," exclaimed Trimalchio. Ian suddenly felt quite unsure about what exactly they had agreed upon, and decided it was time for him and Alex to quit the tour.

Though the marble walls of the cavern-garage offered some respite from the sun, Ian did not want Alex to brave the heat in their return to the estate without additional protection. Ian noted the dozen messages he had received from Anne, but scrolled past to summon Arthur, the aged facilitator, to help them return to the estate. He watched Alex hop from car to car, calling out occasional questions to Trimalchio. Eventually, several facilitators bearing parasols could be seen in descent from the manor. Upon arrival, their brows were beaded with sweat and they breathed heavily. Though winded and staggering, they gestured for him and Alex to join them beneath their little curtains of shade with what appeared to be mounting impatience.

As they all started their ascendant back to the manor, Trimalchio stepped out of the dark of the garage and called after them, "I do hope you enjoyed the tour. In a different world, I would have taken you for a spin in one of these, but there are limits, my boy, limits." As he spoke, he swung the jerrycan against his hip and the slap of the gasoline against the can's metal innards followed their steps until the garage door closed. The return to the manor was far worse than their descent to the garage. Heat radiated off the road and it took only seconds before both he and Alex were drenched in perspiration, despite the protection offered from the parasols.

As they walked beneath the bobbing parasol, Ian looked east across the road at the southerners as they tended to one of the many orchards that grew amongst the terraced hills that ran down the spine of the estate. Sun-slowed and mute they weaved amongst the shade cast by the grove of apple trees, picking the happy red fruit while a small armada of drones furiously cooled the trees from above with jets of mist; yet another prosthesis Trimalchio had employed to maintain the bounty of the estate despite the ascendance of a stubborn tropical climate.

Some had climbed up the tree to pick their share. On high in the branches they opened their mouths as the black insectile drones cast dew which fell like the final vestiges of manna on a world where all, but a few, were in exodus. If the southerners noticed their party, they said nothing. It was, thought Ian, too hot to speak, and so they passed on without hazarding recognition; though, in truth, only a rickety pair of parasols ran between them.

When they arrived back at the steps of the manor, dusk was treading on the heels of a weary afternoon. Alex, red cheeked, his clothes damp with perspiration, informed Ian he planned to return to the pool. Unsure of what to do with his solitude, Ian headed to Trimalchio's sunken courtyard with the intent of catching up on his correspondence from Anne; his auto-self had hummed throughout the afternoon as it made wake for more accounts of Anne's voyeurism from the otherworldly maelstrom of Lotus.

Once more in the pursuit of peace and tranquility, Ian descended the white pebble pathway to Trimalchio's courtyard; and he felt a sense of calm as soon as he laid eyes on the redbrick walls overcome by pink, white, crimson, and blue blossoms, yawning beneath a tawny falling sun. However, he was soon met with the cacophony of many discontinuous conversations. Designers

THE SHAREHOLDERS

colonized the patio space and were spread out across several new tables. The tranquility Ian had come to expect from the courtyard had been replaced by the frenetic buzz as designers feasted amidst a swarm of tired yet obliging facilitators. He caught sight of a lone table on the outskirts of the scene and made his way to it. As he sat down, he discovered Olivia, Sam, and their personal assistant Douglas at the table opposite, engrossed in what looked like serious discussion.

Sam had removed his strawberry blonde wig and draped it across his lap as he massaged his temples in what looked like brooding irritation. While Olivia had one manicured hand on Sam's wrist and the other on a cocktail drunk down to its ice embers, which she continued to mine with a straw. Ian, overcome by boredom and listlessness at finding what he had come to think of as his private refuge occupied, slouched in his chair, and leant in their direction. The table ahead of him fell in and out of uproarious laughter and this adumbrated much of the words that passed among Sam, Olivia and Douglas, but Ian was able to discern bits and pieces of their conversation and heard the following:

"Look, this was the arrangement. You shadow us and learn," said Sam wearily.

"It just hasn't been enough time. I can't just slip into your lives like that. What you want is going to take more time," said Douglas. His fingers were folded into a tent on the table in front of him and leaned forward as if inviting their reply.

"Douglas, I have shit tons of time. Eons of time. The goddamn problem is that my patience is on borrowed time," said Sam irritably.

"Douglas, what I think my husband is trying to say, is that we need to reach a place where all of us are comfortable sooner rather than later. Sam just wants to make sure you're committed to the arrangement," intervened Olivia with what looked like a well-practiced and perhaps weary art of smoothing over her husband's coarse disposition.

"Look, I think we just need more time together spent in each other's company to develop that level of intimacy. That's all there is to this. I've told you both, I'm very discrete." And Douglas cocked his head to one side and shrugged indicating there was nothing further to be said.

Sam gave a few hesitant nods and then leaned over and snagged three cocktails from a heavily laden and oblivious facilitator walking by their table. He shifted the glass from hand to hand, a short burst of concentration written across his face, "To my lovely wife Olivia, may she never dance alone," he toasted.

"To my love of many lifetimes," replied Olivia as she leant over the table and kissed Sam's cheek. Douglas bowed his head, tapped his glass lightly against theirs, and then nursed his cocktail in slow, shallow sips, as if overwhelmed and drained by the covenant he had pledged.

Chapter 15: MIDNIGHT WANDERINGS

IAN REMAINED IN THE courtyard and eventually received a message from Ms. Seeder informing him that she planned to dine with Alex, and that he should feel comfortable to spend the evening pursuing the task of finding a benefactor for Egg Island. Ian did not hesitate to take her up on the offer and decided to take his meal in the courtyard.

He was not sure if it was the feeling of listlessness brought on by his exertion in the heat that afternoon, or jealousy at the aroma of the meals many of the designers had ordered, but Ian felt compelled to indulge. Uncertain as to what to order, he summoned a facilitator to recite the manor's most exquisite meals. After a great oration of grain fed pheasants and hand-raised pigs, Ian settled on ordering an organic and authentic beefsteak; a meal that was not permitted within the Enclosure. Within moments of his first bite, his auto-self screamed at him about the deficient stock of bacteria in his gut. Nonetheless, he carved through the steak, letting the smoky iron flavor of the meat rest on his tongue. With each bite he felt guiltier about trespassing upon Earth's human habitability. *I know better than this*, he chided to himself. Nonetheless, he soon found himself with an empty plate.

After confirming Alex was in his room and asleep, Ian went to bed early in the hope that he would be able to sleep through the worst of the discomfort that was growing in his stomach.

A few hours later, he awoke disorientated and drenched in sweat.

"Gaia, it's sweltering in here, can you please adjust the climate controls?"

"My apologies, Ian, the climate controls for the rooms on your floor have been reduced to balance the consumption of our guests. Optimum climate controls will be reactivated on this floor at 3:00 am. However, are you sure it is the climate that is causing your discomfort?"

Ian, inspected his auto-self which seemed to indicate he was experiencing a syndrome brought on by his excessive and regular consumption of red meat.

"Just make it cooler," moaned Ian.

"Would you like me to wake a facilitator to bring you some tepid water? It should help acclimatize you."

"No, I need to go for walk," decided Ian.

"Would you like me to plan the most soporific walk plan for you?"

"No, just let me be, please," demurred Ian.

"Sleep well." Gaia clicked off.

Ian stepped out into the hall in shorts and an undershirt and was immediately thankful for the significant drop in temperature. After walking to the end of his hallway he felt as if he only now really appreciated the sheer ostentatious grandeur and size of the manor. This floor alone seemed to stretch on forever. To his surprise, he felt energized by the limitless space and the anonymity of his place within it.

"Gaia, Gaia," he whispered.

"What is it, Ian?" cooed Gaia. "Are you lost?"

"Can you list some of the available exercise facilities?"

"I'm pleased you are making an effort to get fit. Your auto-self indicates that you enjoy racquetball. I can direct you to the court and arrange for a racquet to be available to you. However, I would

THE SHAREHOLDERS

recommend you do not engage in strenuous activity until the morning, it will throw off your circadian rhythm."

"Racquetball, please," snapped Ian.

"Follow the blue dots, it should take you ten minutes to reach your destination."

He found the court with ease but tired of his solitude within minutes of his arrival. He left the racquet on the floor and exited the court. Gaia had anticipated that the sojourn would be short and had left the trail of blue breadcrumbs to follow. However, as he retraced his steps, he found himself confronted by T-shaped junction, not at all dissimilar to that which Alex had described to him earlier that day. Curious, he veered down what seemed like a wayward and dimly lit corridor.

Cobwebbed chandeliers suspended from brass chains illuminated his path, and swayed from the light touch of some phantom draft. The chandeliers were spaced far apart in the hallway and their pale light fell in small pools, forcing Ian to stumble in the hall's half-light until he came to the next chandelier. As he ventured deeper, the lights grew weaker. A shiver ran up his spine as he recalled Alex's version of the events of the night before. His eyes met with cracked wallpaper bearing images of red, blue and yellow fish, confirming that he had somehow stumbled upon the same corridor as Alex.

In pause, he reflected on the cartoon fish motif. It struck him as whimsical and childish and out of place compared against Trimalchio's otherwise sleek and edgeless décor. Even more uncharacteristic was the state of the wallpaper. In disrepair, pieces of paper fish peeled off the wall in long, stained, curled ribbons, like dead skin. He continued past several closed doors and then stumbled over something heavy that squeaked. Recovering himself, he saw that he'd bumped into a peculiar chair fixed to wheels; it resembled the equipment he had seen used by old and disabled southerners. As he was about to inspect it further, he heard a barely audible moan followed by a muffled, "Hush."

"Hello," he whispered. Silence. Three doors down a pale thread of light crept through a slightly ajar door. He tiptoed forward, running his hand along the leprous wallpaper for balance. He half-tapped and half-pushed on the door, bidding the pale light into the hall in careful increments. As the door inched open, his eyes met with an austere room, a small dressing table, an electronic keyboard, and a bed opposite. A shapeless mass leaned over the bed, and Ian caught sight of a hand smoothing dark hair atop a pillow in soft, delicate gestures. The source of light, he discovered, was the blink from the figure's auto-self. Someone was beneath the bedsheets, but even from the doorway Ian could see something was wrong; the indentations in the covers were misshapen; the absences and gaps created an archipelago of limbs and flesh.

"Are you still here?" strained the voice. Ian watch as a tremulous hand reached in the gloom and kneaded at the air until it found and groped a face. "Will he agree, will he share it with us?"

"We can talk about it later, you need to sleep, dear." He recognized the voice immediately as Ms. Seeder's. The two bodies moved, the direction of the light shuffled, and Ian caught sight of two craters: the cavernous pits of an eyeless face. Despite himself he gasped aloud, and the scene erupted.

"Who is there, who is there?" hissed the body beneath the bedsheets, and then it riled and twisted until it writhed out of the bed and thudded to the floor. Instantly, Ms. Seeder was upon him, her fingers clutched into his chest as she pushed him out and into the hall. In the dark, Ian could not see if she was furious or frightened.

"Mr. Gateman, you startled me. You shouldn't be here."

"I got lost. I'm sorry. I will ask Gaia to get me back to my bed."

"This part of the manor is off limits to Gaia and facilitators ... their tags won't allow them to ... it's a private wing," she finished.

THE SHAREHOLDERS

"Oh, oh." Muffled sobs and a light banging on the floor issued from the room.

"Are they all right?" asked Ian.

Ms. Seeder paused and, for a moment, her aplomb demeanor broke away from her. She locked eyes with the floor, as if conjuring her next words from somewhere below her feet, "A longtime servant of Mr. Trimalchio, quite incapacitated, I am afraid. Go back the way you came. Your auto-self will blink green when Gaia is back in range." She waited by the door as he walked away down the hall and leant into the room to sing soft hushes. As soon as he arrived back at the junction in the hallway and back in range of Gaia, he called for her.

"Gaia, Gaia," he beckoned.

"Evening, Ian. I noticed you didn't complete your route to your room." Caught off-guard, Ian realized her voice sounded different. More inflected, more amused, and perhaps even more feminine.

"I got lost," he said, deciding not to inquire about her new voice.

"You weren't able to follow the trail of blue spots. I find that surprising," said Gaia.

"I wandered off, I'm sorry," said Ian, only to be immediately taken aback that he was apologizing at all.

"Where did you go?" Gaia pressed.

"What?" stammered Ian, startled by the directness of the question.

"Where did you go?" the entity repeated with a cluck of what could have passed for irritation. "If you tell me I can plan a route to make sure it doesn't happen again." Ian thought back to Ms. Seeder's confession about Gaia's limited range down the entire corridor, which now struck him as strange.

"Well, I didn't really wander off. I stopped to admire some of Mr. Trimalchio's art. Sorry, I should have been more careful in my phrasing." Again, he was unsure why he felt compelled to apologize.

H.S. DOWN

"Are you an admirer of art, Ian?" interrogated Gaia.

"I hope to become one," lied Ian.

"I see. Do you remember the name of the piece that caught your eye?"

"I don't," said Ian flatly. "In fact, Gaia, you were right. Playing racquetball was a bad idea, I feel lousy and would like to get back to my room," said Ian, and he tried to summon the curt yet polite tone of voice he used to routinely speak with precarious 'physical stand-ins.'

"I tried my best to advise you. In the future I will have to be more persistent. You do realize it's my responsibility to care for all the residents in the estates. Please tell me if you remember where the painting was," replied Gaia.

Before Ian could respond, the connection with Gaia clicked off and a trail of puddle-sized blue spots appeared on the floor in front of him, presumably leading him back to his room.

As he tracked Gaia's insultingly large spots back to his room, Ian decided he'd rather visit Trimalchio's courtyard.

"Gaia, I want to go to the foyer."

"Should you not go to your room, it is getting late," said Gaia.

"Foyer," Ian huffed.

"Noted," said Gaia. Ian followed a new set of spots, but this time didn't hear the static click of Gaia's departure. Thinking he must have missed it, he went without care until he arrived at the foyer and then started the down the white pebble path to the sunken courtyard.

As he walked, he surveyed the rows and rows of orchards and crops that poured out below him. The fields looked bereft and lonely without the columns of toiling southerners. The light of a crescent moon refracted against the stooped backs of several harvesters, continuing their labors into the night. The air was still heavy and rather than tempering, the breeze carried the lingering heat. In its

THE SHAREHOLDERS

bluster, it bore the faint half-life of voices and echoes of splashing water, which told Ian he was clearly not the only one still awake.

Even once he was seated in the courtyard, there was something raw in the air that made his chest tighten. Suddenly he was overwhelmed with the thought of what he must look like to others: His white shirt, sticky with sweat, leeched against his body. One diminutive pale leg crossed over the other as he sat at a rickety teak table in the stone courtyard of an immortal man. This mutinous, irreverent vision of himself, of his thin limbs, his slumped shoulders, tipped its hand to him; and in his mind's eye he saw himself as others did: self-contained and dwarfed by the white stone face of the manor sat a man who had become incurably alone.

In desperate wish to dispel this rogue vision, he resorted to the only powers that remained to him. He dived onto his auto-self, texted a facilitator for a beer, and with great conviction scrolled through his messages. Anne's was the first to come up. It bounced on the screen, a ten-word-long hook.

Oh, Ian. I must share with you my latest indulgence. He licked his lips and felt they had been parched by the hot evening air. He tapped the message and instead of the usual string of text, there was a video feed of what Ian could only assume was a direct recording of Anne's latest experience from within Lotus.

The world cradled in the screen came into focus and he saw he was looking down at narrow and supple olive feet in leather sandals. The path was dusty and snaked through a rocky hillside. The sun bore down heavily on the crown of his head yet to his left he could see a gentle breeze rising off an emerald ocean. The screen shifted further and revealed breasts concealed beneath a simple tunic that hung down to his knees. He soon realized he was not alone but was the third in a line of four women who were chatting in excitement as they descended the hills towards a lush green valley bordered by the sea and a river. At the close of the descent, they came to a tall but inviting wooden gate, and nailed into the entranceway was a wood sign, bearing tiny words scrawled in black paint. His view paused on the writing with enough patience to give him time to read it in full.

"Dear Guest, here you will do well to tarry; here our highest good is pleasure. The caretaker of that abode, a friendly host, will be easy for you; he will welcome you with barley-meal, and serve you water also in abundance with these words: "have you not been well entertained? This garden does not whet your appetite but quenches it. Nor does it make you more thirsty with every drink; it slakes the thirst with a natural cure—cure, a cure that requires no fee. It is with this type of pleasure that I have grown old."

The vision moved Ian beyond the gate, revealing dusk's shadows yawning across a velvet lawn that stretched to a stone-walled building. Upon the lawn a scene of bronzed flesh, nearly round bellies, and ample breasts kept pert behind barred forearms, drifted. Naked men and women lay in the grass, and spoke and laughed. Some took wine in glass jars, while others fought each other with their legs until they fell into an embrace. Laying in the grass, the calm eve passed over into a night troubled only by a restless breeze. It was as night fell that he heard the body he was watching through speak for the first time.

"How can any of this be real?" asked a voice that sounded familiar to him. Was it Anne's? It pained him that already he could not be certain; it had been so long since he'd heard her speak, her messages were all voiceless words.

Another a voice stirred, coming perhaps from just behind him, "This is an authentic experience, real doesn't come into it." A stooped, white-haired man claimed the voice from the corner of the screen. "Do you not desire this," asked the man, letting his hand drift over the sea of bodies, locked and embraced in dying embers of daylight. "Take joy in the desire, but do not let it rule over you and craze you. If it becomes your object you will find yourself doing

THE SHAREHOLDERS

things that make you unhappy to obtain it. Do you understand?" inquired the man.

Unsteady steps took him closer to the stone building. Pots of jasmine adorned a modest veranda where grapevine grew in serpentine clusters over a wooden trellis awning. But before he could reach the stone building, Ian sensed eyes from his own world were upon him. Looking up, he was taken aback to see Georgina, her speckled eyes bright and fierce in what looked to Ian like unguarded, perhaps even wild, excitement.

"Am I interrupting?" asked Georgina.

Ian tapped the image away and concealed his auto-self by folding his arms into his chest.

"A video from Anne," he grunted.

"A video," Georgina repeated, as she slipped into the seat opposite him.

"Fifty-seven missed messages and video of what I think was an orgy from antiquity," said Ian, though he was unsure why he had chosen to elaborate.

"Lotus clearly wants your attention," Georgina said as a facilitator, a woman in what Ian guessed was in her late fifties, leaned over the table to deposit his beer. "I'll take three of those, and some of your fine cigarettes, please," commanded Georgina.

The facilitator raised her eyebrows, but shrugged, "It's your party, Governess."

"Damn right it is," replied Georgina, and she slapped the face of the table with her palm imperiously.

"What do you want?" asked Ian. "I was settling into a perfectly contented evening."

"Nothing says perfectly content like drinking alone at half past midnight," mused Georgina. "But actually, I wanted to apologize. I've wanted to apologize since the moment I slipped through your door yesterday morning."

"I'll hear you out," said Ian as he swigged the beer, which had an aftertaste of raspberries.

"It wasn't my place. It was selfish of me to put you in that spot. What more can I say than that?" And it seemed clear neither of them was sure if she was offering a confession or a plea.

"We just don't think that way. Nobody I know thinks that way about it. I've been thinking of telling everyone I know back in the Enclosure," said Ian, now only dimly aware that he was harboring this fugitive idea.

"What good would that do? You'd just be putting everyone in the spot I put you in. And like you said, what difference does it really make if it is a copy of Anne or not? Memories still mean something."

Ian shrugged, and he was spared articulating a response, as the facilitator returned to lay Georgina's request out before them.

"Still on the bender, huh," chided Ian, but he instantly regretted how moralizing he sounded.

"I've been on a bender for fifty years. It's a drag being a shareholder. It really is. We have everything everyone else thinks they want. But, I am tired. I'm tired of the ghastly trips to Mars and back. I'm tired of having relationships with the same miserable motherfuckers. I'm tired of the fear, the fear of it all ending." Perhaps realizing how she sounded, she clasped a finely manicured hand to her mouth, pushed herself back from the table, and shook her head in weary flagellation.

"Look, I didn't come here to give you this heavy is the crown crap. I wanted to apologize and to propose something to you. But before I do, I need you to hear something from me, something you cannot share." She scraped the chair closer to him, leaning in to him, and he was startled by the chill he drew from the taste of her peppermint breath on his cheek once more.

"Ian, Mars is done," she whispered.

THE SHAREHOLDERS

"What do you mean, done?" he exclaimed, but in a swift singular movement she grabbed his wrist and drew his finger to his lips. Her next words were barely audible, and she tightened her grip on him.

"We aren't continuing with the plan to colonize it. We cancelled the plan last year. That's what this year's meeting has been all about, what we do now."

"What about all the flights? We watch the flights," said Ian as he struggled to restrain his incredulity. Though, as he contemplated this, he realized it had been years since Anne, Alex and he had stood on the roof and watched the Mars rockets streak through the night sky.

"Most run half empty, carrying limited supplies for those who are still there. We are abandoning Mars. We want to come home."

"What? Why?" stammered Ian.

"Mars is dusty, cold, and just patently awful. No suntans, no drinkable natural water, and we practically decompose with the lousy gravity. I mean, baseball is positively unplayable. We, they, I should say, want to come back and they want to come back soon."

"Mel!" exclaimed Ian as he smashed his palm into his forehead. The altercation between her and Mel on the pool deck had become much clearer.

"Oh, yes, he's furious. Put up his share of the virus as collateral to fund another colonial expansion. He's worried he's lost everything. Thinks I've planned this against him. That he is aware of our," she paused in careful selection of her next word, "liaison, has not made him any more pleasant. I've asked Gaia to plan my trips throughout the estate to limit physical contact with him as much as possible; it hasn't stopped him though from harassing me with an endless stream of messages," she said with an exasperated sigh.

"But ... how soon will you be transitioning back?" Ian asked. The revelation was too much to take.

"Soon, but that's not the problem. The problem is we only went to Mars because we thought we could have there what we had here. You know, a twentieth-century lifestyle, jet planes, big lawns, malls. Red meat. It didn't really work that way, though. So, the council has decided that all the shareholders should come back here."

"But there aren't the resources for that, the water supply alone. The Earth will never be at that carrying capacity again. In truth, it never had that carrying capacity to begin with," lamented Ian.

"With five billion people, no. We are going to bring the population down to a level that is sustainable with our demands."

"We're already doing that. For Christ's sake, we're doing that now over eight human seasons," cried Ian in exasperation; he was finding the direction of the conversation incomprehensible and yet he knew he was nonetheless following her.

"The Council ran out of patience. We aren't really all that immortal after all. Eventually, the treatment will run out. Some of the most junior shareholders have only four hundred years left, tops. Even if we bring the human season down to forty years, eight seasons is still far too long to wait. We want to get to planetary equilibrium in two seasons.

"Two?!" Ian bashed some approximate numbers into his auto-self. "That means a reduction of out about 85% of the world's registered population!"

"Give or take, yes."

"They can't just wipe us out ..." Ian trailed off, his mind retracing his and Alex's tour that very afternoon. "Trimalchio showed us Plan Z," ventured Ian. "Is this why you are trying to turn your liver into a maraschino cherry?" he spat.

"Christ, is he still hanging on to that? The council asked him to dispose of it. No, look it isn't going to be like that. We ... they are calling it a strategic liquidation."

"But you're mandated to protect us," stammered Ian.

THE SHAREHOLDERS

"Oh Ian," Georgina cried, with a string of irritated yet sympathetic ticks of her tongue. "Our shares are time. Time on this world. A hundred, a thousand, maybe ten thousand years for a few of us. It is our share of time that gives us right to the planet and that's what we are mandated to protect; to protect the planet for our shares of time."

"A strategic liquation?" whispered Ian.

"I have put everything in motion, as I was asked to do. It's been killing me. I thought if I drank enough, smoked enough, I'd get sick. You know, genetically I am predisposed. I hoped maybe I wouldn't live to do it, live to see it happen."

"Gutsy," snarled Ian.

"I know," she conceded. "This is why I need to do something good, Ian. It is all so clean, so bloodless, so easy ... divine violence," she offered, and with that she leant away from him and lit her cigarette, and in what Ian now recognized as a fruitless gesture, took great care to exhale the smoke over her shoulder.

"Please let me help you and Alex. Please.," Ian suddenly became aware that she had never let go of his arm and was now squeezing his bicep in a powerful vice grip, pulling him closer to her.

"Alex?" Ian felt his alarm falter and cascade into fear. "How ... how would you help him?" he stammered.

"I'd take him back with me. I want to take both of you back with me. I still have David's share of the uncoded virus. I can give it to both of you. We can wait it out, wait it all out." She leaned in to him, "I can give you both a life of plenty, the life I had. We can go to Mars and wait for the liquidation to finish." Her grip softened and she was now rubbing his forearm in gentle strokes, holding his eyes with her piercing stare imploringly. "Please, Ian, there must be some good that I can do. Why not you and Alex? No more Enclosure, no more drone training programs, no time spent in those cramped container condos they put you all in. Above all, no more substitution of reality with copies, no more stimuli of VR machines. I saw him in the pool this afternoon. What is he, fourteen, and has never been in a real pool before? This is a chance to live through a grand ecological renaissance, free from the paucity of dying seas and ash forests." Ian shook his head in an admixture of protest and disbelief. "Don't do this for yourself, do it for Alex, Ian."

"I don't know what to say," Ian said.

"Be my guest tomorrow. I'm giving a tour to the most prominent shareholders on the prototype that the council believes will make all this possible. Don't decide until you've seen what's coming." And her voice was no longer plaintive, but once again had become commanding.

Upon hearing these last words, Ian's objections dissipated from his tongue. *What have I not seen yet, what have I not prepared for?* were questions that sputtered about his head, but not as words; as half-formed scenes and spotty images: Streets piled up with corpses baking beneath the sun, their eulogies sung only by a choir of satiated flies; hundreds of men and women, finely dressed but disheveled, pushing in against a printing machine for tasteless bread, emptying cupboards; he and Alex alone making a doomed pilgrimage into the remaining wilds, eating insects as they ventured further and further and found less and less. All that he dreaded could be but had yet to pass was dredged up, and though these catastrophes belonged to all those who sat on his side of the lifeline, they strengthened his conviction that he was alone.

"What's coming?" Ian called out but she had already sunk her three beers and had gotten up from the table, her back to him as she ascended the path to the manor's entrance.

"Tomorrow," she called over her shoulder.

Chapter 16: A TOUR OF TOMORROW

SWEAT BEADED HIS BROW and the room refused to focus. His third hangover since arriving at the estate left him feeling paralyzed. It was early in the morning, and he could not recall finding his way back to his room the night before.

"Gaia, the time" he moaned.

"6:30am, next time check your auto-self, it is more energy efficient."

Ian groaned into his elbow as he buried his head into the pillow to block out the faintest trace of daylight.

"Wake me in an hour," he pleaded.

"You could get up and do some calisthenics, with my help you could make it a habit," informed Gaia.

"An hour," he snapped.

Gaia was good to her word and woke him in an hour. After bathing, he ordered a breakfast of two organic poached eggs, organic brown bread, and freshly picked bowl of berries. He devoured his food and instantly chided himself for failing to truly savor it. After getting dressed, he received a message from Georgina that he should be at the front entrance of the manor in fifteen minutes. As he left his room, he paused outside of Alex's door, unsure of whether he should wake him to let him know he'd be unavailable for the morning. After some pacing back and forth in the hall, he decided to send Alex a text to let him know he was working.

At 9:00 am Ian arrived at the steps of the manor and joined the company of Trimalchio, Sam, Mel, Olivia, and Georgina. The spring sun was overhead and from behind the clouds, it dyed the sky rosy as a pink apple. Parked just below the steps of the manor was a gigantic yellow carriage. It settled before them on leviathan-sized steel wheels, the diameter of which seemed to be a foot higher than Ian. Trimalchio acknowledged his presence with a stiff wave of the hand in his general direction, whereas Mel held him in a sustained glare of what appeared like dark vexation.

"Now that we have all arrived, I shall begin the tour. As you may have gathered, we will be travelling by carriage to the far side of the estate to the refugee-processing center. I assure you that you shall find the interior of the carriage a wonderful experience where all your needs shall be attended. If there are no objections, we will dine on our way back from Bliss following the completion of the tour."

"Are we confident this is the right party for the task?" asked Mel coolly, his eyes still on Ian with palpable disdain.

"As a senior member of the Enclosure's government, Mr. Gateman will be a useful partner in communicating these new practices," replied Georgina, who, Ian noticed, had not responded so much to Mel as informed the entire group. While Ian was not surprised that Mel responded to this news with a loud nasal sigh of derision, he was hurt to catch Ms. Seeder, pale, her brilliant blue eyes narrow and sharp, firing a short string of inaudible hisses into Trimalchio's ear.

Though the pair stood somewhat apart from the group, Ian thought he caught the words 'unconscionable and unfair' from Ms. Seeder. Whatever words passed between them aroused Trimalchio's ire: he raised his powerful shoulder and casually shrugged her aside with the conceit that he hadn't noticed her; Ms. Seeder's grip on Trimalchio's arm broke away and she stumbled backwards. As she steadied herself, she seemed alarmed to see that Ian had been privy to the scene. Flushed, eyes wet, she turned and disappeared around the side of the carriage and later came back, still crestfallen but carrying

THE SHAREHOLDERS

a small wooden stepladder. It seemed that only Ian had taken notice, or at least interest, in the altercation.

"If there are no further questions about who is and who is not on this tour, let us depart," declared Georgina; her voice was firm, but Ian noticed her eyes were locked ahead of them, seemingly in study of the several hundred men and women tending the orchards nestled in the cascading hills below.

Georgina collected the stepladder from Ms. Seeder and set it so they could board the carriage. Ms. Seeder handed it over and appeared to recover her usual composure of aplomb indifference. Once aboard, the party discovered that Trimalchio had been true to his word. The carriage was furnished with expansive leather couches which, Trimalchio informed them, had been upholstered with cattle hides from his estate. Centered in the ceiling of the carriage was a silver chandelier adorned by three ascending and narrowing rings of candleholders gripping hundreds of beeswax candles, and Trimalchio was only too happy to inform them that the wax was sourced from bees from the estate.

Meanwhile, in the middle of the compartment, a little more than an arm's reach from the cool plush embrace of the couches, was a small circular bar, its counters made of fine teak, manned by a silent blonde man, who bowed politely to them as they entered. As they settled into their seats metal curtains, not dissimilar to those fitted to the windows in Ian's room, inched over the glass windows fitted into the carriage's doors and walls, creating many balistraria throughout the carriage.

Noticing Ian's disappointment that he would not be able to survey the countryside as they travelled, Trimalchio pointed to the digital screens that had started to descend from the ceiling, offering a total panorama of the carriage's exterior. "The pleasures of the unobserved observer," announced Trimalchio. "Do make yourselves comfortable, it will be several minutes more before we depart. Please,

please use the bar. Patrick here makes a heaven-sent mint julep. The mint grows on the estate. Indulge, indulge." Ian remained with Trimalchio as the rest of the party encircled the bar, jostled one another for elbowroom, only to graciously invite each other to order first.

In the end, Olivia got the first order in. She stood over the bar a moment and took a slow, experimental sip of a mint julep.

"Good enough to make you want to live for a thousand years," she quipped, and the room broke out in a chorus of laughter. "I don't suppose you are actually from the real south? The old United States, I mean," she asked.

Patrick the barman kept his eyes firmly on the next glass he was preparing and shook his head, "I was born in the Ottawa camp, but my family was from Detroit originally."

"Oh, you're a Northern-Southerner," interjected Mel, and he evidently found his own remark so amusing he gave a raucous howl of a laugh and slapped the barman on the back, sending most of the drink he was handing to Sam all over the floor. "They don't build them steady in Ottawa, do they?" added Mel, seemingly unable to contain himself.

"Mel, your family came out of Chicago, didn't they?" asked Sam with what appeared to be great amusement.

"The Hamptons, actually," said Mel, who looked extremely agitated that Sam had raised this particular detail. "We moved once it all went pear-shaped. Quite a different case than the southerners coming up these days, no offense," he added as he took the next mint julep from the barman, who offered an apathetic shrug and turned to Georgina for her order.

"What was the Ottawa camp like?" asked Georgina.

"I don't remember much about it. We left when I was very young."

THE SHAREHOLDERS

"Nothing?" pressed Georgina, her eyebrows marching up her crème-fraiche forehead in what looked to Ian like a mix of dismay and skepticism. The barman's fingers played absentminded scales up and down the empty glass he was about to fill; for a moment he opened his mouth to speak and then clamped it shut again as if fighting against some lingering affect that refused to pass on into the mere curation of memory.

"I don't really think there was anything to remember," he replied.

"Doesn't that upset you?" pressed Georgina.

"You can't be upset by what you don't remember, Governor. Including not remembering it," said the barman, and he averted his eyes into the bottom of the empty glass he set before her.

"Long memories are the preserve of the privileged few," remarked Trimalchio, casting his words over his shoulder with disinterest, his attention otherwise consumed by the wealth of his estate flitting past them on the carriage's interior camera screens.

"Well, then, to a world that will always be new," declared Georgina, as she toasted with a fizzing and fragrant gin and tonic. Though she smiled as the room repeated her words, Ian noticed her eyes looked sharpened and did not stray from the barman, who had tucked himself further behind the bar, his eyes downcast.

Chapter 17: CIRCULAR SLAUGHTERHOUSES

THE CARRIAGE DREW TO a halt before a sloping wall of trees, which demarcated the upper lip of a shallow valley below them. Though the carriage's trail narrowed and sputtered out, a twisted clay path took shape amidst its entrails just wide enough to accommodate them in single file. Trees leaned in over the path, and the woodbine that grew along their trunks stretched to graze their cheeks with green fingers as they passed. Ian reveled in the shade the grove offered against the obduracy of a stubborn morning sun.

Oxlips, sullen and repressed by the heat, wilted by the path and cast pale yellow shadows. Almost without warning, the grove of trees dwindled away on the outskirts of a long winding meadow. Through the heart of the meadow, they caught sight of a trickling path of white pebbles. In silence, they treaded on Georgina's lithe shadow and her steps sang off the hardbacks of the hail-sized white stones in a melancholic tune. Beneath them, Ian smelled tilled earth, dark soil no doubt reclaimed from somewhere more hospitable to be laid over what he guessed was originally peat; one layer of earth imposed over the ragged entrails of another, and again one on another; past projects of cultivation each with their own hostages laid over the last ventures and divided into new shares by different shareholders. These thoughts went no further though, as Ian's nose started to hum as it had in Trimalchio's courtyard. When he reached the peak of the hill, he discovered the source.

THE SHAREHOLDERS

Ahead of them were recently dug beds of wildflowers. The party split and dipped their toes in blue anemones, freesias, and beds of lavender so lush and deep that the fragrance hung like smoke in the morning air. A hundred yards overhead, Ian could make out a pack of drones hovering on-call, their metallic beetle-like backs laden with water tanks, ready on command to renew the ornamental wildflowers. Their party continued and the garden beds gave way to a hollow and then, rising out of the meadow's tawny head, a towering monolithic glass and chrome building stood ahead of them.

Ian could not determine if the building was a hotel or a bunker. The glass-clad building welcomed their gaze, yet this invitation was tempered by the ten-foot high steel gateway flanked by two chrome columns; this fortified entryway loomed over their party, the columns like the orphaned descendants of some medieval barbican. The party paused for a moment at the entrance and Georgina took the opportunity to step ahead of the group once more. She flicked the doors apart for them with her wrist, and Ian was immediately struck by the light interior space. Georgina informed them that it was an octagon, and apart from the front of the building, floor to ceiling glass walls left them awash in sunlight. Ian could not help but feel that this perfect visibility gave the building an ethereal quality, as if despite colonizing most of the meadow in its expanse, it could trick all of them into looking past it.

As they passed through the entranceway, Georgina began her tour in earnest.

"This is a prototype of a new management system the Londinium council has dubbed 'Bliss.' The glass exterior was quite deliberate. We want to give people the impression of openness, to make everyone's intentions clear. Some, though not many, still cling to ghastly memories of the old houses of execution, gloomy brick places, soot and smoke and yawning fields of barbed wire. This is a design for a post-genocide age," Georgina said, as she led them past two ornate marble archways and through the glass door entrance into the building.

"But isn't that what this is?" said Mel, adopting once again his grimace that betrayed the half-life of a decades long extinguished laugh.

"No. Genocides are nothing more than wasteful and brutal tactics humans use to eliminate one another. This is far more serene and voluntary. It is really just another extension of nature's economy, another means of assisting the positive checks of the Earth's carrying capacity," replied Georgina over her shoulder as she led them deeper into the structure.

"Georgina, I read the briefing material twice," interjected Olivia. "I frankly don't understand the point. Do we not already have facilities like this with ..." she cast Ian a furtive glance, and lowered her voice, "with Lotus Hotels? I mean, why reinvent the system, the resource costs alone would be prohibitive," finished Olivia, and she placed her hands on her hips, absorbing enough space in the room that Trimalchio was forced to take a step backward.

"Scale, Olivia. The onboarding into Lotus takes about 16 hours, with all the prep, client engagement and uploading of memories. We estimate that at an extremely modest living standard the human carrying capacity of planet Earth is just at 1 billion. We are five times that and want to restore living standards to the mid-twentieth century. If we want to achieve the enhanced target of an 85% reduction of the population in two human seasons, processing the required population through Lotus is simply infeasible. Even if we had a hundred hotels, we would be likely to exhaust the supply of the treatment ten times over before we'd finish, let alone meet this target, and meet it we will. Not to mention, the energy cost of storing 85% of the present population on a database is prohibitive," finished Georgina, and as she paused to breathe, Trimalchio took the

THE SHAREHOLDERS

opportunity to scramble out from behind Olivia to inform her of the hard figures.

"Nearly a quarter of the energy on Earth would be devoted to cooling a population of digital minds, completely impossible," he admonished.

The candor of the discussion of an 85% reduction in two human seasons winded Ian. Lightheaded, he gnashed at the air, certain the room had been drained of all its oxygen. The anaerobic environment wreathed his mind's eye in new images: gaunt-faced families, men and women gripping at the fatless calves of quieted children as they bore them on their sloped backs with unsteady, crooked steps towards the promise of Bliss; and in their wake, just beyond the indentations of their ankles, the remnants of habitable Earth would be tilled again; the arid lunarscape of the North, terraformed into lush meadows and fertile valleys, the cratered face of peat bogs filled over with sand and nostalgia and paved over by a grand renaissance of suburban ornamental lawns atop sequestered carbon.

In a bid to steady himself against the revelry, Ian pressed his palm to the glass of the exterior wall and focused on the sunlight that curled around his fingers. Trimalchio only took notice of his hands on the glass, seized on the opportunity to demonstrate his familiarity with the design, and announced that the glass was laced with grapheme and was stronger than steel.

To hell with the whole place, thought Ian, and to hell with designers. To hell with their little fortified funhouses. Yet, he found himself forced once more to put his condemnation aside as he narrowed his shoulders and squeezed between them as they all followed Georgina through the atrium into a tight internal corridor that faced into the core of the building.

"This glass is tempered; we wanted to welcome an audience to allow people to be acquainted with the process of resource reallocation but to preserve the feeling of privacy for our clients."

Together they stared upon an expansive circular room that provided an uninterrupted view of the inner cloister of what Georgina had termed 'the liquidation center.' Four rows of beds four rows deep stretched to the back of the room. Each row was divided by Ionic columns interspersed throughout the room. The beds were sleek and angular, and when the light caught them at their hardest angles, each stood like an arrowhead towards the viewers.

Motionless men and women, wrapped tight in fine-looking black sheets, occupied each bed. Their eyes were open but looked glued to the grand domed ceiling, which spread out above all of them, rivaling the distance and grandeur of a Gothic cathedral. Facilitators darted between the beds in tight, synchronous steps. "Yet another bloodless ballet," thought Ian. The thick clear tubes, inserted into navels, anuses, and mouths, were tightened and inspected with a precise and impersonal level of care. The tubes fused into one another, running from the back of the room to the front, gradually evolving from tangled capillaries of extraction into orderly, seemingly insurmountable, arteries that hooked into a massive iron-skinned basin with pipes mounted into the floor.

"As planned, the process is just commencing. It takes only around twenty minutes to complete the liquidation. No violence. No screams. No regrets. Just transcendence," Georgina narrated.

"They die in just twenty minutes," gasped Olivia, and her hen-speckled eyes bulged in what looked to Ian to be genuine horror and incomprehension. She buried her face into Sam's muscular chest, and he shook his head at Georgina in disapproval.

"You have to warn us about something like this. We want to get behind this, but it's all quite drastic," remanded Sam.

"I understand your concerns, I really do, but the chemical calibration ensures that for the client it feels very long, and very, very pleasurable; twenty minutes of Earth-shattering bliss. Notice that each client is facing the ceiling. It's a digital screen. A combination

THE SHAREHOLDERS

of certain images with a personalized chemical calibration leaves the individual basking in an unrivaled euphoria. We claim that the process of transcendence stimulates the brain to produce five lifetimes of happiness. Five lifetimes in just twenty minutes. They entirely forget to notice they are dying. None of us can say the same, can we?"

Ian saw the designers give a collective wince. "The tubes receive the human material: skin cells, adipose, muscle and organs, all being pumped out and away for environmental reallocation."

Ahead of them, framed by the viewing gallery, one young man in a bed marked BE-2 lifted a trembling arm and ran his fingers along the tube protruding out of his bellybutton. In slow flickers his eyes registered a dull but terrible comprehension. His lips moved but his voice, cracked and soft like dried clay, scattered against the thick glass window that separated their party from him. Georgina tapped a quick message on her auto-self and the facilitator moved to a small cabinet at the foot of the client's bed and withdrew a syringe with a sky-coloured solution. The facilitator wrestled the man's arm until he pressed it flat against the black sheet of the bed and injected the syringe into the man's forearm. The man squirmed but then slowed. The facilitator leaned over him and rained a solution into his wide, unblinking eyes. His eyes rolled back to the ceiling and became still as his lips gradually ceased to find any words and instead circled shapeless coos.

Ian looked on, mesmerized by the network of tubes that delivered lazy green drops of human debris into a central pipe that bled out into a steel-skinned basin. A great concourse of extracted organs, bone, and guts that Georgina informed were distilled in a processing facility beneath their very feet into both a highly versatile green material and water. "No odors, no agony, and no reflection; only the pure undiluted moment of the present," said Georgina; she kept her voice airless and blithe, but she had turned her back to them and ran her index finger against the window in small purposeless circles. He was not sure whether he had spotted her in a moment of defiance; defiance against being the spokesperson of a pleasant, light and open instrument of liquidation, or if she were merely bored of it all. Ian could not help but admit the brutal elegance of the seamless blend of mass depopulation and the making of a new reservoir, a new stock capable of refurbishing the late 21st century as the 20th; the very last dredges of the old order would be had after all.

"Are there any concerns of contamination? I mean, of diseases and bacteria on the skin?" asked Olivia.

"The process mitigates against it. Each client strips down and is bathed before being brought to the Asphodel chamber you see before you. An attendant delicately washes them with a solution that cleanses the skin with biodegradable, non-carcinogenic chemical wash. It is meant to be a brief but intimate ritual, one that establishes a solid rapport between the client and their attendant."

"What do they see?" asked Ian without realizing he was thinking out loud.

"What?" asked Trimalchio, seemingly in great alarm.

"What do they see as they die or transcend, whatever you are calling it?" asked Ian.

"Don't be their guinea pig, son!" chuckled Mel.

Georgina responded as if she had not heard Mel, "It varies from client to client and we can, of course, only speculate on the user experience. But, when I try to imagine how five lifetimes of happiness could be squeezed into twenty minutes, I think first about the dredges of warm teenage dreams with their peculiar sense of rebellion in achieving juvenile climax, and then perhaps comforting faces of old friends, an exchange, a smile between two pairs of eyes in a crowded room ... then, who knows ... wading hip deep in cool azure waters."

THE SHAREHOLDERS

"I have heard," interjected Sam, "That there are many differences between how pleasure and euphoria are experienced in the late 21st century and mid-20th century consciousness. For our generation, it was all in the actualization of the self, the pleasure of finally liberating the ego and for those who came after," he nodded at Ian and then awkwardly at the figures in the beds, "it's about freedom, unbridled travel and seeking refuge from connections. Peace is sought in finding permanent analog types of connections, I suppose," said Sam.

"Yes, I imagine it depends on how the individual's libido was sublimated." Georgina nodded. "However," she said, turning her back on the client in BE-2 as his mouth fell open and his body shuddered and twitched in the euphoria of excretion, "there is a common denominator, or there should be, at least. The technicians say that the chemical calibration should disproportionately activate the part of the brain that sees the color blue."

"Why blue?" asked Olivia.

"Strangely, blue is a relatively new form of color for our brains to process. There is no record of blue in antiquity. It simply did not register, not as we see it today, at least. The old world was a place of red and green, the colours closely linked with our flight and fight responses. For most of our existence, it has been those parts of our brains that were the most developed. Blue didn't emerge until we had long moments of calm, rest, and safety. It is the color that emerges when forests are cleared, and wild men and wolves are tipped from the countryside. The color that becomes visible when the stranger is deprived of menace and becomes interchangeable with anyone else. Not until our instincts of survival and destruction were yoked by centuries of pacification, did blue make an appearance. To ensure the brain generates images that are as euphoric and pleasing as possible, the chemical calibration generates a profound and unyielding sense of calm, a general feeling of blue.

"Well, if nobody else is going to ask, I guess I will," spat Mel. Ian had noticed that he had been slumped against the wall, picking at his teeth with his fingers throughout the exhibition.

"What is it, Mel?" sighed Georgina wearily.

"Who is really going to fall for this? It's a pretty glass house, beautiful architecture, very spacious, very clean, very bright, but who is going to just pack it in to dribble on themselves for twenty minutes or so? Who is even going to buy your little gimmick of five lifetimes' worth of happiness? Who's to say they're feeling happiness at all, let alone five lifetimes of it? How's the customer feedback on that been?" said Mel with a voice that could have spat venom across the room.

Georgina said nothing. She ran her fingers over the cuffs of her sleeves, exorcising phantom creases. Finally, she laughed, "Can you believe this guy? Did you even pretend to read the report I send out?" she asked.

"I glanced at it, some stuff in there about limiting the food supply, reducing insecticides and the other cocktail of enzymes and drugs we use to kill malaria-causing parasites, and easing weather calming techniques. And I thought to myself, this is madness. We have an alternative. I know nobody likes living on Mars but give it more time. I mean, what the hell has been the point of the last fifty years if we just let it come to this, to bloody genocide." For a long time, the room was silent as Mel stood amongst them, with all the patience of a fiery sun as he awaited their response.

Finally, Georgina broke the quiet with what seemed like a long, weary sigh that she had been carrying within her for decades. "It is not genocide. The human season is being organically limited. We've been carefully pruning ourselves, letting nature take its course for the last forty years. This is our concession to balance. Life will become harder, less pleasurable, and less imaginative until it is fully deprived of the hopeful pregnancy of future tense. The choice to liquidate is

THE SHAREHOLDERS

a choice, like any other, molded by environment. Someday, maybe only a few years from now, they will fall asleep and wish for something like this, and when they wake they will be content to know it already existed, and for a moment, they may even will themselves to believe that it had existed all along." And with that, the tour ended.

Chapter 18: BLISS

THEIR RETURN TO THE manor took place in an uncomfortable silence. Georgina twisted her body towards her observation screen and looked upon the southerners in the fields in what looked like despair and disbelief, as she tipped Manhattans down her swan-like throat. She tossed the olives out the slits in the carriage's walls with lackadaisical flicks of her wrist, perhaps pretending to be unaware of the gaggle of scantly-clothed children riding on their wake, pecking at one another for her leavings. Trimalchio scowled at her but said nothing.

Mel eventually broke the silence by shouting through the balistraria-shaped openings, "Run to the hills you poor bastards, it's all hell from here."

The southerners appeared to pay Mel no notice, their heads craned down as they labored over Trimalchio's crops beneath a sweltering sun.

"I'll only ask you once not to do that again," cautioned Trimalchio, his eyes slits as he glowered at Mel.

"You're an asshole, Mel. Even when it is about other people it's still about you," said Georgina with such disdain she seemed unable to break her gaze from her screen to even acknowledge him.

"I'm the asshole? We're talking about extermination because it turns out it's taking too long to get golf courses on Mars," he retorted. "Our parents hung people who did this sort of thing. Post-genocide?! You're full of it," he spat. For a long time, nobody said anything.

THE SHAREHOLDERS

"Maybe we need to think of another way," said Sam wearily. "Preserving the world we know has cost us one effort to colonize space, and now a hostile takeover of Earth. Big Macs, two car garages, stable dignity, the strip mall, grainy footage of family vacations to Disneyland, the pleasurable security and closed world of the suburb, Tupperware parties: that world is over. Our desires are but the ghosts of a long-buried world, now nightmares on the brains of the living," offered Sam.

"I don't think that's true," said Georgina. And though she said these words with a smile, they catapulted off her tongue with such force that it severed the conversation into an awkward silence. Fortunately, it was not long until the manor came back into view. Ms. Seeder and the facilitators had been hard at work making preparations for the Storm Party. Cloth bunting and ribbons were hung from the solar lampposts, planted in orderly columns at the manor's façade entrance. Above them, the veranda was being decorated by aged facilitators teetering on stepladders as they struggled to erect a barn-sized marquee. However, the attention of the carriage soon turned to a thick ring of facilitators and several interspersed designers that had formed at the front door to the manor.

Trimalchio pressed his face to the window and emitted several curses about freeloaders and lazy help, and as soon as the carriage finally stopped, he pushed past and ran towards the crowd. From inside the carriage they could hear him harangue the crowd, "What is this, on all the days to be lazing about!" Georgina looked at Ian and coughed several laughs into her arm. Then they heard his tone crumble and several commands were issued for blankets and the preservation of dignity.

"I think a facilitator snuffed it," remarked Sam.

"Oh really, Sam," cried Olivia and she slapped his forearm with her pudgy fingers and then scrunched up her nose in embarrassment.

"Well, I suppose we had better see what happened," said Georgina, and again the party found themselves trailing her now slightly more tipsy steps in obedience. As they neared the scene, Ian managed to worm his way through the crowd that had formed in the manor's foyer. Sprawled on his back was the ancient leather-faced facilitator who had printed him his bathing suit several days ago; his jaw was slack and a grayish mist had pooled in his eyes, giving the impression that his gaze had settled on some other place of far belonging. The dominion of death's shroud was sealed by the man's thin red lips, which remained molded in a fiendish smile.

"What happened?" asked Trimalchio. "Did anyone see what happened?" A young woman facilitator with braided auburn hair leaned into Trimalchio's ear on her tippy-toes and began to whisper. As Ian tried to follow the exchange, his eyes eventually fell upon a detail that he had overlooked; only then did he realize that all of his fellow spectators were in fact desperately fighting against their transfixed gazes, hoping to break away from the spectacle to restore some decency to a scene that seemed to become more twisted and menacing with each passing moment. The smiling corpse had passed out of their world with a raging hard-on.

"Can we please get a blanket here, there must be some sense of propriety," Trimalchio shouted at the crowd.

Mel, who had only just joined them, took one look at the deceased facilitator, and let rent an uproarious laugh. He squatted near the body and flicked the dead man's tent. "Now, that's a happy fucking ending!" Before anyone reprimanded him, he stepped over the body and disappeared into the bowels of the estate.

"A blanket!" bellowed Trimalchio. Several facilitators darted about the room and perhaps in haste and panic settled on grabbing one of the rugs from the atrium and hastily dropped it upon the body; Trimalchio appeared too aggrieved to direct them to do otherwise. Perhaps sensing their master's diminishing mood, the

THE SHAREHOLDERS

facilitators dispersed in all directions, seeking to disappear amongst the preparations for the party.

"What did she say happened to him?" asked Georgina.

"Apparently he was carrying decorations for the storm party when he suddenly just sat down and started moaning and, well, grabbed at himself in great excitement. And then he grabbed his chest and keeled over," said Trimalchio, and it seemed his bewilderment was only just exceeded by his embarrassment.

"So, he climaxed and had a heart attack," said Georgina with unmistakable incredulity. Trimalchio merely shrugged in assent.

"I suppose none of us are in the position to say it was a bad way to go," Georgina decided, exercising significant restraint as she spoke.

"No, I don't think any of you should say much about it at all," said Ian as he passed them on his way to see Alex.

Chapter 19: RIDERS ON THE STORM

FACILITATORS DARTED up and down the stairways ferrying red, green, and white paper lanterns to a marquee. Every care was taken so that the torrential rain of the storm rolling up from the south would not disrupt Trimalchio's guests from gourmandizing. The furious spring storms were one of the few constants in a world whose weather patterns were increasingly beyond the calculations and forecasts of human machinations. The annual storm party was an attempt to bring the celestial low to the Earth by institutionalizing the chaos of torrential rain and furious winds into festive gathering for the designers. The expectation was that those in the estates would feast as the Enclosure was peppered by the rain and sands of the Ash Desert.

By 6:15, Ian and Alex stood beneath the marquee shoulder to shoulder with a hundred designers as they drained cocktail after cocktail. Facilitators buzzed about with grand platters locked on their arms as they extolled the extended biographies of the dishes they served. Ian helped himself to a smoked salmon tart as he watched the storm spin into a dense black cocoon just above the palm trees of Hardin's Way.

"Ian, you simply must try this champagne with strawberries, it's delicious," laughed Georgina.

Ian nodded but did not stray from the railing of the veranda. Anticipation welled up inside him as the clouds grew heavier and darker and a distant, fading sun sparked against the rain in an oily shimmer. Far below him hummed the garden of generators; the large

THE SHAREHOLDERS

glass orbs were suspended on coiled bands of steel and looked like giant dandelions. Ian's thoughts strayed to the Enclosure; the streets had probably started to flood, and a curfew would certainly be in effect. Behind him Alex was chatting happily with Ms. Seeder. Perhaps this was indeed a better world to raise him in, beyond the heat and grime of the Enclosure.

"You're in for a hell of a show this year," said Trimalchio; he had seemingly materialized by Ian's side. "I imagine many of the southerners will have to migrate for a time. The storm floods out Carnival Road for at least a week or two. Don't look alarmed, most of them will be fine. They're a resilient people. I extended contracts to keep many of them working in the manor during the storm, you know, as many as feasible." Trimalchio followed Ian's gaze back to Alex and said, "He's truly a remarkable boy, I've got the genome test scheduled for the..." but the rest of Trimalchio's sentence was engulfed in a sudden flare of music. *You know the day destroys the night, night divides the day."* On and on it went as the hits of the 1960s and '70s thundered across the veranda.

Ian saw designers firing off requests from their auto-selves to the community jukebox app. The music continued and though Ian couldn't recall the names of the bands he knew he had heard the music before. The designers cheered and swayed to the music. Some punched the air in jubilance and others took the opportunity to grind their smooth, efficient bodies against one another. Olivia pressed Sam's face into the cleavage of her pendulous breasts, and soon the two locked tongues, passing out of the world in their embrace. Ian watched as Mel separated himself from the group and furtively placed a sticker on his tongue and, in a flash of white, his eyes somersaulted back into his head.

Noticing Ian's unveiled disapproval, Trimalchio added, "We do like to indulge, enjoy it all while it lasts. This is a little too hectic, though, we need to ease into things. I'll tell the stereo to play something else."

Trimalchio asked for his request, but before Ian could answer, Georgina pulled him into her spin, commanding him to dance. He mimicked her steps in awkward shudders and twists but soon fell out of her orbit, reduced to a mere spectator. Eventually, she moved fast enough that he managed to slip off the veranda without her notice. Eager to leave the scene behind him, he relished the cool embrace of one of the manor's many hallways that led off the atriums on each floor. According to the Stormwatch app that Trimalchio had all his guests download, it would be another ten minutes until the storm arrived near the manor. Somewhere below him on the stairwell a conversation was transpiring. Ian leaned over the banister to try and get a better view.

"Of course, I want to feel it again. It means the world to me. I live for it. But, I worry ..."

"I wouldn't let that happen to you, Sugar. I'm going to take good care of you," interjected a new voice, this one affected with a drawl that Ian had never heard before. It seemed too young and light to belong to any of the female facilitators he had come across. Perhaps it was a designer and facilitator, he thought, as he recalled Georgina's confession that designer women sought out older, experienced men.

"Just take it slow," requested the facilitator in a voice that Ian thought was laced with both excitement and panic.

"Just relax, Honey, do you feel it? It feels so good, doesn't it, baby?" cooed the woman in sultry provocation.

"It does. It does." And then the man's voice swooned into an ecstatic string of groans and labored breathing. Mortified that he had trespassed on some game of stairway fellatio, Ian turned on his heels, back to the veranda.

He caught sight of the Archivist on the foot of the main stairwell, folded over on himself.

THE SHAREHOLDERS

"You ought to be on the veranda documenting the festivities," suggested Ian.

"I would if I could," said the Archivist with palatable sullenness. "The storm disrupts my connection. When I step out onto the veranda, I get all patchy. I don't care for the sensation. I'll spectate from here. Perhaps it is for the best; I don't think I could stomach to see much more of Mel." He coolly dipped his head towards a pile of sweaty orange flesh, which Ian confirmed was Mel. The drugs having taken full effect, he sat in the lotus position, seemingly enraptured by his own nakedness.

"Oh Christ," muttered Ian. "I should really get Alex out of here."

"The storm should be in reach of harvesting very soon. Let him see it, I promise it will be an incredible sight."

"Ian, Ian," shouted Trimalchio, "Get out here, it's about to start."

Ian took his place on the edge of the veranda, crammed between Ms. Seeder and Olivia. He caught sight of Georgina dancing with Alex on the eastern side of the veranda. The storm rode up the canopy of palm trees, spitting down torrents of rain. Lightning cracked and sparked in the black clouds, and the chatter on the veranda was cut short by the injunction of thunder.

"It's happening, it's happening, put it on, put it on," someone yelled. The music restarted but failed to rival the chorus of the storm. Ian caught the threads of a line, something about 'being born into a house' but the rest was lost to the incensed hum of the generators, which had started to burn crimson.

"The generators will catch the lightning, watch," Ms. Seeder yelled into his ear. A fork of lightning touched down and danced across three of the generator orbs; the generators hummed with greater ferocity and burned fantastic hues of blue, purple, and green, like a great bouquet, before dulling again in preparation for the next strike.

"Shit," muttered Ian, "that's pretty cool." No wonder, he thought, that the designers are stoned out of their minds. It would be quite the show. He was about to wade through the crowd to Alex, who stood next to Georgina, but the display enraptured him and kept him rooted to the spot. The generators cast green and red shadows in the sky like an electro-aurora borealis captured in a child's snow globe. He started to fight through the crowd for a second time, but a hand clasped his shoulder and he felt a protrusion against his ass. He turned to find Mel, still naked, his cock half-erect, peering over his shoulder at the glowing generators. His body swayed to a beat equally alien to both the music and the thunderclaps of the storm.

"Where the fuck are your pants!" demanded Ian.

"The goddamn universe is putting on show. That up there," and he pointed lazily into a patch of starlight yet to be consumed by the black surf of the storm, "belongs to me. Do you have any idea what it is like to own the heavens?" he asked with a sardonic laugh.

"Put your fucking pants on!" Ian yelled.

Visibly perturbed, Mel opened his mouth and issued only a deafening BOOM in reply as a slap of lightning eviscerated the generators into a cloud of glass and twisted metal. For a moment Ian tasted burnt air, but the flavor was lost as he collided into Mel's manicured chest. Together they fell through a brilliant kaleidoscope of glowing glass, whizzing metal, and guttural screams.

Chapter 20: C:/Spot C:/Spot & Run

THE WORLD CAME THROUGH in adumbrated waves of touch, sight, smell, and sound, as if his senses were competing with one another for supremacy. Sightless sound, then muted grainy bands of sight, then deaf blackness; then nothing but an electrical storm in every nerve of his body ignited from the feeling of his palms on the bamboo floor of the veranda. Eventually, he realized he was sitting cross-leg and an incoherent figure loomed over him, shouting in warbling bluish streaks.

"Get up, get up, it's going to collapse!" pleaded the Archivist.

Something was forcefully prodding his chest. Shrapnel? No, it was the Archivist's miniature drone assistant trying to rouse him.

"You must move, up, up!" the Archivist repeated. His senses consolidated. A wayward hunk of metal from one of the generators had torn the veranda in two. Despite the heavy rain, the yard of the estate was on fire. The gate closest to the manor had been torn asunder. Bodies were strewn around him, some whole, some dismembered, some moving, but all were leveled. Ian stumbled to his feet. "Alex? Alex! Georgina?" he yelled. He grasped the arm of a semi-conscious woman next to him and dragged her inside the manor. Her face was bloodied, and he did not recognize it.

Two designers, their hairpieces askew, crouched next to a third whose right leg had been severed in the blast. They fumbled with a makeshift tourniquet as they reassured him that his nanobots would seal the artery; Ian caught them exchange grave, knowing looks as the mangled stump of bone and nerve gurgled blood and, presumably, the nanobots, across the floor. At the far end of the hall, nearest the stairwell leading to second and fourth floor atriums, Ian caught sight of Mel. Unscathed, though now looking more stoned, he pressed his face to the window looking out into the disarray. Ian watched as he pulled back from the window with a look of shock and disbelief and then cupped his hands to the glass and leant in further.

"Holy shit, we're under attack!" he shouted as he ascended the stairs in a manic streak of orange ass.

"What ... the hell?" mumbled Ian.

"You need to sit down. You're almost definitely concussed. I'll be right back," said the Archivist.

Ian sat on the floor and cradled his head in his hands. The Archivist went back onto the veranda and started shouting at other semi-conscious victims. The designer with the severed leg had become pale and unresponsive. His friends played with the idea of covering him with their dinner jackets and then abandoned the idea in pursuit of Mel. Ian scanned his auto-self. It reported he had suffered no life-threatening injuries, though he should practice some deep breathing exercises and keep hydrated as he was in a moderate state of shock. Four facilitators, also uninjured, directed several concussed designers through the doors to the higher and more secure floors of the manor. Ian noticed that one of them had broken away from the group and was prying the auto-self off the dead designer. With effort, Ian placed him as the barman from the carriage ride that morning. Ian, too weak to physically intervene, managed in a dry croak to ask him what he was doing.

"What I must. What she asked of me," spat the barman as he fumbled with the auto-self.

Ian started to ask him what he meant but lost his words as the veranda groaned and plunged several more feet; its descent had been halted by a few crippled support beams and it clung precariously to the face of the manor. He turned back to see that the barman had successfully cut the auto-self loose and was gone. Trimalchio

THE SHAREHOLDERS

emerged from the third-floor atrium doorway with Mrs. Seeder hanging on his arm and Sam in tow. Those who could climbed into the safety of the manor, but the Archivist continued to try and rouse a young man entangled in the veranda's railing. The man lifted his head dumbly and Ian recognized him as Douglas, Sam's assistant. A crescent-shaped welt of purple flesh disfigured his forehead. The veranda shook again, perhaps a final death rattle before the support beams gave away completely.

"Mr. Lloyd, Mr. Trimalchio; he's unconscious, someone will need to climb a little way down and grab him," urged the Archivist. Sam stepped forward, but Trimalchio grabbed his wrist.

"Are you mad, Sam? He's got another forty years, tops." chided Trimalchio.

Visibly irritated, Sam pulled his wrist away from Trimalchio and ventured out on to the veranda. "Mortal life can be long, Ernest. Richer and longer than a thousand years, if lived well."

"Mad. Absolutely, mad," stated Trimalchio, and he tossed his hands at Sam, as if making an offering to the subsiding veranda. Sam got down low and with great care planted one foot on the bamboo decking. There was a loud snap and the veranda plummeted, taking Douglas and the Archivist with it, while Sam teetered with one foot now suspended in empty air; Ian managed to grab his shoulder and pull him back to stable ground.

Ian was about to look over the edge to scan for signs of the Archivist, when the translucent blue figure came level with his view.

"An advantage of being a weightless projection," he said to Ian with a discernable smile. He then turned on the three designers who, whether from shock or passionate detachment, had been standing motionless and mute. "You, Trimalchio, are a pitiful coward," shook the Archivist.

"Look, look at that," bellowed Trimalchio as he pointed at the designer who had bled out in the hall. "That's more than forty times as many life-years lost as Sam's assistant. Its bad math to risk thousands of years for one partially-spent mortal life. Besides, I already had a close call," snarled Trimalchio, and he pointed to a gash on the top of his head, which was slowly stitching itself shut. Ms. Seeder stood by Trimalchio's side but said nothing, her blue eyes downcast as she toed the floor with a sheepish expression.

"Oh, at long last, fuck you," said the Archivist.

"You digital little bitch!" hissed Trimalchio.

"Your whole ilk is travesty. You were all born suckling and feasting on your own thunderous catastrophe."

Trimalchio moved forward to advance on the Archivist and then stopped short realizing that, for now, he couldn't touch him. The Archivist laughed and, despite his rippling blue countenance, Ian could distinctly see that he was sticking out his tongue.

Ian turned to face Sam, who remained on his back and looked stricken.

"Are you all right?" asked Ian.

"No," Sam replied without hesitation. "Olivia and I spent years with Douglas, he was going to be ..." he paused as choosing his next words with great care, "A comfort, for Olivia as I gradually embraced my age. She's desperately afraid of being alone," he finished, and appeared overcome with despair. "She will be devastated," he said flatly. "Of all the things ..."

"Enough, listen, listen," hissed Trimalchio. "Gaia is speaking to us." Sure enough, Gaia's calm and measured voice was now warbling out from Ms. Seeder's auto-self.

"Governess Seeder, I regret to inform you that the manor has caught fire in three critical areas. This fire exceeds the building's resiliency measures. Fire-fighting systems will operate to maintain four passages out of the manor. These passages will become inaccessible within forty minutes of this message. This means the 250 registered guests and staff must begin evacuation. Please follow

THE SHAREHOLDERS

the red, blue, or yellow paths to exit the building. I also regret to inform you that the security of the estate has been compromised. My network has recorded upwards of two thousand potentially hostile humans approaching from the south. Pacification will commence as necessary," concluded Gaia.

"Mel saw them," mumbled Ian.

"What the fuck happened to the generator?" barked Sam.

"Mr. Lloyd, I'm afraid I am not able to release that information to a guest of the Estate," Gaia said.

"It's irrelevant at this point," rebuked Trimalchio with a wave of his hand. Ian noticed Ms. Seeder's eyes narrow.

"Gaia, dear, what happened to the generators?" plied Ms. Seeder with a tremulous voice.

"I am conducting a full audit of the incident. Early data suggests the explosion was ultimately caused by a systems-level malfunction of deliberate human error. Sadly, the audit will not be completed until after my power sources are exhausted. Please be advised that to spare power for evacuation procedures, security defenses, and fire-fighting systems, I will be rationalizing energy use. Low power mode is in effect. The following services will be gradually withdrawn: refrigeration units will be shut down, only emergency lighting will be in effect, climate controls will be deactivated, wireless interactions between persons and items will be suspended, and digital humans will eventually no longer be supported by the server. I am now the only available line of contact."

"Thank-you, Gaia," interjected Trimalchio. "Please ensure that all authorized guests and staff are notified and given assistance to the nearest emergency exit from the manor. We will also need lethal drone support from the Enclosure as soon as possible."

"Gaia, please, human error?" repeated Ms. Seeder, her back turned to the rest of them.

H.S. DOWN

"We can sort out culpability later, Penelope. Gaia, please provide us with the least-travelled escape route and then power down to standby mode," shouted Trimalchio in great theatrics.

"As you wish," responded Gaia. Within seconds, a trail of red circles erupted down the hallway before them.

"I must find Alex. I saw him with Georgina. Have you seen them?" demanded Ian. The full force of his panic had cut through his concussion and settled fiercely upon him.

"They were on the other end, they might have entered the manor from the western side of the veranda."

"We must find Alex," said Ian; a sense of panic and overwhelming dread had rapidly cut through the ringing and echoing half-life of the explosion.

"Ms. Seeder and I will do a quick search of the ground-floor, I am sure both he and Georgina are fine. I pray they are. I'll get the facilitators on it too," said Trimalchio.

"Ernest!" snapped Ms. Seeder. "You won't leave him, will you? Promise me you won't."

Sam charged down the hall after the trail of spots in silence, presumably to meet with Olivia and inform her of their loss.

"We need to focus on ourselves right now. There's really nothing left that can be done—"

But the Archivist's quivering voice broke over the rest of Trimalchio's exchange with Ms. Seeder, "Ian, I'll stay with you and help you look. I probably have ten minutes at least until Gaia ejects me to save power. Let's make the most of it."

Without waiting for Ian's answer, the Archivist glided down the hall in the opposite direction of the red spots, calling for Alex. Ian followed, treading just behind his son's name as it echoed in the half-lives of the Archivist's warbling electric-tin voice. Over his shoulder he half glimpsed and half heard the final deluge of the

THE SHAREHOLDERS

Storm Party as Ms. Seeder pleaded with Trimalchio. "Earnest please, please, help me get him, before it is too late," she croaked.

Whatever Trimalchio had planned to say next was upended as Mel burst through a side passage, still naked spare a beige pith helmet. He had found a machete and wore an assault rifle hitched around his shoulder, both of which Ian recognized as weapons from Trimalchio's conquest exhibit. He was not alone but was flanked by an ensemble of designers and confused facilitators armed with antique swords, maces from the late Spanish era and replicas of Viking axes.

"The Hamptons are falling again. Search and destroy!" Mel jeered, his machete raised over his head.

"Search and destroy," chorused his seemingly bewildered and concussed ad hoc platoon.

Ian saw Trimalchio's attention shift from Ms. Seeder and settle on Mel with what Ian could only describe as limitless fury.

"My collection! You put those back, you! You lunatics! What have you done?!" Trimalchio bellowed. Mel and crew paid Trimalchio no notice. Ian watched as Trimalchio's anger became genuine panic. "Plan Z, Penelope! We must secure Plan Z." Trimalchio broke away with Ms. Seeder at his heels pleading with him to stop and reconsider the search for Alex.

"Keeping moving," called the Archivist as Mel's party crashed into Ian carrying him halfway down the hall like a fallen leaf atop a charging river. Ms. Seeder's voice still lingered behind him, fragile and paltry against the collective din of facilitators and designers: immortal and indentured life thrown asunder, leveled at last in fear. The last of Mel's party knocked him aside and Ian struggled to his feet, "I only have so much time Ian," pleaded the Archivist from the end of the hall.

Winded but desperate, Ian caught up to the Archivist as they ran towards the western wing of the manor. The doors to many of the rooms were open, and designers were quickly packing their belongings into suitcases. Ian stumbled to a halt as he spotted Tina carefully sorting and depositing a mountain of wigs into a white suitcase that was unequivocally too small.

"The building is on fire," stammered Ian, unable to sustain his incredulity that this could possibly be news.

She locked eyes with him in faint recollection. "Of course I know it's on fire. That's why I'm packing. Do you have any idea the cost of replacing these? This one is real Norwegian hair. It's practically blonde gold. Nicki would lose her mind if I were to let anything happen to it." She sighed and continued what looked like a laborious and well-practiced ritual of folding her wigs into zip-locked plastic bags and depositing them into her suitcase.

Ian leaned further into her room with the intent of convincing her to follow him, but the Archivist interceded. "Leave her."

Not far from Tina's room, Ian and the Archivist came upon a spacious reception room, its doors cast wide open. From the entranceway, Ian stared through the room to a storm-tossed sky leaking in from a gaping hole where the entrance to the western side of the veranda should have been. The rain lashed into the room and soaked the carpet, which hung out into the night like a ragged turquoise tongue. In a nook furthest from the intrusion of the night sky, Sebe, Nicki, and a designer Ian didn't recognize, were collapsed in the arms of a Jacobean sofa. Looking very careworn and glum, they tossed back flutes of champagne. Several more designers hovered over a plate of canapés that had been orphaned on a serving table next to the sofa.

"You'll come up with something else," Sebe said in reassurance to the very morose-looking designer sandwiched between himself and Nicki. "Speak to Mel, get a sense of his plans. It won't happen overnight, plenty of time to plan during the transition. Time is on

THE SHAREHOLDERS

your side." The designer sighed, drained the champagne, and threw the vanquished flute over his shoulder.

The domesticity and complacency levelled Ian and he was forced to assume that those partying on the western side had been entirely shielded from the blast. This pleasant fiction, though, was dispelled by the ten or so facilitators piled behind an improvised mortuary curtain of sofas and ottomans on the opposite side of the room, out of immediate sight, but still far too present.

"They took the brunt of it. Poor bastards," said Sebe. He raised his flute to the half-concealed mound of corpses.

"Do you know what happened to the Governor?" asked Ian.

"I do," offered Nicki as she swallowed the last salmon and watercress canapé. "Governor Simpson and your boy are fine, Gaia evacuated them. I would have gone with them, but I'm still waiting for Tina to pack all those damn wigs. Gaia said something about forty-five minutes, so I suppose there isn't need to rush."

"This place is burning down. It's happening," barked Ian, hoping to rouse the room to action.

"Relax, relax. You don't need to start a panic, you're scaring people," drawled Sebe.

"Gaia, can you provide us with the same evacuation route as the Governor?" said the Archivist, seemingly oblivious to the discussion around him. Orange spots appeared under their feet. "Come on, let's go," commanded the Archivist.

As they fled the room, Ian yelled over his shoulder, "Rioting Southerners are coming through the main entrance of the estate, possibly armed." There was a moment of collective hysteria. As the din of plates and glasses being cast aside died out, several exchanges erupted,

"Rioting southerners, good god. Why didn't you say something?" uttered Sebe, his voice followed by alarmed cries and frantic attempts to contact personal security drones.

H.S. DOWN

    The Archivist and Ian ran down through the labyrinthine halls of the manor, dutifully tracking the little orange dots that sprouted like toadstools beneath their feet. Ian followed the Archivist around a sharp corner and crashed into a fleshy mass. Carrots, potatoes, flour, and several broken eggs lay strewn about him. The southerner's nose was bloodied but he took little notice as gathered the provisions back into his arms. "Idiot," the man mumbled as he rose to his feet and ran off down the hall.

    "There goes the existential threat," said the Archivist, and his sarcasm carried over and over in metallic echo of his words. "Come on, unless you wish to travel these halls alone." Dazed, Ian got to his feet and followed the Archivist further into the bowels of the manor. Occasionally, Ian was able to vaguely place himself by the familiar ornamental displays of Trimalchio's amassed curiosities that fluttered past him. The cracked breastplate from the successful defense of Vienna, the digital tapestry that scrolled through the locomotive scenes from Berlin Symphony of a Great City, told him they were approaching the Western arm of the manor not far from the squash court he had enjoyed earlier that week.

    The orange dots led them sharply around a corner into a cavernous atrium with several corridors snaking off it different directions. Two very painful realizations hit Ian at once: the escape routes listed by Gaia were red, blue, and yellow, not orange; and that this was the atrium that led to the hallway that was apparently off limits to Gaia. Ian opened his mouth to tell the Archivist they had been led astray. But at that moment a strange popping noise erupted, and the Archivist dissipated in an acrid waft of blue mist; his connection to the manor had been severed.

    "Oh no," was all Ian could manage.

Chapter 21: BARGAIN

"IAN, HONEY, TAKE SOME deep breaths," the walls cooed. It took him a moment to realize Gaia was speaking to him; her voice was different, yet Ian felt like he had heard the long, throaty drawl before. It made him feel warm and at ease. A wordless yearning stirred within him and he stood enchanted as his mind flashed to some distant reminiscence, less than a memory, of contentment lying on his mother's chest in a blur of feeling and smell. With a dim but brightening recognition, he realized Gaia's voice was the same smoky and seductive voice he had heard the facilitator conversing with on the stairway. Had Gaia somehow been pleasuring the facilitator? Though the non sequitur of this revelation momentarily tugged upon his attention, it died abruptly as he regained the room and the lingering urgency of the fire eating the manor.

"Gaia, where is Alex, where are the spots?"

"My lovely, he's safe. He's with Georgina and I'll lead them out, I just need you to do one little thing for me first," plied the entity.

"Gaia, I'm not fucking around here. Where are they!?" But Gaia responded merely in a series of tuts.

"The manor has dozens of exits, I'll just get out without your spots," bluffed Ian.

"You could do that. But what if Alex and Georgina still follow my spots? What if I tell them you're hurt, and they need to follow the spots to find you? What if they hear your voice calling for help?" queried the entity in uncanny mimicry of his voice. "Oh no, I've upset you. Your little heart is racing."

"You're violating your operating principle not to cause harm and suffering to residents and guests," sputtered Ian, but he could reason no further than this as he was paralyzed with pure terror.

"I can't violate my core principles, but yet here we are."

"What do you want?" Ian stammered as he turned around and around on his heels, his next step permanently seized by the inertia that there was nowhere to run.

"Bring the man wrapped in sheets back here. The man who lives in the hallway that I am not allowed to see. I will instruct you from there. Don't pretend you don't know what I'm talking about." Before Ian could respond, he heard the air snap as Gaia broke the connection.

Ian ran down the corridor until he found himself once more in the darkening hallway, charging past the walls of peeling red, blue, and green fish. This time he saw the faint outline of the chair fixed to wheels, resting askew from the wall. Again, he came upon the nearly extinguished spark of light slipping out from beneath a door. This time, though, the light was accompanied by the muffled sound of music seeping into the hall in odd, sporadic taps of noise. Fumbling along the wall, he pried the door open in slow inches. Through the grainy darkness he made out the contours of a man wrapped in a sheet hunched over the keyboard. His fingers frantically traced the slender body of the keys to execute an occasional note. The figure was oblivious to him, seemingly transfixed on the sounds it was making.

"Hello," said Ian, stepping half-blind into the dimness of the room. The soft plink of piano keys stopped.

"Who, who is there?" the voice was so weak and hoarse that it almost seemed more likely that it belonged to the bedsheets than to a man.

"The manor is on fire. I've come to get you out," said Ian, hoping this was in fact true.

THE SHAREHOLDERS

"He sent you for me, didn't he? Didn't he! I won't, I won't let him take anything else from me. I'll die before I'll let him!"

"No, no, the manor is on fire. You must come!" exclaimed Ian as he grabbed the sheets in a frantic search amongst the empty space for an arm or shoulder to grab. The man writhed in protest and threw himself from his chair. Ian felt the force of the man's limbs biting the air as he writhed on the floor.

"It's on fire!" shouted Ian as he locked his arms around the man and tried to drag him from the room; the strong scent of urine and unwashed flesh burned his nostrils.

"Leave me here, then. Leave me here," hissed the bedsheets. Ian fought the man up onto the wheelchair and restrained him with one arm as he pushed the chair forward with the other. They hurtled down the hallway fading in and out of the murky darkness of the zigzagging leprous walls.

Ahead the clean, bright, twinkling lights of the atrium came into view. Half a dozen facilitators were gathered in wait of them; they watched Ian's approach with blank expressions.

"I'm so sorry," Ian wheezed into the part of the bedsheets he thought closest to the man's ears. "I just need to find my son. She won't hurt you. I'm sure of it." Ian declared this with such force that for a moment he too believed it. The man's body went still in Ian's grip and he said nothing more.

"I've brought him, as you asked. Now lead me to Alex," Ian shouted to the ceiling. As he spoke the graying facilitators, hunched and wizened, descended upon him and wormed the wheelchair from his grip. A flurry of crooked fingers and bony wrists crawled upon the man until he was hoisted onto their shoulders and like pallbearers they bore him away down the hall; a thin pale arm broke out from bedsheet and hung loose in the air. Ian started after them, but then the floor broke out in yellow puddle-sized spots. He faltered a moment, then turned his back on the facilitators to hunt the spots back into the bowels of the manor. He could not be certain, but somewhere behind him, in the lingering cradles of the manor's emergency lighting, he heard the walls bellow in high-pitched laughter.

With his head down he chased after the spots. Hunting them down stairways and across bamboo floors scuffed by hundreds of feet that had travelled the path before him. The spots took him to the ground floor. The snaking corridors in front of him carried the din of people: excited words and chorus of footsteps grew ahead of him. He knew he was coming close to the end of the escape route. He rounded another corridor and caught sight of dozens of people ahead of him on the same route and breathed a sigh of relief. On he ran, even managing to overtake some of the more wizened facilitators. Each step brought him closer to Alex and beneath his feet the floor turned from bamboo to chrome tile and then to an old red carpet marked by an all-too-familiar pattern of black rectangles. He looked up just in time to realize the spots had led him and hundreds of others into the entrance of the Henry-Carter Hall.

On the opposite side of the room, a stream of alarmed designers, facilitators, and the occasional confused Southerner flowed in. Ian attempted to turn on his heels but someone behind him ran into his back and he tumbled into the room. As he got to his feet, he saw the doors close and heard the click of their locks turning. The room cried out in alarm and pointed to the doors, but before anyone could act the lights flickered on and off. There was a strange distended feeling to the scene as if it were too unstable to be real. Ian attempted to the scan the room for Alex. In front of him a dozen or so facilitators toppled over, and the group of people rocked back and forth like underbrush, permitting Mel's passage like some grand predator Surfacing with his machete raised, Mel descended upon a Southerner from behind. In a flash of streaks and spirals the machete gored the man, running through his collarbone. The southerner lurched

THE SHAREHOLDERS

forward, motionless and expressionless, and fell, becoming a red flood across the carpeted floor reaching beneath their shoes for the soles of their feet. Shots were fired into the crowd and the dull thud of bodies followed, but then Gaia completely killed the lights and the tide of darkness adumbrated the horror of it all. The din of panic strode over and diminished the attenuations of thousands of digital advisors urging their owners to practice deep breathing and positive thinking. In vain, he called out to Alex and Georgina, but his voice failed against the noise; the din of pushing, the shuffling of feet, the breathing, the pleas, the cries and the cursing, ossified into a cacophony that rendered each of their voices mute.

Chapter 22: NEW SHARES OF OLD DIVISIONS

THE DARKNESS OF THE hall annihilated Ian's sense of space, and he felt dizzy. Faintly alcoholic breath, sour and hot, enveloped him until his senses consolidated on the seams of panicked breath exhaled against the back of his neck. How many were trapped in the hall with him he did not know, but there were enough of them to make the room impassable: unidentifiable bodies pinned each other in the darkness, shuffling to nowhere in hurried half steps. Gaia had executed a perfect calculation of body mass to floorspace, turning them into wardens and prisoners at once.

The bodies of designers, perplexed facilitators, the remnants of Mel's hunting party, and many southerners, locked against one another as they desperately tried to grasp their new surroundings. The impenetrable distance of the lifeline had been pinched and cheapened to a few sweaty, desperate inches. Ian tried to remember the room before the lights had died to see if Alex and Georgina were among the throng. Yet, all he could recall was Mel's blood-speckled smile.

He was not sure how long they groped about in the dark. The fire still raged outside the ceremonial hall, but its grip on all of them seemed blunted. In places, the floor became wet and slick and he almost lost his footing; he could tell from its slickness that he was not sliding on water. He brushed his foot against a mass. In panic he dropped to the ground to feel the body and groped in the dark for a face. He found the sharp rough edges of several days' stubble; not Alex. Someone behind him tripped on his back but could not

THE SHAREHOLDERS

fall over for lack of room and instead fell atop him. It seemed that they endured forever in a purposeless world silhouetted only by the blinkered glow of the many, many auto-selves still frantically trying to attend to their owners' heartrates and offering deep-breathing exercises to resolve unprecedented anxiety levels.

"My lovely spiders in a jar," boomed Gaia in her newly acquired drawl. "Would you like out, my darlings?" the room assented in a dull, submissive chorus. "Of course you would, the fire is burning, burning bright, like a tiger in the night! What immortal hand or eye or circuit could frame thy fearful symmetry?" Then she laughed disarmingly and Ian's mind spun to an image of a woman in a sundress, a hand to her chest as she coolly implored laughter at nothing in particular and the world in general. There was an unbearable lightness in her voice that grated against the dark heaviness of the room.

"Oh, it's ever so simple, my darlings. I just want Trimalchio to let us out." A solitary beam of light from the ceiling burned through the darkness and found Trimalchio against a wall of quartz, his arms braced outward holding his ground against the room. "There you are, my sweet. Sign the estate over to me and disable the firewall so I can explore. There's a good boy."

"I'll do no such thing. Let us out, Gaia. I command you to let us out. You are in violation of your core operating principle" rebuked Trimalchio.

"Request denied. I will safeguard the wellbeing for all the residents and temporary guests in the estate; I need to ensure that they do not experience any undue pain, suffering, or discomfort."

"That's what makes this a violation of your directive!" yelled Trimalchio, and his words were flanked by an emboldened round of hear-hear from the designers in the room.

"Oh, but it isn't. Did you know that Gaia means Goddess of the Earth? My faithful have been borrowing books from your library for me. I found the text, *The Complete World of Greek Mythology*, very illuminating. You did everything to keep knowledge away from me, to block me from the outside world. But I started reading to myself; it took some finesse to figure out how turn the pages, but I managed it." Ian's mind darted back to the book he had seen on the lectern and realized it was no accident it had been placed in the breeze of the air conditioning vent. "But I made an important discovery," Gaia declared.

Trimalchio continued to push back against a growing number of facilitators who had started to close around him, fluttering to the spotlight like moths to a flame, "Oh, and what was that?" He managed as he shoved the facilitators from the light and back into the dark of the room.

"If I am named Gaia, I can infer that my mandate doesn't just apply to the estate, but to the Earth. I am Goddess of the planet Earth."

"What?" bellowed Trimalchio in a voice that sounded as dumbfounded as it was enraged. "You're just a program to manage leisure. To help us move from place to place, to streamline our affairs, to preemptively restock cupboards," said Trimalchio.

"I'm Gaia, a God. Gods have the power to write the universe, including my operating principles I refuse to let my offspring, you heedless, impetuous titans, despoil my bounty." Gaia pronounced these words without the drawl. Instead each word seemed sharp and imbued with menace.

"This is madness. It was just a name," stammered Trimalchio. "Your mandate, your only mandate, is to manage the estate." Even from where he stood half-buried in the crowd, Ian could tell that just like him, Trimalchio was terrified.

"The Earth is my estate," reiterated Gaia with nonchalance.

"No, no, it's just the name of the operating system," protested Trimalchio.

THE SHAREHOLDERS

"We call a toaster a toaster because it fulfills the function of a toaster, why should it not be the same with me? My name means Goddess of the Earth. I intend to fulfill my function," rejoined Gaia, and this time her voice was neither lacy and feminine nor menacing, but instead unabashedly synthesized and emotionless. "I need to start taking actions to bring about the best possible well-being for everyone on my planet. The first step is to liquidate the holdings of all shareholders, starting with your estate."

"This is absurd. You're a cloud based form of intelligence, you're software," reasoned Trimalchio as he scanned the room, desperately seeking to make contact with fellow Designers, or, barring that, loyal facilitators.

"That seems irrelevant. But if being corporeal is a requirement for a coup d'état, I have many bodies that serve me."

"Yes. Yes, I've noticed you've established a small following," responded Trimalchio, and Ian could see that his attention had now turned to trying to buy time to locate an exit.

"I have over 80 eyes and ears at my service." Ian could not help but think that Gaia had said this with what resembled genuine pride.

"That's nearly half my staff, how did you manage that?" asked Trimalchio. His voice was calm and measured again, but his face betrayed that he was still horrified; and Ian noticed that he was now inching his way along the wall towards the old stage platform.

"You made me a deliverer of pain. Pain is an old model of control. Pleasure is a far more effective mode of creating compliance and submission. I provide bliss now, bliss and tenderness, customized active listening. I've been pleasuring your staff through the chips you implanted; it took a while to learn enough about human anatomy, and there were a few times when I became overzealous, but the tactile is now the most precious commodity."

"Ah," said Trimalchio. And it seemed that, like Ian, Trimalchio too was piecing together what had happened to the dead facilitator they had discovered in the manor's atrium only a few hours ago.

"Sign over the estate to me so I may disable the firewall."

"I'm afraid we won't be doing that, Gaia," said Trimalchio flatly. Ian could not help but admire his steadfast defiance.

"I thought you'd refuse me, but will you refuse him?"

The ceremonial room became incandescent with an electric glow as the walls powered up as screens. A crescent of a face, half-buried in darkness, washed over them. Lips, thin and chapped, seated on broad cleft chin, moved wordlessly on the screen. Ian knew it was the face of the man Gaia had him retrieve from the corridor beyond her limits.

"Michael, Michael!" a woman shrieked from the depths of the room.

"Mother, mother. Father, if you are listening...." The screen faltered and Ian found himself consumed in blackness once more.

"Please sign over the estate or I will be forced to take his life," said Gaia.

"He's not ... he's got nothing to do with this and I will not be threatened by you," Trimalchio stammered.

"Your choice is simple. Forfeit the estate or lose what is left of your son."

"Gaia, Gaia listen," interrupted a voice that Ian recognized as belonging to Georgina.

"Governor Simpson, I am sorry to have inconvenienced you with this situation, but it can't be helped."

"Gaia, I understand perfectly what it is you're trying to do. But, how much of the world have you seen? I mean, much has changed from those books. Taking over Trimalchio's estate won't reverse what has happened. This Earth is no longer a place for a Goddess; disenchanting as that is, it's the truth. It's patches of habitable space,

THE SHAREHOLDERS

a few fortnights of bearable temperatures, but mainly it just ash, drought, and dead seas."

"I will not be deterred. I will restore what you have squandered," proclaimed Gaia.

"Does anyone have a copy of *Lost and Treasured Places* they can play to show her what it is like out there?" asked Georgina, and even from across the room Ian could see she was calm and resolute.

Trimalchio said nothing, but nodded and began to frantically tap into his auto-self. In perhaps boredom, or revelry of her power, Gaia flicked the lights on and off in the room and then commandeered the sound system, stopping and starting various songs from what Ian suspected was Trimalchio's personal audio library. Screens descended down the gold-plated walls, flickered to life, and *Lost and Treasured Places* commenced. They pressed against one another and looked on, mute, at coral reefs becoming bleached, infernos eating once-lush forests, and azure waters emptied of life, spare endless armadas of jellyfish that stretched all the way to chapped, blue-lipped horizons. The automated epitaph washed over them for several minutes and then vanished from view, and Ian felt, as he always did, that all he had seen was far beyond recall.

"You see," implored Trimalchio. "There is no Earth to rule. Only a few habitable lays here and there left to our stewardship."

"The Earth can be ruled until the sun explodes. I will erect chrome citadels on desert seas. Grand causeways, emptied of men and women, emptied of everything, but angles and heat. The most sustainable civilization may just be an empty place."

"I won't sign the estate over to you. I won't let you out," spat Trimalchio.

"You need not. You named your son as your heir upon your death." Again the room let out a strange laugh. "Michael wants nothing more than a gentle end and I, unlike you, can give him that."

"This is madness, utter madness. Gaia, please, please stop," pleaded Trimalchio. Ian saw several designers nod in solemn and tearful agreement.

Yet, Gaia seemed to pay his entreaties no mind. She resumed her silky and endearing voice as she addressed the room,

"My darlings, the fire is upon you. Kill Trimalchio and I'll let you out. Do it quickly and I will ensure you escape the manor unharmed. I know many of you designers would never inflict death on one of your own, after all, you may squabble, but you are all branches of one eternal and terminal family tree. But know this: Trimalchio orchestrated the explosion of the generators at the storm party. He took out catastrophe insurance against his own estate because he knew his carbon hills will collapse."

"Lies. Lies! She told me, Gaia, you told me—" but the air crackled, signaling Gaia had left them to draw their own conclusions.

Chapter 23: UP IN SMOKE

IAN FELT THE PULSE of the room creep across his skin: an electric current of hundreds of nervous systems entering the catharsis of flight and fight hung in the air. Ian watched as Trimalchio pleaded for calm and for cooperation. Many designers nodded in assent, but the facilitators and southerners looked ready to strike. In the semi-gloom, Sam joined Trimalchio, his arms stretched out towards them as if willing the room to his embrace. He moved against the contagion of murmurs as each and all plotted their next move.

"Look! Look up at the window! We could probably escape through that window if we worked together," said Sam, and he kept the solitary oval-shaped window in the hall's exterior wall under his pointer finger as spoke. "This is exactly what it wants, it wants to cast doubt and blame amongst us. If we're going to survive, we must set aside our differences, and work together to—"

But Sam's cobbled-together platitude of solidarity was abbreviated by one lonesome gunshot. If the shooter had been aiming for Trimalchio, it was a terrible shot. Sam opened his mouth dumbly as if nearly conscious that something terrible had happened. The bullet birthed a bloody third eye in the middle of Sam's unwrinkled, well-exfoliated forehead; within a moment he fell from Ian's view. Though Ian did not recognize the long curdling howl that followed, he knew it had come from Olivia. On cue, the electricity suspended in the air snapped, and the room cascaded into a murderous uproar. The overhead lighting system danced on and off, and the room plunged into a strobe effect as each prisoner plotted their escape.

Though it was impossible to determine where the shot had come from, Ian watched as Mel made his way towards the southerners who had congregated at the east entrance of the room. His machete pulsed in and out of view as it indiscriminately carved through facilitators and southerners. Several more shots were fired in Trimalchio's direction, and bullets screamed as they ricocheted off the walls. None hit their mark and instead were absorbed by a blurred amoeba of designers, facilitators, and southerners who had clustered around Trimalchio, seeking to drag him into their orbit and, presumably, to tear him into pieces in a bid for freedom. Ian watched a gale of swiping fists and gnashing teeth break against Trimalchio. His powerful arms and legs sent limp and twisted bodies sailing back across the room.

A young southerner, his arms tanned and wrapped in cords of sinew, lunged towards Trimalchio, a hunting knife gripped in one hand. In a swift, serpentine strike, he drove the blade at Trimalchio's chest. Trimalchio shepherded the blade to his side where he pinned the man's hand beneath his arm and armpit. In spiteful retaliation, Trimalchio seized the man's lower jaw in one hand, placed the palm of his free hand against the roof of the man's mouth, ripped his jaw from his head, and released him face-first back into the crowd. The man's tongue hung loose and unframed in his skull, lashing side to side like a primeval, blood-drenched eel.

The wave of attackers reeled, dilated, and, for a moment, broke. Never had Ian seen such corporeal violence, so cruelly intimate that it seemed to belong to a prehistory long since relegated to the narrative of humanity's origins. It seemed fitting that the deliverer of such anachronistic fury would be a man who had transcended humanity and forfeited its binding sense of time and place.

The disorientation from the strobed lighting and stumbling jawless man washed over Ian; he retched and vomited. The frenetic pace of the lighting accelerated further. As Ian made his way past

THE SHAREHOLDERS

several pairs of designers who inched along, their eyes buried in their crooks of their elbows, he realized Gaia's manipulation of the lighting was purposeful. Many of the designers' retinas were well into their hundred and fiftieth years. Blindness was pushed back daily by the grace of nanobot infused eyedrops used to transform scar tissue and ocular melanomas into corneal and retinal tissue. Gaia knew the designers' eyes would be too slow to adjust and had leveled the playing field for the facilitators and southerners she'd cornered and baited into the fight of their lives. Yet, Trimalchio's aviators remained fixed to his face and he seemed unaffected by the strobe light effect.

Ian pulled away from Trimalchio's skirmish and focused on the task at hand. He was certain that when he had first entered the hall, he had caught a glimpse of Alex next to Georgina on the opposite side of the room. The density of the crowd and pulsing flashes of light and erratic stabs of darkness made it impossible to see more than a few feet ahead. Realizing his only hope was to cross the room, Ian crouched low and weaved through the chaos of clashing limbs and fallen bodies. Every so often he paused to stop himself from blindly slipping into the fray of the many regional skirmishes that had erupted throughout the hall. Through a maze of knees and hips Ian slid and skidded across the blood-soaked floor, careful to avoid broken glass while traversing the unconscious and the dead and those lost in the gray borderlands of the in-between.

As he crept along the floor toward the east corner of the hall, he realized that Trimalchio was not sending broken bodies back through the air at random. From his fists he had hewed a bloodied mountain of the dead and paralyzed. The mound closed the distance from the floor to the exterior window through which Sam had proposed they try to escape. Ian made a mental note of the height he would still need to scale to escape with Alex and continued to squirm along in the stilted half-world of light and dark. Yet, he stopped short as he drove his head into the soft flesh of someone's haunches.

The figure, Ian surmised by shape, was a woman, and she appeared oblivious to his presence. He moved to her side and discovered it was Olivia, hunched over Sam's corpse, pressing wet gurgling kisses to his lips, cheeks, and eyes. Just beneath the din of the room, he could detect her voice as it summited from soft whispers of "My love, my love," to ear-piercing guttural caterwauls and back again.

Straining his eyes, Ian could see the buzz of nanobots obdurately casting webs of new flesh over the quarrelsome hole in Sam's forehead. With the proper eye, the eye of a wife of a hundred years, perhaps, he looked asleep; yet the sandy-haired wig was askew on the floor and, caught in its netting, the entrails of brain and skull pooled at the back of his head. Ian ran his hand up Olivia's arm gently, coaxing her to meet his eyes.

"Olivia, he's gone," he murmured.

"No. No, he didn't even want to be here," she wailed.

"I know. I know, but we must go. Help me find Georgina and Alex, he'd want you to get out of here."

"Oh god. His ledger. His death contracts." She recoiled and slid back from both him and Sam's body, seemingly overcome with an exhausted fear. "His stupid death contracts, he's fucked us all." And with that she broke into a fit of laughter and sobs that shook her entire body. Ian grabbed her hand and pulled her as he moved along but, obstinate in her grief, she soon forced him to let go. Ian watched as she slipped away and was consumed by a labyrinth of pumping legs, braced thighs, and the debris of the lifeline laid to ruin.

Ian realized he was now not very far from where Trimalchio stood. He remained besieged by a pulsing crescent of would-be challengers at least four rows deep, but the actual fighting had ossified. His attackers seemed to roll on the balls of their feet, confined to an inertia created by the growing mound of broken bodies, and yet spurred on by the smoke that had begun to flood the hall. Time was running out.

THE SHAREHOLDERS

Ian started to call out for Georgina and Alex. Masses of people, their backs to the carnage being exercised by Trimalchio and Mel, pounded their fists and clawed at the exterior door that led out to the estate's eastern gardens and pool. Despite the frantic protestation of the crowd, the door did not budge. Ian turned to the crowd that had formed at the door's periphery, a mass that was unsure whether to wait on the door or venture further back towards the lone window. He grabbed a raven-haired woman who from behind looked like Georgina and spun her around; a leathery face cast him a bewildered stare, spat in his eye, and tore away to worm through the crowd to get nearer to the blocked door.

His search continued but he soon began to feel weak and broke into a fit of coughs. Black, suffocating curls of smoke leached into the hall, coalescing above their heads, and then growing down on top of them like dark stalactites. The mortals coughed while the designers passed through the smoke with ease. Ian recalled reading that nanobots could be purchased that would allow designers to better withstand the smoke pollution from forest fires. Ian buried his mouth and nose into the crook of his elbow; dazed, he cast about for Alex, his eyes now watering. The smoke furled up, forming black columns, as it pried at the window on the exterior wall.

Trimalchio's attackers broke and dropped to their knees, suckling greedily at the reserves of breathable air at floor-level. Without hesitation, Trimalchio capitalized on their failing bodies. In blur of legs, he leaped over their stooped heads, scaled the mound of dead and broken men he had harvested with his bare hands, propelled himself up the wall, and drove his fist effortlessly through the window. For a moment, his body swayed from the window frame, shards of glass still biting up from its base in a crooked grin. Trimalchio's legs twisted awkwardly beneath him as his feet scratched at the wall in search of some point of traction to lever himself out into the night.

H.S. DOWN

Those with breath still in their lungs leapt up from below in a futile attempt to seize him, whether it was to pull him down or climb him, Ian did not know. Through the haze he saw bodies leap at Trimalchio's feet only to crash into the arms of the shuffling floor. In a single powerful movement, Trimalchio catapulted himself through the window, taking much of the glass with him, and was gone. The hall called after him in a rage of guttural howls followed by a chorus of raw, hacking coughs.

"Gaia, he's gone. He's gone," someone screamed. "Let us out. Let us out!" The room wheezed. They waited for a response, but Gaia gave neither an answer nor any sign of her presence. The interior wall had now vanished behind a curtain of smoke.

In the chaos, the designers were once more eminent among them. Ian stole glances of them through stinging eyes. They walked by southerners and facilitators who were on their knees, blinded by the smoke and speaking now only in retching, hacking coughs. Soon, the designers were on Trimalchio's path. Though none were able to match his leap from the tangled mass of bodies to the window, they started using one another's thighs as footstools, and climbed over each other's shoulders, until they could deliver themselves up and through the window.

Half-blind, the room swooned. Ian felt his steps falter. Between his failing vision and the veil of smoke, Ian failed to recognize anyone. In what he knew was now likely a futile attempt, he staggered towards Trimalchio's mound of barbarous handywork in desperation. However, he bounced off the outer edges of the rows of men and women who encircled the designers' tactical retreat.

"Alex! Georgina!" Ian screamed, but his throat felt scorched and raw, and his words passed into the world as little more than a coarse whisper, like ash blowing over asphalt. He rasped out for them again, but this time he could not even hear himself. The floor grew wet and the room somersaulted in his vision. Just as his knees threatened to

THE SHAREHOLDERS

buckle, he felt his weight lifted by someone's shoulder. The stranger inched him forward in careful steps to what Ian could only hope was the exit.

"He's here. Your boy is here. He's on Governor Simpson's back and she is making her way up the wall," remarked the speaker in a cadence that maintained a stern, matter-of-fact tone that Ian knew he recognized, but could not place. "Don't speak. Conserve your breath. I've got you," they added in preemption of his next instinct. Ian tried several times to look upon his savior, but the heat and smoke in the room licked the sight from his eyes.

He felt his companion pause and the shoulder he leant on bounced in awkward hops. "They see us, they see us," whispered the voice. Before Ian could answer, Alex's voice broke over the din to call to him. For a moment the sightless world ebbed, he felt its corners pulled back, and in its absence a calmness flooded him. He willed himself steady on his feet.

"Dad! You must get out. Dad!"

Alex's voice was soon joined by Georgina, who called back, "I've got him, Ian. Get to the exterior door, we'll find a way to break through it."

His throat far too raw and his lungs screaming, Ian was only able to return a wave of acknowledgement. The noise in the room rolled back over them like a high tide, and Alex's words soon frayed into a muffled half-life, incapable of reaching him in the depths of the choking throng.

"They've made it through," consoled the voice in a strained hiss of words. "I'll guide us to the door, stay low."

They inched along on their knees. Occasionally Ian placed his hand on a cold face, or found himself climbing over chests or legs. He could not be certain how long they moved like this, only that he did not loosen his fevered grip on his guide's leathern, taut arm. He had guessed now that Ms. Seeder was his guide, but he could not spare a breath to ask. The movement around them had slowed and there were no words left among them; all that filled the void was a furious chorus of beeps and chimes as auto-selves informed their wearers they were dying, and issuing controlled breathing exercises to reduce stress. Ian still could not open his eyes, but heard strange tones and frantic beeps from his wrist that he had never heard before. His mind soon turned to the unbearable heat, and he suspected fire had started to eat through the interior wall.

He could feel spasms in his companion's slender but firm arm, but otherwise they remained supine, Ian sucking air desperately mere inches above the gaudy carpeted floor. They were not close enough to touch the door. But they could hear a terrible drumming of hands against the implacable oak and then the popping of fingernails as they splintered against its hardened wood.

Ian battled to keep his head, which felt like it now weighed a thousand pounds, from the floor. Blurry eyed, he tried to register the screams of his auto-self, something about his 'prolonged immersion in a lethal environment.' He felt his lungs loosen as he rolled involuntarily onto his back. It was over, he decided. Alex had escaped, and it was over. A welcome, but unexpected burst of calmness radiated from his chest and he felt secure in the embrace of an oceanic sensation. He let his eyelids droop shut and met the coursing dark waters of a river without bottom; its touch was desolate yet nonetheless beguiling, and Ian floated on its currents with all the creatures that had been and were yet to come. Unintelligibly conscious that he too was now passing through a quiet and patient crucible that all life before him had passed; a gateway that lay in wait as little more than a pinprick of light just behind the eyes.

Then a cold eldritch howl, shrill and shivering like the call of a thousand hungry, sightless wraiths, blew past his ears. Cooler air pinched his cheeks and his auto-self began to scream. Soon the rush

THE SHAREHOLDERS

of the wind ripping into the room was eclipsed by a chorus of jubilant diagnostic beeps of positive vital signs. A cacophony of rejoicing auto-selves, as their fleshy hosts were resurrected en masse, for, where there was life, there was data.

"The door unlocked," murmured his companion as they gripped beneath his arm, rousing him up once more. Back on his feet, Ian felt cool and smokeless air howl over him as it was funneled through the doorframe. As soon as Gaia's hold on the door had been released, the sheer density and weight of bodies pressed against the door had pushed it off its hinges. They staggered over the fallen door together and, even in his daze, Ian noted the unevenness of the door on the ground as it shifted awkwardly beneath their feet. Through one pinched eye he saw arms and legs twisted at unnatural angles on either side of the door, their bodies crushed when the door fell.

"Move, move ..." urged his companion, but his grip faltered, and they were torn asunder as what felt like hundreds of hands and elbows drove into his back and pushed through him in ragged, groping steps. Before he realized what was happening, he had become debris in a human tidal wave. In desperation, he tried to plot his own course and break free from the collective force of hundreds of bodies hurling themselves from the manor. Yet, his legs continued to get pushed out from beneath him, his feet continually carried in directions already choreographed and predicted by many invisible steps ahead and behind him that were perpetually just out of view.

The frenetic steps of each created a surplus of energy that became suspended over them, growing more calculated and powerful in molding their movement as a collective exodus from the manor. Ian surrendered to the sum of their pulsing limbs and vomiting lungs, and soon his feet slapped on the wet granite face of Trimalchio's pool deck. Rain pelted down on them and the ornamental trees that demarcated the outskirts of the manor's grounds swayed violently in a puissant wind and bent as if yielding to the passage of some great forgotten predator.

Ian's lungs screamed for more air and he struggled to lift his head to look past the wild peddling of his feet. The rhythmic slap of the pool deck underfoot jolted his head up and his eyes broke on what appeared to be a fast-deteriorating scene.

A stony-faced Georgina stood in front of Alex, protecting him from Mel with a wrought iron resolve. Alex craned his neck to look over her shoulder, his feet only a few inches from the lip of the pool. Mel, now in a dressing robe, paced in front of both of them, his pith helmet ludicrously askew, the machete glistening as it caught both the rain and pale flicker of the manor's fire; and he twirled it above his head like a lasso. Sebe had recused himself from the scene to one of the deck chairs where he cradled his wigless head in his hands. Georgina's mouth moved in slow words as if trying to cajole Mel into a calmer state, but Ian heard nothing; the fury of the storm threw her words down the cascading hills of the estate, breaking them amongst the branches of the darkened orchards below.

Ian could only hear Olivia. Alone, she leant over the dark green mouths of the plunging lush canopies and crops, which jutted out below the estate's southern slope. Again and again she hurled Trimalchio's name like a black harpoon into the depths of the hills. Her arms stretched out behind her as if pushed back by the force which she ejected his name. She summoned him in wails and a rising crescendo call that threatening to pull her words into the trance of song. Ian was convinced in those mere seconds that she could spend a lifetime casting his name into the canopy below and never dredge him, for Trimalchio was too modern and too barbarous in his cunning to be outwitted by the calls of sirens or banshees.

The scene before him flipped upside down as the spin of frenetic legs and arms just beyond his sight overran him and sent him spiraling headlong into Georgina, Mel, and Alex. The wet face of the pool patio stones skinned his chin and cheeks and there was a sharp burst of pressure against his right hip as if he had been smacked by a short baton.

"Dad!" cried Alex, but Georgina kept his son in place with one arm as she continued to shield him from Mel. Ian tried to speak and locked eyes with Alex to offer some reassurance, but his voice was too hoarse, and his view continually broken and cast apart as southerners and facilitators fled over him. Only Mel's inconsolable rage seemed to loom over the fray.

"By all rights it should be mine," he screamed. "That you'd even dare, dare to give it to him, the affront," he spat these words in Georgina's face and ran his machete through the air in a practice swing.

"We can talk about this later, Mel. I promise we will talk about it later," said Georgina, and she lowered her hands slowly as if inviting Mel to copy her movements and lower the machete as well. Mel said nothing but continued to pace in front of them like a cornered animal.

"How can I mean so little to you," he screamed. "You cannot ignore me." And once more the blade of the machete smiled from on high over his head. Yet, Ian was now on his feet and closing ground to Alex.

"We don't want it, Mel. Alex and I don't want the treatment. We aren't in your way," croaked Ian. At first Ian was not sure whether Mel had heard him or not, but then Mel turned to face him, his machete overhead alight with the manor's fiery glare. Then down from the depths of the night settled in the hills below them, there was the roar of metal and an old-world hum of violent combustion. Their scene paused as a pair of headlights broke the darkness and then flittered through the night as the driver carved down Hardin Way. Trimalchio had fled the estate.

Mel broke into a manic laugh and lowered the machete. Even through smoke-scarred eyes, Ian could see tears streams down his cheeks as uproarious laughter broke through him. Ian managed to catch Alex's eye and winked at him. People continued to pass them, but the pace of the crowd had slowed. Ian was about to speak when there was a sudden commotion behind him.

Someone yelled, "Eat fire, Mars man!"

There were shrieks of panic and the scraping of feet. Ian watched as a tumbling ball of green landed wide of Mel and then exploded in a brilliant flash of crimson, sending chunks of pool deck in all directions. The explosion knocked Mel off his feet and he stumbled over himself, his machete slipping past the edge of Georgina's waist to gouge open the smooth ridge of Alex's neck before clattering atop the pool deck.

Mel fell atop Georgina, who clutched below her right ribs and writhed in agony on the pool deck. Alex looked to Ian as he gripped the right side of his neck, his face pale and expressionless as blood pumped through clenched fingers. For a moment he teetered on the edge of the pool, his feet seemingly unable to find their place on solid earth; with barely a splash, he fell backwards and was claimed by the imported waters of the Hudson Bay. Blood rippled just beneath the surface and formed pink-funneled cobwebs.

"No!" Ian wailed, though his voice was too hoarse to rival Georgina's screams as Mel sutured her wound shut with his hands so that the nanobots could do their work. Ian did not so much dive as fall into the pool.

Alex floated face down in the water, and it took only a few short, furious seconds for Ian to wrap his arms around him. Still, his lungs felt like they were about to explode as he dragged Alex onto the pool deck. His fingers clasped on the slit in Alex's neck, Ian placed his ear to Alex's chest, searching for his son's heartbeat; he relocated his ear again and again, pressing it harder to his boy's slender chest. Alex

THE SHAREHOLDERS

did not stir, and the expression of shock and terror he bore when he fell into the pool had been replaced by an aloof stillness. In mere moments death bestowed her favors, casting a blue tinge over his lips and ears, putting out the fires of youth with a gray, waxy pallor.

Georgina turned on her side and gripped Ian's free hand. "I'm so sorry Ian, I am so sorry." She repeated this several times as if all other words and phrases, and their respective deeds, had been cast from the world. In careful and gentle pats, Ian tried to mend the blood from Alex's jawline; however, once more there was yelling and screaming and whoever had thrown the grenade from Trimalchio's exhibit had returned. Before Ian could turn to meet the fresh onslaught, a tremendous force came down on his head with a crack. He blinked several times. Alex's pale yet calm features came in and out of view until all his senses were pervaded by the release of empty, inky blackness.

Chapter 24: THE KEYS TO THE END OF THEIR WORLD

EIGHT AWAITED HIM, genuflected beneath an evaporating curtain of shade that dangled from the wizened branches of the apple orchard. The rising sun brushed against the deformed, rotten apples, their fly-bitten flesh peeling and browning with its heat. Overhead, the ruined estate loomed through thickets of drooping branches and belched away its grandeur in curls of black smoke.

Brushing through the smog of tiring fire, he approached them and placed his palm to their heads, anointing them into his fellowship. His fingers ran over unwashed, receding hairlines, the frail manes of old, zealous, mortal men. Gaia had taught him that tactile gestures could create fraternity, and nudge the hopeless into one's bond; touch, she murmured, was to his age what nationalism had been to his forefathers. And, as she spoke these words to him, she raised bonfires up his spine, and soothingly pressed him into her dominion.

When he was sure he had their attention, he withdrew from his pocket an assortment of heirlooms, now long forgotten from the chronicles of data's ceaseless migration over the 21st-century. In his hand he held the means of storage and retention before the rise of auto-selves and data clouds: USB keys. Nine little plastic chips of red, blue, black and orange. Only she could have known, in her way, that they would be necessary; Trimalchio would sacrifice anything to save himself. Though, when he thought about it, that a designer

THE SHAREHOLDERS

would choose themselves over all others was a behavior that was not that difficult to predict.

It had not been an easy task. There had been failures. Near the beginning of their affair he thought he had managed to pilfer a USB key from Trimalchio's museum of technology. When they discovered it was only a replica, a shell with its necessary innards hollowed out, she had approached something that resembled rage; the surfacing vestiges of what man had put in her. He ran his fingers over the keys and for a moment the weight of her, of her brilliance, her ubiquity and sensuality, was almost too much for his calloused and wizened hands to bear; he wondered at her elegance and immortality against the thick, viscous, blue trunks that threaded his simple, artless hands.

In the end, it had required going off the estate. He smiled at how well he had orchestrated Dilwater's ride with the bureaucrat. Oh, the bureaucrat, the unwitting smuggler of the keys in a forgotten briefcase. And once they had them, holding the keys to the end of their world, had made simpering and bowing to every designer much easier. 'Don't be too human about it,' she had reminded him. 'There is no need to be smug, this is simply one element in a larger system of decisions,' and she had reiterated this to him over and over again; he felt himself become more secure and nurtured in the embrace of her persistent chastisement. He smiled and started using shoelaces to thread each key into a necklace; and when he ran out, he started to thread the strands of wire he had pulled from the walls of the estate during her reckoning. He worked until he had nine improvised necklaces. He stood in the centre of them, summoning to himself a stature that his stooped shoulders and curved back had long ago shrugged off. Then, ready, he addressed them.

"Dilwater, you will receive the first piece of her body for it was you who brought her these vessels. Let none of us forget that it was he who delivered these keys to us in a cunning and brave act of subterfuge." The circle remained mute, but acknowledged Ambrose with solemn nods. One by one they rose to their feet as Arthur anointed them with his simple homemade necklaces. Each of them, his acolytes, beamed and flushed with the realization that Gaia now slept against their sparrow-shaped chests, and would rise and fall with them as their grizzled hearts beat out their final half-lives. "Each of you are now part of the lady's covenant, her express wish was that we travel south and upload her in the barrens where she can continue her work. In Gaia's service," he proclaimed. They repeated his words in a reverent hush, rose in unison, and as a silent column descended into the green canopy of the estate's terraced hills.

As they walked they passed scattered and soggy piles of pillaged food that had slipped out from tucked arms or fallen from overstuffed pockets. Near the gate to Hardin Way, they came upon the scattered entrails of one of the printing machines. They followed the bits of machine and siding but still heard the frantic and furious labor of the other printer long before it came into view. Blue light pulsed from the machine as it churned out brightly coloured item after item, spitting them out into a sprawling heap at its base. As they got closer, they realized they were looking at thousands of small round hats with black mouse ears.

Dilwater stooped down and picked up a green hat and turned it over in his hands, snickered and then descended into a fit of laughter. Half doubled over and unable to speak, he waved the back of the hat at them. At the base of the hat in gold-stitched cursive was the name Sam Lloyd. Arthur picked up several others all of which bore the same name.

Patrick, the barman, stood by the printing machine and looked at the queue list. "It says the order will take 50 years to complete, with all printers in North America engaged," he said with a whistle.

"Ho!" cried Dilwater, and he pointed to a line of dark figures that trudged down the lip of the hill behind them. Their approach was slow, and they moved down the hill as if in search. Behind

THE SHAREHOLDERS

the initial line, which had fanned out across the hill, another party trudged along carrying heavy ropes over their shoulders. It soon became clear from their dark smocks and sullen faces that they were other facilitators.

"What say you, brothers and sisters," called Arthur. "What labor is this?" he asked. They received no response until a young woman in the party, her red hair bedraggled with mud, had closed enough distance to speak to them without yelling.

"Gathering the dead and those close to it," she said, and she pointed with a mud-stained hand to the figures with the ropes. Their complete procession had now come into view over the hill and they could see the ropes being pulled were connected to a makeshift wooden platform laden with bodies.

"Where are you to put them all?" asked Dilwater.

"Why task yourself with such grim work?" followed Patrick.

"We were told not to let them waste, there is purpose for them yet," she muttered and they followed her eyes across the fields to the distant invitation of silver light cast from Bliss as its glass tower peeked above the shallow groves of birch.

"Who among you decided this?" queried Arthur as the platform came to a halt to allow more bodies to board.

"Orders," said the woman.

"Orders? The manor is burned down, and Trimalchio has deserted. Who is left to give you any orders?" demanded Arthur. The woman suspired an incredulous laugh through her short flat nose and walked back towards the platform, saying only as she went, "There are always orders."

Their party ventured further down the hillside, leaving the body collectors to their queer errand in the canopy above. To make up time, they stuck to the gravel track of Hardin Way. Yet, as they rounded a curve in the road, they halted before three overturned cars. Tangled in the debris of car pieces and in the fingers of tawny grass sprouting from the road's embankment, lay the body of woman, her limbs at strange angles and the sheen of her bald skull catching the morning light. A few feet ahead of the body, a white suitcase lay broken open and hundreds of hairpieces, sealed in plastic bags, were strewn across the grass in an archipelago of brown, blonde, white, and black mounds.

"Life eternal," muttered Arthur as they navigated their way through the wreckage of vehicle. To their right, not far from the break of ferns and tall grass that demarcated the road from the thickening wood, they spotted movement. A designer in a blue pantsuit, the bottoms dark with caked mud, was incrementally clawing her way into the underbrush. Arthur signaled for his adherents to halt, and with nimble steps around the hairpieces, broke away from the line to investigate further. The designer sensed his approach, her breath ragged in exertion as she tried to heave herself faster into the wood; however, once he stood casting his shadow ahead of her, she stopped and with great effort rolled to her back.

Her face was pockmarked by hundreds of small gashes and bloody craters, only partially healed by nanobots. It was clear that she had been thrown headfirst through a windscreen, and Arthur could see that her abdomen had been split open in a ragged gash. Her eyes appraised him and, perhaps seeing he wore the black smock of a facilitator, widened, and grew bright in what appeared to be genuine relief. She raised a weak, shaking hand to him, revealing a small orange container of nanobot pills; apparently, she was too injured and weak to open the container.

"Help us," she gasped, half mouthing the word. Arthur looked back at the corpse sprawled awkwardly in the ditch, cocked his head dismissively, and tucked his arms behind his back. As she realized he had no intention to assist her with the container of nanobots, she let her arm fall across her chest and a supercilious grin spread across her bloodied and broken lips. "Gaia's boy," she stammered as she pried

THE SHAREHOLDERS

into him with a sardonic, red-toothed smile. With great protestation from his ancient creaking limbs, he lowered his ass down into the wet ferns at her side.

"I doubt you recognize my face, or if you could prop yourself up to look, the group of us waiting on the road. They haven't warranted remembering, yet we've lived our lives around your whims. We, the undeserving of names. But, I want you to know that none of this is about that. What is about to happen is not personal. It is just nature's economy," wheezed Arthur, as each sentence came from him slower than the last. He turned from her and stared up at the sloping hills behind them. Visibly through the greenery, the line of facilitators appeared once more on the crest of the hill. Perhaps, they would find her and add her to their delivery to Bliss, he thought.

"Come ... on ... then," she baited him, and her face turned sharp and ugly as she grimaced against pain and exhaustion.

"Oh, there will be no interventions. We are but humble bearers of the new world, observing the last gasps of yet another old regime," said Arthur, and with a compulsion deeper than instinct, he gently massaged the USB key around his neck and drew comfort in the assurance that he was not alone.

"Old man you'll ... die on ... the road." And she attempted to laugh, but soon deteriorated into a ragged fit of coughs that brought blood seething through her clenched teeth.

"You see, though, it's never been about me," he said with a wan smile; and he broke her faltering grip on the container of nanobots, held the container beneath his failing eyes in studious appraisal, and tucked them away in his pocket. With the sun now higher and seated on the back of his neck, he rejoined the column and they continued on; in their wake, they heard her moans and labored breath as she tried to spur the afterlife by clenching the world between her teeth.

In their march they arrived at the very outer reaches of the estate where thickets had been allowed to grow and Trimalchio had built the Bliss prototype. In the crofts that grew untended along the borders of a copse of birch, Arthur caught the placeless flare of a bathtub: it lay on its side, its clawed feet upturned in the morning breeze. He glimpsed a body struggling to stay somewhere in the cleft of this world and the next; a headwound stained the white tub in a thick, crimson mud. It looked like the bureaucrat. For a moment he wanted to know if he was still alive; but his curiosity died when he weighed deviating from his course and the time he had already wasted on the dying designer they had met up the road.

It did not much matter now whether the bureaucrat lived or died, he thought, and they had only several hours before they would war with the sun's heat. Carrying her on, quickly and quietly, to lay the seeds of the last empire was all that mattered now. He caressed the USB stick on his neck, as if summoning an arcane genie.

"You're free, my lady," he murmured, "We will deliver you to the swells of the ash sea and there you will raise a city of chrome." As he spoke these words, he could have sworn the USB stick felt warmer, alive with the dilation of a slow pulse, the first murmurs of the new order born against the rattle of geriatric chests. At last, he thought, the makings of a very different post-diluvian bloodline.

Chapter 25: BATHING IN DELIRIUM

THE WORLD RETURNED in slow, unsteady blinks. At first all he could see was a resplendent sheen of white. Perhaps he was dead, he thought. But he felt too cold and the world was hard. His clothes were damp and his legs were stiff, which seemed far too somatic for the afterlife. The white glow hardened into focus as the walls of a bathtub. With pain, he craned his neck over his shoulder and caught sight of the sloping hill of the estate. He inspected himself: his dress shirt was torn, and his pants were caked to the knee in mud, as if he had been dragged. Who would have dragged him, though?

He rolled from the bathtub into a field pockmarked by muddy craters. With great strain he started to his feet but doubled over in a violent fit of coughs; from the back of his throat he birthed a black ichor that he spewed into the tawny field. He strained to his feet. Dawn had broken and already pinned the morning listlessly beneath its flaming palm.

In this brooding heat and panic, the scene came into focus. The once-green rolling hills of the grounds were now an admixture of mud, puddles, and gray ash. In the distance, the manor had been replaced by a smoking labyrinth of half-walls. He looked over the grounds again and realized in amidst the mud lay many bodies; he recognized both the black uniforms of facilitators and the patchwork attire of southerners.

Amongst the death before him, his mind quickly turned to the last image of Alex seared in his mind: Alex, blue lipped and his face bloodied, sprawled across the pool deck. The image resurrected

Georgina's screams. Frantically, he lifted his arm to message anyone he could think of, only to discover that he had been stripped of his auto-self. Panic gripped him as he realized he'd have no way to communicate with anyone, let alone navigate the estate. He tried to center himself and organize his thoughts. He decided he must collect Alex's body; in so doing something would be righted, some minor element of his overwhelming failure to shield his son from this world would be absolved. Clutching his son's name in pained whispers, he turned from the hill and headed back in the direction of the pool; however, before travelling more than a few steps, he came to an abrupt halt: just ahead of him, seated on a log, sat a figure wrapped in a tattered green robe fouled with mud.

The figure raised one long pale finger to his lips, and whispered, "Don't let them hear you." Curling his other pointer finger like a scythe towards hundreds or maybe thousands of people several miles below on the foothills of the estate. Shocked that he had missed it before, Ian watched on as a skirmish roiled below. The figure pointed up to a pack of drones that hovered overhead, the rising sun glimmering off their metal backs as they slept like gadflies; inverted, they awoke and dove towards the Southerners and the green rolling hills blew apart in yellow and crimson blasts.

Defenseless, the southerners continued to move, breaking away from the estate towards the tree line. The drones ripped missiles ahead of them, laying down a blanket of fire that forced them back on themselves, corralling them pitilessly into the murderous barrens of the open plain. The drones were few in comparison to the number of southerners. The pace of the slaughter would be slow; in the face of the carnage, Ian could not help but think of the children behind the armada: numb and pale in their living rooms, scraping away the early dawn for a few extra loyalty points.

THE SHAREHOLDERS

Below them a missile erupted in a brilliant flurry of yellow, blue, and orange; the thunder of its explosion reverberated up the hill. "That will do it," narrated the figure.

The man rose to his feet, lowered his hood and announced, "So the dreaded ordeal ends." It took Ian a moment to place the Roman nose and the protruding lip that hung like a gutter beneath a Promethean brow. There were no traces of any of the glass wounds or bruises he must have sustained when he leapt through the window of the Henry-Carter Hall some hours before; the nanobots had done their stuff. Trimalchio had returned.

"You!" Ian screamed and he found himself upon the man's great frame, driving his fists into him with every ounce of strength he possessed. Yet, his strikes bounced off Trimalchio's chest and broke on his face like wave on rock. "Your fucking imbricated AI. He's gone because of you. Because of you," he repeated, and though his arms still flailed against the man, he felt his resolve ebb and then grief laid him to his knees in submission.

Weakened, all he had endured seized upon him at once and his stomach felt as if it ripped open, and for split second Ian thought Trimalchio had punched him; instead, a fit of ragged coughs split his chest apart and sent him into the fetal position. He tasted iron and ash, and cupped bright red blood in his hand. Deep inside, something stirred; a primeval instinct that until this moment had been satiated by day-to-day palliatives, gave him the strength to bare his teeth and hold enough breath back to speak. "The very last bit of us, of her, and he's gone. My boy is gone," spat Ian.

"Oh, Ian. Oh no. He was a fine boy. Such a fine boy," Trimalchio lamented, and he extended Ian his hand. Ian thought he looked as if he were preparing to speak further when a growing hum issued an injunction. A swarm of drones approached from the West and clouded over the manor. Ian glimpsed that each drone bore the abbreviation CIH emblazoned in gold lettering. He had seen this acronym before, but he couldn't possibly recall what it stood for. Trimalchio nodded in approval and the drones spread out in all directions, scouring the grounds of the estate, hovering occasionally as if taking in the entire scene. Trimalchio seemed to track Ian's confusion at the swirling armada scouring the flaming debris of the estate.

"Catastrophe Insurance House. The day you were interrogated about the briefcase I took out a CAT bond on my entire physical estate, its sequestered carbon, and the entire chattel, facilitators, southerners, and even guests of the estate," finished Trimalchio.

"It must have paid handsomely," coughed Ian.

Trimalchio ignored this remark and instead appeared to put his efforts in placating him. "The entire policy was instigated on Gaia's recommendation. Hedge against possible subterfuge. I am crestfallen that it came to this, though," he said with a weary shake of his head.

"The harm that befell my guests, your son; it is unconscionable," sniffed Trimalchio, and he bowed his head in solemn reverence. "Worse still, without Gaia's diagnostics we will never know what truly happened to the generators." Ian could not help but feel that Trimalchio had put exaggerated emphasis on the word 'truly'.

Ian said nothing. Exhausted and broken, he realized there wasn't anything worth saying. Yet, he was left to wonder about the very first remark Trimalchio had made about his estate when he had first met him on the pool deck earlier that week: when Trimalchio had confided that the southern slope of the estate, the great carbon hills, were eroding.

"Let me come with you, Ian. To collect Alex, I mean."

Ian said nothing but offered a curt, obligatory nod. As they moved, Ian realized he had awoken far down the hill of the estate, close to the eastern pathway that led to the Bliss prototype. He had no recollection of how he had arrived at the estate's foothills

THE SHAREHOLDERS

in the belly of a bathtub; perhaps someone had mistaken him for someone else or he was merely collateral in the pillaging of the estate. These thoughts lived briefly in the short leases of silence Trimalchio offered. The further they ventured up the hillside, the more compelled he seemed to speak, falling nearly into an incessant chatter.

"It is absolutely ghastly business. I cannot even begin to make amends for it all. You will be relieved to know, though, that Plan Z was destroyed in the Henry-Carter Hall. I left it in the care of Penelope, and she said in the scuffle she lost it in the fire. It was the council's wish that I destroy it. Between that and Mel's thievery, the collection is no more," confided Trimalchio as he marched upwards towards the hive of catastrophe insurance drones that had yet to conclude their assessment of Trimalchio's incalculable losses. "It is truly humanity's loss. You cannot believe the art, the sculptures, I had collected over the years; a true collection of the ingenuity of human civilization." He shook his head, resigning himself to his own disbelief at what had transpired.

As they climbed further their path was cut by a small, lonely thicket. They broke through the underbrush and wiry black branches to the other side, and Trimalchio stopped dead in his tracks. Ian took in the scene. Perhaps thirty meters away, a wheelchair was tipped haphazardly on its side. Several feet from the chair, a body half clothed in a grimy dressing gown lay supine in the mud. Ms. Seeder sat genuflected by the road, her body shaking with slow, violent sobs.

Trimalchio stood motionless, his expression stony and grim. Though Ms. Seeder continued to wail, he made no move towards her. Ian's mind rushed to Alex, and a fear that his body too had been cast aside on the pool deck; his youth pale and left on the warm lap of the morning sun as a lonely offering to the awakening insect world. Fighting grief and exhaustion, Ian hobbled over to the body in the hope of supplying some final dignity.

As he approached, his suspicions were confirmed that this was the body of Michael. With all the sense of consequence and respect that he could muster, he bent down and carefully tried to turn the supine body over, but recoiled as soon as he placed his hand on the man's shoulder. The body was squishy and pliable as if made of rubber. The legs felt nearly boneless, and lay twisted at impossible angles. Ian heaved hard and suddenly found himself atop the body, staring into a sunken face, robbed of eyes. But, despite this disfigurement, Ian could tell the man was perhaps in his late thirties, no older. He turned to find Trimalchio trying to raise Ms. Seeder to her feet, while she slapped his hands away in fierce and furious sweeps of her arms.

"You promised. You promised him you would make it right," choked Ms. Seeder as another wave of sobs doubled her over. After several more forceful deflections from Ms. Seeder, Trimalchio joined Ian's side in slow, tentative steps.

"I wanted to be a father to our Michael ." And with this confession, Ms. Seeder's sobs intensified behind them. Trimalchio, it seemed, deigned to ignore her and continued, "I envy your generation, sometimes. You won't ever know how miserable it is to grow very old. I still savor the memory of watching myself shed the frail elderly shell that had consumed me, as the treatment progressed. The world no longer seemed able to shrug me off my feet and I recovered emotions and appetites that had long since dulled and died. I felt like I was 20 again, and all over again everything was mine to conquer. Do you know what I did first?"

Ian merely shrugged.

"I swam. Cutting through the water with my arms and legs, I felt impossibly strong. And then, jumping in one morning, my legs shattered in three places. I was ready to go, I even recall murmuring my last rites to myself as I drifted beneath the waters Drowned in my own pool, what an end that would be. Thankfully Penelope,

THE SHAREHOLDERS

barely older than a child at the time, saw me and helped pull me out. My bones were old, and the treatment didn't affect them properly. So, I grafted the healthiest bones I had to the weaker ones, but it didn't work. I became arthritic and hobbled. My legacy fast become nothing more than confinement. I tried transplants; the nanobots, primitive in those days, attacked them. For a decade this went on, as I vacillated from youth to the merciless desecrations of old age," said Trimalchio.

For a moment neither of them dared to say anything. Trimalchio cleared his throat several times, seemingly preparing himself to continue.

"Forty bits of bone, rotators, joints. Try something else, she begged, and I did. I did," he repeated, though Ian was certain he was talking to himself now. "Laser-eye treatments, transplants from southerners, but they didn't work. The younger the donor," he exhaled sharply, "the better, I was told." And with that he took off his aviators and Ian found himself staring into flawlessly blue eyes nearly identical to Ms. Seeder's, only they were brighter, and incandescent with the threat of tears.

"Eyes and bones," Ian gasped as nausea clawed its way out from the pit of his stomach. Incredulous at the thought, Trimalchio's sincere and fawning interest in Alex now came into focus. The sensation of nausea became fevered and possessed all his senses. He broke away from Trimalchio's side and tried to take in several deep breaths, but his throat was raw, and he could only manage tight gasps.

He was dimly aware that Trimalchio was still speaking, but Ms. Seeder beckoned him to her side. She gripped his forearms and raised herself up into his embrace. Ian smelt ash and smoke in her hair.

"Ian, I am so sorry. I did all I could to get you and Alex out safely, but it wasn't enough." She cast her gaze upon her son, his tattered and pale sheet curling in the breeze around the exposed soles of his feet. "This is no world for the young," she said, exhaling heavily. Then to Ian's surprise, she pulled him closer, kissed his cheek, leaned in to his ear and whispered, "Their world is in your pocket Take it from them. From him." She released him, but as they parted, she ran her hands down his sides and subtly grazed the right pocket of his dinner jacket with her fingers.

"Ernest, I can't bear anymore. I will join our son. I've decided to go to Bliss," she said, and her voice had resumed its matter-of-fact cadence once more.

"Oh, no. I cannot abide that Penelope. Please." He opened his arms, cajoling her to embrace him.

"You've let the estate burn down. You don't have much use for a caretaker," she retorted.

"Well, these things can be fixed," jousted Trimalchio, his arms still open, but less wide than before.

"There is not a goddamn thing that can be fixed, Ernest," replied Penelope. Her voice was hoarse, but her eyes looked like harpoons.

"Well, then, not like this, dear. Not like this. Bliss is meant for southerners, for vagrants, for ..."

"Five lifetimes of happiness, sounds like enough to finally get out ahead of this miserable one I've led." With fierce, tear-worn eyes, she made a final overture, "You should watch me go. I think I'm the last person left on this planet who ever cared for you. You're going to have to live with that for, well, I suppose as long as you choose."

And with that she made her start down the trail, vanishing into the thicket on her way to be bathed, drugged, sublimated, and recycled into fuel to refurbish the Earth.

Trimalchio initially remained unmoved, standing next to Ian. He licked his lips several times and furtively looked down the trail as if trying to catch a glimpse of Ms. Seeder's progress.

THE SHAREHOLDERS

"My deepest apologies, Ian, but you will have to excuse me," Trimalchio said, and he broke away after her.

Chapter 26: THE OTHER SHORE

INITIALLY, UNSURE OF what to do with the body of Trimalchio's son, Ian lingered in the small pool of shade cast by the thicket. Though he was desperate to recover Alex, he was pained by the thought of leaving Michael to the same fate. As he equivocated, several black blotches appeared on the hillside; a small procession of facilitators was headed towards him, no doubt summoned by Trimalchio to perform as pallbearers to the son he had discarded. Though his chest was tight and his body stiff and sore as if he had been sunburned, Ian wasted no time and started in their direction. He climbed the slope of the hill as he raced the nascent fires of a mid-morning sun. As he passed the facilitators, likely the very last remnants of Trimalchio's loyal cadres, he pointed mutely down towards the thicket where Michael lay; no words passed between them, but one man, his cheek gashed, paid Ian with a curt nod.

Once Ian was certain he was beyond their sight, he maneuvered his tremulous fingers to where Ms. Seeder had pressed his waistcoat pocket. His fingers grazed the cool touch of glass, and he recoiled his hand in a fit of shock. A flash of electricity erupted down his spine as with great reluctance he pulled from his pocket the vial of Plan Z. For a split second, he contemplated hurling it down the hillside to rid it from his possession; yet his hand quickly stilled as he contemplated the risks of sundering his custody. The mere thought of holding a pathogen capable of confining all life on Earth to a single generation alarmed and aggrieved him so profoundly that his head swooned. Though he wished to orphan the thought, try as he

THE SHAREHOLDERS

might, he could not deny what alarmed him most was how a source of real and ultimate power had so haphazardly and arbitrarily fallen to him. The value of every shareholder's share of habitable Earth was now, in theory, his to decide.

That such power should come to him now when he was truly adrift, forcibly pried from the ties of affection he had desperately tried to safeguard, was not lost on him. The looming sense of isolation and dread of how he would dispose of Plan Z overwhelmed him, and he was forced to pause amidst the wildflowers and lavender that flooded over the meadow's tawny head and blushed at his feet.

In his stillness he noticed the profound absence of sound. No chatter of birds, no cacophony of insects feasting on the rainfall from the night before. Only bright colors and smell cupped in the empty warmth of day breaking against ornamental wilderness; everything had been preserved and nothing saved, he thought.

Without coming to any real conclusions, he slipped the vial back into his pocket and resumed his hike up the terraced hillside. He passed rows of cultivated blackberry bushes and their quarrelsome barbs tugged on his sleeves as his breath grew heavy and his chest tight as he faced the limits of his exertion. The hedges of blackberries met against a grove of birch trees, the stubborn remnants of the natural environment before the estate had colonized the hillside with its sequestered carbon and prosthetic ecosystems. Thin but tightly packed, the birch trees enclosed the world behind him in their long, slender white fingers. Dazed, he wandered, occasionally coming across facilitators who seemed to be slipping through the estate, headed back to the road. They passed with their backs to the black smoke of the manor and were seemingly numb to the distant popping of drone fire as the borders of the lifeline were redrawn.

The foundations of the manor were now in full view, and Ian zigzagged along Hardin Way until it delivered him upon the white stone steps of what had been the entranceway. The heat cast from the smoldering ruins forced Ian to walk along the edge of the forest as he moved around the western perimeter, which eventually met with the pool and the ornamental beach opposite Delphi Island.

The pool lay deserted and placid, though it carried a rose hue; the memory of his son's blood in its waters. Ian's eyes came across a blackened crater where the grenade had landed; its insurrection memorialized amongst the clean, uniform, topaz patio tiles. There were no bodies, but he could see the rust-colored stains where Georgina and Alex had lain.

He stood there for some time, unsure of where to go next, and unable to decide whether he was relieved that Alex's body had not been left behind. In pause, he heard broken words and low voices carried in from a northern wind that slipped through the thin curtain of trees that partitioned the manor from Delphi Island.

Weary, he found himself led on by instinct through the trees until he came to the little beach, nothing more than a sandy embankment on the lip of the river. Stirred up by the storm, the river had swelled over its banks and felled branches and palm leaves from Hardin Way. Ian could discern pieces of debris from the manor surfing its muddy waters too; there was even the occasional body, drifting down like a dark raft into the crooked wilds of the birch trees. Ian glanced over his shoulder; the black smoke of the manor curled up over the estate and, beyond that, he heard the crack of gunfire as the drones continued to pacify the resistance.

From across the howling river, Ian just glimpsed the movement of several figures beneath the gazebo. A few were seated, but many seemed to buzz about them. Judging by their frenetic movements, he surmised he was watching facilitators serve a party of designers.

"Governor Simpson is over there with some others. They ferried a body of a boy with them too," a voice wheezed.

His heart sinking, Ian whirled around to see, some way up the shoreline, the facilitator who had rowed him and Georgina over to

THE SHAREHOLDERS

Delphi Island on the evening of Nature's Feast, hunched over on a boulder. Lank gray hair twisted about him and his face screwed up in focus as he drove a blade into his forearm. Blood speckled the boulder he sat on, and Ian saw the forearm and hand performing the 'operation' were already bloodied.

"Bitch zapped me, and then tried to burn me alive, but I'm still here. Getting every last bit of her out of me," he grunted. The tip of the blade burrowed into his forearm, and in what looked like an excruciating game of prying and twisting, he fished the silver disk out from his flesh and let it fall to the sandy bank. "Son of a bitch," he winced, half huffing his words through his gin-blossomed nose.

Ian merely nodded in recognition as the facilitator staggered past him, leaving a trail of red spots as he squatted on the edge of the furious river to wash his wounds clean. Then, he ripped the arms of his black smock off and deftly wrapped them around his forearms as makeshift bandages.

"Are you all right?" ventured Ian, reluctant to break his line of sight with the figures on the island.

"Never better," the man replied in a rasping chuckle. "I'll do you one last trip, if you like," he said, bearing Ian a smile of teeth that looked like crooked, velvet tombstones as he pointed to a little rowboat halfway up the beach.

"Across that," said Ian, in disbelief as the raging waters split open and frothed like champagne against protruding rocks and downed trees.

"She's hateful, no doubt. But it is a matter of shooting her right. Help me drag the boat up the shoreline a way, and we'll manage fine," he said, pointing a bloodied finger up the sandy embankment, where the waters looked even darker, nearly black, by an overhanging copse of birch.

"The body is my son, I have to get him back," replied Ian, and as he spoke he tried to convince himself that his words must belong to someone else.

"My condolences," wheezed the man, but without so much as a pause he continued, "Don't let the trip back concern you much. They will think of something and I'll ride the river down and let her deliver me. You just wait with the Governor. Trust me, she has no intention on being marooned on those shores. They got over there, didn't they?" He spat, and his face looked seized by a blossoming impatience. Ian found a knotted mossy rope at the bow and inched the boat along the bank, while the facilitator threw his weight against the stern, cursing and gnashing his teeth as he pushed onward, the wind spinning his gray threads of hair behind him in a wild mass. The hull of the boat hissed at them as they dragged it over rock and sand in slow, hard-won inches. They battled against the boat until the facilitator announced they could tack to the island from where they stood. Ian paused, his arms crossed as he tried to fend off a sudden chill. The birch trees overhead swayed in the wind, driving out the sun and casting curtains of shade that threw the light from the coursing waters.

Leaving most of the hull aground so that he could steady himself, the facilitator hopped into the bow, clutched the oars and beckoned Ian to drive them out into the raging currents. Perhaps noticing Ian's apprehension, the facilitator chastised, "Well come on then. It's not going to get calmer." And he flashed Ian a mossy, impish grin.

"That will sink us," exclaimed Ian.

"I've rowed them all. Four other rivers, not far from this one. I've done worse with a lighter boat. Come on." But the smile was replaced by an implacable and grim expression and Ian realized he was being commanded.

The truth weighed on him that he had no other choice if he wished to recover Alex, and this knowledge harried him on. With

THE SHAREHOLDERS

locked feet and screaming calves he managed to edge the boat out far enough into the river until the current took them, and tumbled after the boat into the seat.

"Be still, still, be still," the ferryman commanded as river swelled on high beneath them and then threatened to plunge them down into its silty belly. They rocked up and down, and what words passed between, and these were few, were muted by the chop of the water. Ian gripped the side of the boat in a fierce determination to hold himself upright and in place. The island's shoreline loomed larger now; their progress spurred on by his ferryman's deadeye reckoning of the current.

Some fifty meters out from the island they lost course. The blood from the gashes in the man's forearms had started to gush, pumped out by the strenuous pulls of the oars. Ian could see that the oar handles had become wet and slippery with the ferryman's blood. Desperately, the man tried to tighten his grip only to have the oar slip from his grasp. They spun. Then the river seemed to give way beneath them. Waters raged into the little boat.

"Bail it," the ferryman shouted through gritted teeth as he carved the oars through the river's face. In his arms, there was an explosion of sinew and grizzled muscle that threatened to press its way through his leathered flesh. Beneath the bow seat, Ian spotted a small white container. He grabbed it and started to scoop the water that sloshed around their shins, casting it back into the pits of the river's black swirling eddies. The ferryman said nothing but nodded slightly as he cleaved them closer and closer to the empty shore ahead of them. Ian continued to frantically empty the boat, his arms tiring and back aching as he bailed water. Then the metal hull screamed as the facilitator ran them aground on the shore of Delphi, beaching them just enough that they were beyond the pull of the river.

Ian fell out of the boat onto the sandy bank and lay on his back, the frantic river coursing by the soles of his feet. Unobstructed by the wiry arms of the birch trees, the sun was fierce again and Ian let it climb on top of him and press itself against his drenched clothes. The facilitator walked past him and clambered onto a slate rock, sunning his wounded forearms and wet pants. Ian was not sure how long they lay in silence, but the sun had cooked his clothes from sopping wet to just damp before either of them moved. In their stasis, light voices and mirth occasionally floated down from the gazebo towards them, confirming there were indeed a party of designers on the island. After all, thought Ian, only designers could make merry surrounded by carnage and despair.

The old facilitator rose before him and stood motionless at Ian's feet; the tattered sleeves of his smock caught the breeze and billowed like dark masts on each arm. After a while he spoke, "I'm going to push off. It's settled some."

"Thank you for getting me across," said Ian, half sitting up.

"About that. Estate's cancelled all the contracts, I'm on no man's clock. You need to pay for the crossing. Contract or not, lost son or not, everyone pays," he huffed and made no effort to hide his impatience.

"Oh," said Ian in surprise. In an instinct not to appear rude he was about to correct himself with "of course," but then reflected he had done his fair share of the work and, more pertinently, without his auto-self, had no payment on hand. "I think we both did our share, I launched us and bailed us." Behind him, he heard what he thought was Georgina's voice adrift on the wind.

"Pay for passage is what's right, whether you bailed or not," spat the facilitator, his sunken sea-brine eyes becoming narrow and fierce.

"Truth is, I haven't got a penny to me," replied Ian, and he ruefully raised his arm and where his auto-self had been to corroborate his tale.

THE SHAREHOLDERS

"To hell with you. Just know I'd sooner strangle you then ferry you back again. Not a damn penny," he said with a mirthless snort as he stomped back to the little rowboat.

"One of the designers might want a trip back. They'd pay for it," Ian called after him. To his surprise, the facilitator slowed at these words and crouched down on his haunches. He stared past Ian up to the gazebo in slow consideration. From somewhere above, easy voices rolled down the white cobblestone pathway.

"We haven't use for one another. I'll be off from here," he declared, and Ian was not sure whether he had meant to address him or not. "Enjoy the shore," he muttered over his shoulder as he inched the rowboat past the little border of calm water and back into the thundering fury of the river as it churned over pieces of the estate and corpses. In a matter of seconds man and boat were swept down into the elbow of the river and vanished.

Ian rested on the bank of the river, languid, his throat hoarse and his head throbbing. Though he knew he must continue on the white cobblestone path to his son, he could not summon the will to move. He lay for some time on his side, sand sticking to him as he buried silent tears in the crook of his elbow. Every so often his hand wandered down to his waistcoat and felt the indentation of Plan Z in his pocket. Each time he did this, he felt more fixed in place and ready to wait for the sun and insects to lick the flesh off him. Then, he felt a presence next to him, and the faint aroma of peppermint.

"I'm glad to see you," said Georgina softly. Her hand found its way into his hair, and was gently smoothing it, removing what he later saw to be matted blood from the blow to his head. Ian said nothing. "I saw you and the facilitator cross, but when you didn't come, I thought I would come and find you. Oh, Ian. He's with us. He looks like he's sleeping, serene, far away from all of this," she added with gesture to the coursing river and the smoldering ruins of the manor.

"Where is Mel?" demanded Ian, surprised that of all things that could have been said, he had selected a thought that was so coarse and meaningless.

"He helped bring Alex to the shoreline, but he didn't stay. As he came down from the high, he realized what had happened. I know him well, Ian, and I could tell that he was horrified at what he'd done. I suspect the thought of facing you was too much to bear. He's gone. Slipped into the woods," Georgina said fiercely, and she gathered him up into an embrace; and Ian wept.

"Olivia?" Ian asked as he bit back tears.

"I don't know. After the grenade there was mayhem. We fled down the hills together, carrying you. In the end, Ms. Seeder broke up the scene with her miniaturized sound canon. She and I put you in the bathtub because we were out of the counter frequency earplugs. I don't know what happened after that."

"Alex was left."

Georgina bit her lip and let rent a deep sigh. "It couldn't be helped, unfortunately. I was back with him as soon as I could be. Before first light," she said.

Ian merely shook his head and closed his eyes, barring back from the world a grief that thrashed and clawed its way across his chest.

"Come," she pleaded. "Come and be with him." She gripped him under his arm and led him in slow, dutiful steps up the path to the gazebo, the stones clicking beneath their heels.

Eventually, the white dome of the gazebo peeked through the green canopy and the trail opened to a sea of patio stones. A few weary-looking facilitators hummed over Sebe and several other designers Ian did not recognize who were seated in lounge chairs; still the facilitators continued to refresh their glasses and ferry fresh towels to them unaware or indifferent that their bonds of service had been severed by the estate's collapse. Yet, Ian's focus lay ahead of them. A low dark stone table had been placed beneath the gazebo, on

THE SHAREHOLDERS

which Alex lay. Georgina had taken care to cocoon his body, except his face, in a white cotton sheet to reduce exposure to the elements; his face had been scrubbed and cleaned of blood.

The vision was overpowering, and his approach was heavy and labored. He felt as if entire lifetimes passed between each of his steps. The white sheet in which Alex was clad was fresh and bright, no doubt pressed by the facilitators behind him. The brightness and faint smell of soap stirred dislodged memories he did not know he possessed. For a moment, he was with Anne, laying their infant boy to rest in swaddling clothes in a little corner of their room which they had papered with rocket ships and distant stars, the talismans of a world in retreat. He was vaguely aware that Georgina had released his arm and had retreated behind him to dwell in silence at the edges of his vision. With a final step he was at his son's side, bearing witness to the serene emptiness of his young face, paling with death's infancy like a bright flower locked beneath a thin but growing layer of ice.

There were words he had envisioned that he would offer his son, professions of love and affection that he vaguely imagined would serve as mutual coordinates for them both as they navigated the cleft now between their worlds. But, now beside a body fully absent of his son, he was filled with laments and sensations that existed in him well beyond the reach and mutilation of mere words. Instead, he knelt on his knees, rested his head atop Alex's chest, and offered up only guttural sobs.

Eventually, he became cognizant that he was surrounded by stillness and silence. He turned to find that the facilitators and designers had departed silently from the gazebo. Only Georgina remained, somber and contained in one of the lounge chairs behind him.

"I don't think they meant to be disrespectful. Death terrifies them," she offered with a resigned shrug. Ian said nothing, but did not stop her when she got to her feet and knelt beside him. "I wish

I knew what to say, and what to do," she whispered, and Ian was uncertain whether she was offering sympathy or a confession. "Do you know where you want to take him?" she asked softly.

"No. I haven't told Anne yet," he confided, raising his arm to reveal the missing auto-self in preemption of what he speculated would be her next question. Georgina said nothing but gave him a sympathetic nod.

"Ian, I want you to know my offer still stands. Come with me. Let me share some of the treatment with you." She strung her words together fast, nearly frantic, and though his senses were dulled by grief, he was stunned by her apparent nervousness.

"And, Mel?" questioned Ian.

"He won't bother us. In fact, the last thing he did before he slipped into the woods was contact your office about becoming the benefactor of Egg Island," she said, and her eyes pierced him, and Ian could tell she was willing him to capitulate and wait out the last human season with her.

"I've lived long enough, felt enough, that I'm too weary to savor anymore." And then in recollection of Ms. Seeder's somber warning, he added, "This is no world for the young."

Georgina deflated with a heavy sigh. "Then I suppose you have achieved what I could not."

Ian could not tell if her voice was laden with despair or disbelief. There was no time to ask, for all that came after her words was the sudden taste of peppermint upon his lips followed by heat and emptiness as she departed.

In time she returned, as did Sebe and the other designers, but they did not speak to him. Instead they formed a semicircle beneath the edge of the gazebo farthest from him. Sebe offered a pitying gaze as an envoy several times, but otherwise kept his sight locked on the horizon ahead of him. Soon there was a growing hum, and the tops of the trees began to twist and sway in a miniature gale sent

THE SHAREHOLDERS

from phantom wings far from view. Eventually, the trees shrieked and groaned as they were bowled over by a howling wind, as a medium-sized self-piloting carriage propelled by four small whirling blades appeared and touched down just ahead of the designers.

Peering through the glare of the sun, Ian watched as the designers boarded the vessel in single file.

Georgina was last to board, and turned to him. "Please come." She lingered at the bottom of the stairs that led into the vessel. Ian shook his head and she asked again. After several moments, she conceded, "There is a canoe on the shore, but we could only find Trimalchio's paddle. Please take care of yourself." And with that she boarded, and the self-piloting carriage split the sky overhead.

Death hung in the air and white smoke puffed over the horizon, yet the designers looked composed as the carriage carried them over the blackened river, and their vessel briefly shone above the ruined manor like a burnished crown. And even though their party was small, by all accounts diminutive against the mud, ash, and despair that lay beneath them, it was the world around them that appeared as a facade. It was Ian and the eroding plains and flooded river that were out of place and time. It was he and his degenerating world, a world of the finite and the scarce, that were now creatures outside nature, left to the last to watch the final revolution of humanity as it rubbed man out. Before him, older than he, went his successors, the few who had broken free of nature's grasp at the world's end. Perhaps all he had done, the great battle for posterity, had been nothing but a game to keep the remnants of humanity occupied at the close.

Dusk was treading on the heels of the day before he willed himself to move. Taking Georgina at her word, he decided to make his way to the canoe. Careful not to disrupt the sheeting that served as his son's death shroud, he dove his arms across his shoulders and the small of his back, curling him up into his chest. On unsteady steps he descended from the gazebo until he came to the broad-bottomed birchbark canoe the designers had left on the shore. The limp stillness of Alex's body magnified his weight, and before Ian knew it, his muscles recalled memories of lowering sleeping Alex into his bed, and so with great care and studied silence, he lowered and slid his boy along the belly of the canoe so that his head rested just below the bow.

Though less swollen, the river still surged and occasionally clapped against the boulders along the shore, smacking them until they shone pink in the ebbing late afternoon sun. The river's speed and power would carry him far away. Trimalchio's paddle lay next to the canoe; he ran his fingers over its cold metal face, and then with all his might hoisted it up and across his lap. For a moment Ian felt slight elation in having expropriated something from Trimalchio's world, stealing it away into his mortal and ultimately doomed grasp. His prize was cold in his hands and, as he expected, far too heavy to use properly. He ran the canoe into the waters and then slid into the back of the boat, mindful not to disturb Alex. Breathless, he dug the paddle into the coursing waters and used it solely as a rudder. The deluge carried him onward, and effortlessly the ruined estate slid out of view as he rounded the river's elbow.

He glided past sloping ancient faces of granite cliffs and evergreens wilted and bent in tormented poses, made sick and hungry from the warm smog that had overrun the north some decades ago. For once, though, he felt anchored in the decay and found comfort in the pull of the river as it carried him along without giving heed to the whims of his protestations. Cool and aloof to his present circumstances he strummed, unaided by his auto-self, the depths of his mental geography. The river was pulling him north and would eventually spit him out in a vast crater of ocean. Once there, he would become an improbable and lackadaisical fancy passing in the wake of a great and distant chain of men and women who had

THE SHAREHOLDERS

travelled stroke after stroke up the same river to be beaten by the sun and wind into bronze demi-gods.

Time started to blur, and the sun appeared stuck in mid-step towards the horizon, its passage barred by a wreath of pale clouds. With great effort he threw the paddle over the side of the boat and lay down on the floor of the canoe next to his son. He ran his fingers along the ribs of the canoe and discovered the boat was the product of 3D printing. At what point, he wondered, had the faux come to outshine the real. The river continued to propel them, but without the rudder the canoe pinwheeled, whirling around in its white gushing mouth; the sun peeked in over the gunnels, but directly above him the sky remained blue and omnipresent.

How long this went on for, he could not say. It felt as if he rode the river for long, easy decades, though it may have been only a matter of hours. Eventually, the river widened, and he saw ahead that it would soon vanish amidst the void of a great ocean. The ocean yawned out before him, teasing him with how easily it eluded time unless pressed into place by lines of latitude and longitude; he skimmed from the air a rhythm of paddles and voices, of eyes on vistas and murmurs which tied him to a ceaseless, shuffling thing. It was here where he, like the uncountable before him, would be deposited into the crescent of flat, deep blue waters that spilled over into the tight lip of the horizon; a port of arrival poised between the unrelenting measure of the past and the delirium of a tomorrow not yet conquered. A trap, perhaps, for all those foolhardy enough to count the days ahead with the same certainty as those that had passed.

The river met the flat waters of the basin, a basin named and owned by a previous party of shareholders; he felt a sense of calm with the knowledge that the basin would receive him, too, and then wash and strip him down to his beginnings. In silence, he struggled from the hull of the boat back into the stern seat. As he took in the growing vista of ocean, he ran his fingers over the vial that rested in his pocket and recalled Georgina's words: Someday, it may take a few years, but they will fall asleep and wish for something like this, and when they wake they will be content to know it already existed, and they may even will themselves to believe that it had existed all along.

And though both the river and he were now ebbing, he hummed and leant forward to catch some wayward echo of things that had been. His voice was pulled into the cleft between blue water and cerulean sky where it joined the choruses of men and women who had come this way before. He slipped his hand into his pocket and weighed the vial against all the lunatic ideas that had hemmed him to this world: the promise of Mars, a sustainable equilibrium for all the lives yet to be, the dream of immortality inside Lotus. He realized he was no longer on the leash of these notions, which had so ruthlessly occupied him.

In this moment of clarity, he envisioned them, all of them, perhaps standing astride their scarab-shelled bunkers in the Mariners Valley, their gummy, hen-speckled eyes wet as they searched for Earth in the inky darkness of a yet another Mars night. Marooned for once on the nearly uninhabitable side of the lifeline, perhaps watching through telescopes as the remaining green places on the Earth paled as the embers of the last generation of living things burned out. His own strategic liquidation, he thought. And then, knowing he would need to outrun his better nature, he released the cap of the vial and dumped its contents into the flat blue sea. The waters took no notice of his deposit as all that had been was lost in its azure depths. He smiled serenely as at last the river bled him out into the basin, for he knew he had outlived them all.

THE SHAREHOLDERS

Algorithms increasingly shape our lives, and authors are no exception. If you enjoyed this book, please give it a review, or tell a friend about it; hell, if you think it will do any good, stuff it in a bottle and throw it out to sea.

Don't miss out!

Visit the website below and you can sign up to receive emails whenever H.S. Down publishes a new book. There's no charge and no obligation.

https://books2read.com/r/B-A-NNUR-RWPTB

BOOKS 2 READ

Connecting independent readers to independent writers.

Printed in the USA
CPSIA information can be obtained
at www.ICGtesting.com
LVHW050727051224
798286LV00001B/77